VIRA̶G̶O̶
MODERN CLASSICS
484

Margery Sharp

Born Clara Margery Melita Sharp in Wiltshire, England in 1905, Margery Sharp attended school in Malta and in Streatham. She completed college studies in 1928, thereafter attending Westminster Art School, where she was very successful.

She began her writing career at the age of twenty-one as a contributor to *Punch*, with pieces in the *Saturday Evening Post*, *Strand* magazine, *Ladies' Home Journal*, and *Harper's*, as well as many other magazines and papers. In 1938 she married Major Geoffrey Castle, an aeronautical engineer.

A number of Sharp's stories and novels became popular films, but she remains most famous as the author of the children's series, *The Rescuers*, animated by Disney. She died in 1991.

THE EYE OF LOVE

Margery Sharp

With an Introduction by John Bayley

Virago

A *Virago* Book

Published by Virago Press 2004
First published in the UK by Collins 1957

A CIP catalogue record for this book is available
from the British Library

ISBN 1 84408 030 7

Typeset in Goudy by M Rules
Printed and bound in Great Britain by
Clays Ltd, St Ives plc

Virago Press
An imprint of
Time Warner Books UK
Brettenham House
Lancaster Place
London WC2E 7EN

www.virago.co.uk

INTRODUCTION

Margery Sharp was born in 1905, near Salisbury in Wiltshire, but her family came from North Yorkshire, and she inherited – it can be seen in all her large family of novels – something of that incisive Yorkshire mixture of unsentimental wit and blunt speech. When she was very young the family moved temporarily to Malta, which she loved. Much of the atmosphere and feeling of the island later found its way into her novel *The Sun In Scorpio* (1965), as did the contrast between warmth and sunshine and the cold grey inhospitality of the England to which she returned. There is a distinct similarity here between Margery's own experience, and that of the very young Rudyard Kipling returning aged six from British Imperial India. He too was to put his own experience into a memorable story – *Baa Baa Black Sheep*.

After school days in Malta Margery went to Bedford College in 1925, and from there to Westminster Art School, where she not only studied art but herself became an accomplished painter. She might even have tried to become a professional artist, but she already loved writing too; and common sense, in which she was far from deficient, told her that she was much more likely to make a living with her pen than with a paintbrush. It is certainly clear that the young Margery showed remarkable enterprise and versatility. When just twenty she earned a place on the British Universities Women's Debating Team, a kind of forerunner of our *University Challenge* TV programme, and she went with the team to America, becoming, although not through any particular skill in debating, the most popular and well-informed member of her little group.

Back in England she managed her debut by writing pieces for *Punch* magazine, both in verse and prose, some of which were accepted by Sir Owen Seamen, the kindly but critical editor, and some not. But his kindness encouraged her, and she was soon having success with other periodicals, including the *Strand*, *Harper's*, and the *Ladies' Home Journal*. She had also begun to learn the craft of novel-writing, her goal since she had got her first job and become a typist, sharing a flat in Paddington with two other girls. Now she launched into precarious independence, having worked it out that twelve pounds a month, her fee from the successful sale of one short story, would be enough to keep her going. (This makes an interesting comparison with the kind of sum a freelance writer needs to make ends meet today.) So she allowed herself the luxury of setting down to write a novel. *Rhododendron Pie*, her first, was written in the statutory month: accepted, it must have earned her a good bit more than the monthly sum on which she had planned to live. By 1930 she was launched; but it was another two years before she managed her second novel – always a tricky ordeal for a budding novelist, but fortunately *Fanfare for Tin Trumpets* earned the same praise and rewards as its predecessor.

From then on she was to produce at least one and often two novels a year, as well as children's books and short stories. The excellence of her work became more and more recognised, and the number of her fans and admirers grew steadily greater. Like Jane Austen, or, in her own time, writers like Elizabeth Bowen or Barbara Pym, she never tried to write about a world with which she was not wholly familiar. At the same time all her books have the common touch, as well as a kind of freedom and adventurousness about them. Like all really good novelists, she created her own world, which is itself an aspect of her humour, her sense of fun, and a sense of fellow-feeling with her characters. But she is, as it were, the least 'superior', in herself, of all technically and brilliantly superior social novelists. As a spectator and narrator she knows exactly what she is seeing and doing, and what effects she wants to achieve, but she sees her world, herself too, with as much modesty and amusement as self-possession. As a distinguished and distinctive writer, at home in the world of her art, and wholly its master, she remains none the less wholly unpretentious.

In 1938 Margery married Major Geoffrey Castle, an aeronautical engineer; the marriage was clearly an extremely happy one although they never had children. That was not unusual amongst good novelists of the time who happened to be women. Virginia Woolf was childless; so were Elizabeth Bowen, Margery's friend and admirer, the poet and novelist Stevie Smith, the novelist and philosopher Iris Murdoch. Would Jane Austen have written all or any of her incomparable novels had she married and given birth to the considerable family that was customary at her period and in her circle? We do not know – indeed it is much better not to know – whether these brilliant and talented women made a deliberate choice, or how much was due to accident and circumstance. Their creative work – the novels, stories and poems which are, as it were, their family – speak for themselves. What seems indisputable is that Margery and her husband were very happy as they were, living, as Margery put it in her humorous-sardonic way, 'happily ever after'. There are one or two male figures in her novels – heroes of course – who may bear some sort of likeness to her husband, but as in the case of other writers I have mentioned, her admirable feeling for, and knowledge of, different social scenes clearly contains nothing so crude as a portrait from the life.

The couple were lucky enough to obtain a flat in Albany, just off Piccadilly, an extremely exclusive address since Edwardian days and earlier – Byron, Gladstone and Bulwer Lytton had all stayed there at one time and during Margery's tenure there were two other writers in residence, J. B. Priestley and Georgette Heyer. By the time the couple moved in Margery's earnings from her books, together with her husband's salary, were no doubt quite enough to make such an address possible; but before her marriage Margery had continued to live a happy Bohemian life ('It was a most agreeable time,' she wrote later) with her girlfriends in the shabby little Paddington flat. When war came in 1939, a year after her marriage, she was soon absorbed into a branch of the armed services, becoming an army education lecturer. She worked hard and conscientiously, sometimes giving ten talks a week at military camps and on anti-aircraft sites. But meanwhile she never for a moment stopped writing. *Cluny Brown* and *Britannia Mews* were two notable novels written during the war, both of which later became successful films, the first starring Jennifer Jones and the famous Hollywood Charles Boyer.

Margery's novels, indeed, seem to have turned into films with an almost miraculous ease, and her *Rescuer* series for children was even animated by Disney. But she left all such matters to an agent, and to the film-makers concerned. She never interfered, or wished to interfere, in technical matters outside her own sphere as a writer. Film directors loved her apparently, because she never objected, or tried to influence the cinematic treatment of her stories, however much the needs of a film caused these to vary from the original.

Each of her novels has its own charm, its own virtues and individuality. *Cluny Brown* and *Harlequin House* contain particularly memorable portraits – the latter the hero and the former the heroine. But few of her readers would dispute that *The Eye of Love* is, on balance, her undoubted masterpiece. It is the novel her old readers will be most glad to see reprinted, and the one most certain to attract a new readership who have not encountered her books before.

This must be due to the instantaneous effect produced at the outset by young Martha, and also by Miss Diver. There they are, when we open the novel: to be, as it were, immediately recognised and accepted. We feel that we know them at once, and knowing them, become pleasurably curious: we want to know what will happen to them. The same classic effect is produced by Jane Austen's Bennet family at the beginning of *Pride and Prejudice*. It is rare even in a good novel, although when it comes off, as it does in *The Eye of Love*, it gives the impression of effortless ease, and a self-confidence which has nothing pretentious about it. The novel seems to give itself to us generously in those opening pages, like an experience which is already delightful, and to the development of which we keenly look forward.

The first promise is in the title itself. It is not only a good title but a true one. An 'eye of love' is needed if we are really to *see*: both emotionally and aesthetically. What such an eye sees has its own kind of accuracy, and its own kind of truth. It is with this eye that Harry Gibson sees Miss Diver, his 'Spanish Rose'; and it is with the same eye that his beloved, that so very ordinary little woman, that 'Skinny Lizzie, of a certain age', sees her 'King Hal'. There is a remarkable absence of sentimentality about this. True love by its very nature is never sentimental: it does not need to be. Even more certain than the fact itself – in so far as the art of the novel is concerned – is Margery Sharp's judicious and businesslike presentation of it.

So is her presentation of young Martha, and her peculiar but wholly believable talent. When Martha sees something that she can draw, whether it is the gas stove in the kitchen or the grating in the street gutter that 'the eye of love can turn into a Greek temple', she devotes to its particular kind of reality all her youthful concentration. The success of Martha as a character, and as an important part of the story, may depend to a large extent on the author's own early training as an artist, on her sense of the budding artist's psychology. Within the framing of the novel there is no telling whether Martha's down-to-earth vision, and the abilities that go with it, would have had any success as she grew up, or whether they would have diminished and disappeared, together with the eye of childhood which had made them possible. Margery Sharp is no more sentimental about this aspect of the eye of love than she is about its effects on the emotions. Like Martha herself she notes such matters, as author and professional, with her own unmoved and expert eye.

Martha is very distinctly complete in herself, like one of her own drawings; and it was possibly an error on the author's part, although an understandable one, to be tempted by the success of the novel into following it up, and creating a later career for her heroine. *Martha in Paris*, and *Martha, Eric and George*, written some years after *The Eye of Love*, are, so to speak, excellent working novels, but neither is quite a masterpiece in the sense their progenitor was. At the time, and earlier, during the twenties and thirties, there was something of a vogue for the follow-up novel, which might expand into a whole series, like those created by Hugh Walpole, and after the war by Pamela Hansford Johnson, whose trilogy *An Avenue of Stone* was written at much the same time as *The Eye of Love*. *The Eye of Love* came out in 1957 although its action takes place in 1932 – a year of serious industrial and commercial depression in England, as the author unobtrusively reminds us.

But times and dates are of no great importance to *The Eye of Love*. In its characters and story there is a genuinely timeless quality. There is nothing conventional about them either, in spite of a happy ending, which, although admittedly contrived with the author's eye upon the average library reader at the time, has nothing forced or implausible about it. Indeed, given what happens in the novel, and given the nature of those taking part in its action, what takes place really does seem the most likely way things would have turned out. Virtue is not only rightly but convincingly rewarded. Admittedly it is a stroke of luck that Mr Joyce, a friend and associate in the fur trade of Mr Conrad of Richmond, should discover the latter needs a new manager at the very moment when he has himself no choice but to sack his great friend, and our hero, Harry Gibson. He has to sack Harry because Harry has jilted Mr Joyce's 'unmarriageable' daughter Miranda, whom Harry had undertaken to wed as part of a business deal, and to save his own business from bankruptcy.

The reason for the jilting of Mr Joyce's daughter is of course the heart and the romance of the novel. Miranda Joyce is hardly a character to command our sympathy, but as a personality she is superbly drawn. One of the most agreeably subtle touches in the book is the way in which father and daughter come invisibly to terms with the situation: the one taking comfort from his business sense of a deal which might have gone worse than it did – the other from her naturally vindictive determination to show the world that she herself had done the jilting – or at least the breaking-off – and not her faithless lover.

So she puts it about among her friends – Rachel and Marion and Denise and the rest – that her faithless lover had done 'something really awful' in the course of business, which left her poor father with no choice but to sack him out of hand. What a relief for her, since she'd only accepted her horrid old suitor in the first place because 'Dadda' had been set on it!

This double libel Mr Joyce bore with patience: though he didn't care for being branded as either a harsh parent or a poor judge of character, he felt Miranda in the circumstances entitled to do the best she could for herself; and recognised with pleasure that in the character of a girl who could have got married, but chose not to, she was on to a very nice thing.

Although Miranda and her father are in almost every other way so different, this wishing to be on to 'a very nice thing' is something they cannot help having in common. Did Margery Sharp know anything about fur-owners and the Fur Business? The reader may feel confident that she did, however she came by the knowledge: and also that she was familiar with the upper echelons of the sort of people – to a large extent prosperous and assimilated Jewish people – who ran it. Harry's ancestors came from Moscow and were most likely Jewish immigrants; while in all sorts of unobtrusive ways, the speech, background and ideology of a class and a tribe are warmly, accurately, and delicately indicated.

No novelist of the time could have been more adroit than Margery Sharp at preparing the right sort of climax, and the right sort of conclusion. All tragedy, as the author once truly remarks, is mingled with absurdity, a fact with which Shakespeare himself was as unemphatically familiar as was the author of *The Eye of Love*. Romance itself must depend on the absurd – indeed thrive upon it. King Hal and his Spanish Rose are both romantic, and beautiful to and for each other: but to the eye of the outside world they can only seem ridiculous. Mr Joyce, to do him the justice he deserves, comes, however dimly, to apprehend this fact.

'All moonshine!' thought Mr Joyce . . . Yet what was moonshine but a belittling name for love? Employed only by the envious? 'My poor Harry and his Kiss of Death, they love each other,' thought Mr Joyce uneasily. He gazed earnestly at his friend and tried to make him look like a King. It was no use . . . The eye of friendship couldn't do it, only the eye of love . . . So love it was.

None the less, tragedy in its weariest most commonplace sense – the sense in which Arnold Bennett called life – and by implication the work of art that is true to life, a tragedy in ten thousand acts – is in this novel never far away. All the time he reads the reader has a vivid sense of what *could* have happened, indeed of what could still happen, did the novel, in its own way and for its own purpose, not protect its reader from such grim possibilities. Harry Gibson might have found himself absolutely unable not to marry Miranda Joyce; necessity might have compelled Dolores to accept the hand of her drably calculating suitor Mr Phillips; in the dismal hurly-burly of an equal necessity Martha might have been ground in the same mill of unremitting fate and unhopeful existence. So, too, she might have lost her eye, and its promising passion for seeing and drawing gas stoves and pavement gratings.

All such dire and dreary things *might* have happened; and in life some of them, or all of them, very likely would have happened. But the artificial needs of the novel are not always misleading. The climax and conclusion of *The Eye of Love* is beautifully planned: it is both satisfying and convincing. Thomas Hardy, in his novels, would never have permitted such an ending; but Hardy's insistence that the worst should happen, by contrived coincidence or the sheer malignancy of fate, is in fact often no more convincing than some happier ending would have been. Indeed his endings are actually often *less* convincing, for Hardy's own thumb, as writer and plot-composer, is far more obviously and more pressingly in the scale than is that of the novelist who feels no compulsive urge to demonstrate the evil will towards mankind of the Fates, or the cruelly indifferent gods.

Indeed Margery Sharp has no wish to demonstrate anything. She wants to write a good novel, and a good novel by its very nature teaches and illuminates without any need to spell it out, or administer dogmatic instruction. Nor does she, as an author, ever air her prejudices, assuming she had any; it comes naturally to most good novelists of her kind to seem to have none. If she had any 'politically correct' feelings about the Fur Trade (and in 1957 there were already plenty who did) she does not air them or even reveal them; nor does she drop any hint that women are a drown-trodden sex, or that it was a shocking thing that Martha was not being properly educated at school.

By the time she died, in 1991, Margery Sharp could look back on a long lifetime of literary success. She had written twenty-six novels, stories both for children and adults, fourteen full-length books for children, a stage play, *Meeting at Night*, produced in London in 1934, and a television play twenty years later, as well as having two of her novels turned into successful plays.

She was also blessed with a long and happy marriage which, being a wise woman with an eye of love, she may well have valued more than all her many literary achievements. It was, and is, for her readers themselves to get the benefit of her books; and I should be surprised indeed if the republication of this masterpiece of hers does not stimulate a new interest in her as a remarkable writer, and produce a new set of fans for it, and for the rest of her novels.

John Bayley
2003

PART I

CHAPTER ONE

I

Seen from eye-level, (as the child Martha, flat on her stomach, saw it), the patch of pebbly grass in the back-garden of 5, Alcock Road had all the charm, mysteriousness and authority of a classic Chinese landscape. Tall shot-up bents, their pale yellow stems knotted like bamboos, inclined gracefully before the wind; across a sandy plain boulders in proportion carried a low scrub of lichen to the foot of a mountain shaped like a mole-hill. There was only the right amount of everything, and only one sharp note of colour: pimpernel-red a wild azalea bloomed under the bamboos.

Suddenly the whole composition was altered, the whole land-scape receded, as into the foreground leapt a tiger – drawn to a different scale, in fact life-size. For a moment the round striped face glared with Chinese ferocity, the lips writhed back in a Chinese scowl; then the cat recognised the child, and the child a cat.

From the house, from one of the pink-curtained windows, a voice called high and urgent – Miss Diver's.

'Martha! Come and say how do you do to Mr Gibson!'

Martha remembered it was Tuesday, and reluctantly rose, and dusted herself down the front.

More precisely, it was the second Tuesday in June, 1932: a date to be of importance.

Ladies of ambiguous status have by convention hearts of gold, and Miss Diver was nothing if not conventional; but a child in an irregular household is often an embarrassment. It had been wonderfully kind of Miss Diver to save her brother's child from an orphanage, but not surprising; what was surprising was how well the arrangement worked out.

Martha came when she was six, and was now nine: during those three years the quiet harmony of life at 5, Alcock Road continued unjarred. In part this was due to Mr Gibson's good-nature; even more important, in the daily contacts between aunt and niece, was a safeguard never in fact recognised as such – though it had operated from the start. Little Martha was never allowed to address her benefactress as Aunt. To the latter's ear the appellation lacked romance; romance being of Miss Diver's life the essence, she instructed Martha to call her by her first name instead; the happy if un-aimed-at result was a superficial chumminess putting no strain on the emotions of either. – Also due to Miss Diver's romanticism was the fact that they no longer shared the same patronymic, which was for both, legally, Hogg. Miss Diver's brother, Martha's father, had been Richard Hogg: Martha was Martha Hogg: but even while still vending haberdashery Miss Diver had so sincerely felt herself not-Hogg, so to speak, and practically going under a false name, that in the interests of truth (or at least of verisimilitude), she changed to Diver. Besides commemorating a favourite authoress, it went euphoniously with her initial D. The D stood for Dolores, itself modulated from Dorothy because Miss Diver was a Spanish type.

'You shall call me Dolores,' instructed Miss Diver – actually in the taxi going home from Richard Hogg's funeral.

She had never seen the child until an hour earlier; she had never before visited the shabby Brixton lodging-house in whose shabby parlour the thinly-attended wake was being held. A dozen or so of Richard Hogg's ex-colleagues from the Post Office stared inquisitively; this meeting between the two chief mourners provided a touch of drama, something to talk about afterwards, otherwise conspicuously lacking. (As Doctor Johnson might have said, it wasn't a funeral to *invite* a man to: only one bottle of sherry, and fish-paste sandwiches. Richard Hogg, with his motherless daughter, had lodged two full years in Hasty Street; but a landlady never does these things so whole-heartedly as relations, even with the Burial Club paid up and next week's rent in hand.) Interest naturally focused on Miss Diver, partly because her brother had never mentioned her, and partly because of her appearance. Though the only person present in proper mourning – even Martha had no more than an arm-band – Dolores' total blackness somehow produced a brighter effect than the neutral tints of everyone else. She was jetty, they merely subfusc. Her black Spanish hair gleamed beneath her eye-veil. Her black fur was a black fox. Her black pumps were patent leather. Dolores, for her part, felt like a bird of paradise among crows. . . .

She felt also like an angel of mercy; and so took little Martha home with her, in obedience to a law not so much unwritten as written to excess, in every sentimental novel of that date, which was 1929.

'You shall call me Dolores,' instructed Miss Diver, in the taxi that bore them away.

The child Martha, then aged six, looked placidly co-operative. She was a fat, placid-looking child altogether. Her squarish face, pale under a sandy fringe, didn't appear ravaged by any particular sorrow, as her rather small grey eyes, under rudimentary eye-brows, weren't red with weeping. The bundle of clothes at her feet – her last link with the past – she simply put her feet on, to make her short legs more comfortable. It was Miss Diver, aged thirty-seven, who wept.

3

The arrangement worked out better than anyone could have expected. In Hasty Street, indeed, for many a day to come Martha was looked for back bag and baggage. 'I've seen *her* sort before,' declared the landlady – in grim reference to Miss Diver. 'Give a thing and take a thing—! By which same token, if *she* don't tire, someone else will.' The luscious prognostication proved false. Mr Gibson, he who subsidised the little house with the pink curtains, accepted Martha without demur. He had often feared that his Dolores might be lonely, and trusted her not to let the child become a nuisance. As was inevitable, Miss Diver went through a brief period of sentimentality – during which she bought little Martha a three-legged stool to sit on and a box of beads to thread: fortunately if there was one thing Mr Gibson detested it was treading on a bead. He didn't actually swear at Martha, but the effort not to was obvious, and Dolores was saved from prolonging what might have been a disastrous experiment. She was a trifle let down herself. All children under eight have charm, just as all young animals have, but little Martha had less than most. She didn't *perch* on the stool, she squatted on it. The beads stuck to her fat fingers, when she didn't drop them, and she was always losing her needle. The picture envisaged by Miss Diver had been very different. She was still thankful she hadn't started with bubble-blowing, because heaven knew what little Martha mightn't have done with a basin of soapy water . . .

After this preliminary fumble, however, Miss Diver managed very well. She realised at once that if the child was unacceptable as a fixture, she would be even less acceptable – how to put it? – dodging about. From dodging about, therefore, Martha was above all things discouraged; but the situation wasn't dodged either. Whenever Mr Gibson arrived, Miss Diver summoned her to say how do you do and shake hands; thus not only avoiding any tedious pretence that she wasn't there, but also giving the signal for her to lie low.

Martha soon learnt. She didn't mind. Solitude suited her temperament. If it was fine enough, she lay low in the garden. It wasn't at all a pretty garden, the tiny lawn was rank and all the flowers nasturtiums; but Martha discovered landscapes in the wild grass, also after rain, or heavy dew, one could collect from the round nasturtium-leaves, employing a teaspoon, whole egg-cupfuls of liquid quite possibly medicinal. If it was necessary to stay indoors, an attic bedroom afforded delights of its own: a fresco of rabbits (legacy of Miss

Diver's first enthusiasm), a window overlooking the road, a whole year's back numbers of the *Tatler*. . . . For the epicurean enjoyment of these last Martha often put herself to bed, especially in winter, immediately after giving herself tea; a supper of milk and doughnuts to hand on the historic three-legged stool.

In Brixton she'd slept on a box-ottoman at the foot of the land-lady's bed. Ma Battleaxe, (Martha at least knew no other name for her), was a noisy sleeper. Snores half-articulate and vaguely threat-ening equally disgusted and alarmed – as did the set of false teeth in the beer-mug on the night-table. Any bedroom of her own would have made Martha happy, even without the *Tatlers*.

Solitude suited her. She had no other children to play with, and didn't want any. She didn't go to school. The point occasionally worried Dolores, but it didn't worry Martha. No education-officer spied her, and Dolores kept putting the matter off – reluctant to ask Mr Gibson for fees, reluctant also to encounter local officialdom. Martha slipped through the net of education as an under-sized salmon slips through the seine. She learnt to read and write – Dolores could manage that much; otherwise her mind was beauti-fully unburdened, and she had plenty of time to look at things.

For three years, in fact, the child Martha was perfectly happy. Whatever her temperament portended, it was being given full play. She had no regrets for the past. She couldn't remember her mother, and her father had never attached her. Dolores didn't interfere. Mr Gibson, as a sort of deity to be placated, fitted neatly into a child's pantheon: that one could placate him so easily, by one's mere absence, was a stroke of pure luck. Martha was lucky all round. Not a half of her solitary pleasures has as yet been described; seeing a tiger turn into a cat was a mere trifle.

She dusted herself down the front and stumped towards the house.

4

'How do you do, Mr Gibson?' asked Martha politely.

She couldn't shake hands because Mr Gibson, who was helping himself to a whisky-and-soda, had his back to her; he replied merely by a chuck of the head. Martha looked enquiringly towards Miss Diver. The latter was obviously feeling specially Spanish, specially Dolores; there was a high tortoiseshell comb in her hair, a shawl embroidered with peonies about her shoulders; that she reclined upon a settee covered in Rexine didn't, at least to Martha, spoil the effect at all. The Rexine was a good solid brown, against which the brilliant colours of the shawl glowed like the best sort of Christmas-cracker; the obtuse shape of the cushions threw into relief the attenuated shapes of Miss Diver's neck and forearms. It wasn't like the picture the thin grass made, but it was equally satisfying . . .

Miss Diver moved. Martha, once more alert to the moment's social necessities, re-focused an eye of enquiry. She was more than ready to return to the garden. But Dolores' nod wasn't, as usual, dis-missive; it enjoined remaining. And Mr Gibson, though he had by now proportioned whisky-and-soda to some ideal of his own, didn't say what he always said.

('Hey, Martha! Where's Mary?'

'In the Bible,' Martha always said.

'Best place for her,' Mr Gibson always said back.)

But he didn't say it now. Something was different, and therefore wrong.

Instinctively Martha glanced about the room for reassurance. It was mostly Art Nouveau, except for the settee and big arm-chairs. These were there because Mr Gibson needed to be comfortable after working so hard all day in the fur-trade, but Miss Diver had done her best to sophisticate them with black cushions, so that even they were fairly Nouveau. Martha admired the cushions extremely – as she also admired the splendid stained-glass galleon sailing across the upper panes of the bay-window, and the bowl of glass fruit that lit up from inside. Indeed, the whole room was a perfect treasure-house of beauties. Within a black-and-gold cabinet, for instance, frisked a family of stuffed ermines. The little table where Dolores kept ciga-rettes was inlaid with mother-o'-pearl. Upon it knelt a porcelain pierrot, holding the ash-tray, flanked by his companion-pierrette with the matches. Could the eye be offered more? It could. Best of all was the lady in bronze armour, a figure some eighteen inches high, her face and arms ivory, the bronze here and there gilded, a very ikon of luxury and refinement, from the Burlington Arcade.

She was still there. Everything was there, just as usual. But Mr Gibson hadn't said, 'Where's Mary?' Martha looked back at Miss Diver in search of the reassurance the room hadn't given her.

'Mr Gibson has come to say good-bye to us,' said Miss Diver in a low voice.

5

Martha's first thought was that now if ever was a time to shake hands. She admitted it freely: Dolores was right not to let her go before the ceremony had been performed. What annoyed her was Mr Gibson's unco-operativeness. He still stood with his back to her, swallowing noisily – and if he was still swallowing whisky-and-soda he was deliberately, in Martha's opinion, making it last.

'Good-bye,' said Martha pointedly.

Mr Gibson started; and at last turned. (The glass in his hand, as Martha had suspected, empty.) He always affected a certain bluff jocularity with her, and it was now more marked than ever – even lamentably so, in the circumstances, and in a man of fifty, large and going slightly bald.

'Toodle-oo, parlez-vous, good-byee,' declaimed Mr Gibson.

'Harry!' cried Miss Diver.

'As we used to say in the Great War,' added Mr Gibson uncontrollably. 'Good-bye, old thing, cheerio, chin-chin—'

'Harry!'

He managed to stop himself. It was like seeing an old car, or an old steam-engine, at last respond to the brakes. He shoved a hand out towards Martha – or he might merely have been gesticulating. In any case, Martha got hold of it.

'Aren't you going to say you're sorry?' prompted Miss Diver reproachfully.

Actually Martha did feel quite sorry. Nor was it from any apprehension as to the future, though this would have been justified. She felt sorry, saying good-bye to Mr Gibson, simply because she was used to him. But what she chiefly felt was embarrassment. For the first time she sensed, between these two elders, an emotion as strong as her own for the bronze lady (or for the ermines, or the pierrot). Dolores' head drooped against the Rexine like a nasturtium with its neck snapped. The ponderous frame of Mr Gibson was held erect only as a tomato-plant tied to a stick is held erect.

Looking from one to the other of them, Martha recognised, however obscurely, a distress she didn't want to be drawn into. She felt a more than usually urgent impulse to disappear – and further than the garden.

'I'm sorry. Can I go and look at the shops?' asked Martha.

'Go anywhere you like,' sniffed Dolores, beginning to cry.

Martha was out of the house before you could say knife.

CHAPTER TWO

I

As soon as they were alone again Mr Gibson sat heavily down beside Miss Diver and took her in his arms. Through the Spanish shawl he felt her sharp collar-bones; she, through his tweed jacket, A.S.C. tie and solid chest, the beating of his heart. Her tortoiseshell comb scraped him uncomfortably under the chin, but he would not ask her to remove it. He knew why it was worn – like the shawl.

'Remember the chappie who fell into the drum?' asked Mr Gibson tenderly.

They had met for the first time at a Chelsea Arts Ball – Dolores dressed as a Spanish Dancer, Mr Gibson as a brown paper parcel. He could thus hardly, even if he'd thought of it, have matched her gesture, but he appreciated it nonetheless.

'Of course I remember,' whispered Dolores.

'Remember those young devils who started to unwrap me?'

'It didn't matter. You'd pyjamas underneath. . . .'

'I shall never forget how wonderful you looked, pulling me out of the cardboard. . . .'

'I couldn't bear to see you laughed at,' murmured Dolores. 'You were too big. . . .'

They had revived the moment many times before, but never so tenderly.

'Then we danced together all the rest of the evening.'

'Of the night,' corrected Dolores.

'And then I lost you.'

'I got held up in the Cloaks.'

'And then I found you again. What a chance that was! – Just popping in to buy a tie, and there you were!'

'I'm sorry, Harry, but I can't bear it,' said Dolores.

She huddled closer against his solid chest. It was his solidness she'd always loved, as he her exotic frailty. For ten years they'd given each other what each most wanted from life: romance. Now both were middle-aged, and if they looked and sounded ridiculous, it was the fault less of themselves than of time.

To be fair to Time, each had been pretty ridiculous even at the Chelsea Ball. Miss Diver, in her second or third year as a Spanish Dancer, was already known to aficionados as Old Madrid. Mr Gibson, who had never attended before, found the advertised bohemianism more bohemian than he'd bargained for. To the young devils from the Slade, unwrapping him, his humiliated cries promised bare buff rather than pyjamas. Naked, indeed, he might have made headlines by being arrested; in neat Vyella, he was merely absurd. . . .

Dolores, Old Madrid, not only pitied his condition but also lacked a partner. She'd have been glad to dance with anyone, all the rest of the night. But though rooted in such unlikely soil their love had proved a true plant of Eden, flourishing and flowering, and shading from the heat of the day – not Old Madrid and Harry Gibson, but King Hal and his Spanish rose.

So they had rapidly identified each other – he so big and bluff, she so dark and fragile: as King Hal and his Spanish rose. Of all the couples who danced that night in the Albert Hall, they were probably the happiest.

'I can't help it,' sobbed Dolores. 'I mean remembering, now . . .'

'Poor old girl,' said Mr Gibson.

He didn't even eye the whisky. It was an effort, but he didn't. Instead he arranged Miss Diver more comfortably against his shoulder, and got out his handkerchief. – He could have used it himself, but for the strong-man rôle it was necessary for him to play.

Dolores didn't use the handkerchief either. She used, to Mr Gibson most touchingly, the fringe of her Spanish shawl.

'Harry. . . .'

'Yes, old girl?'

'I do understand, truly I do. I'm not going to make a fuss. But just because you're marrying to save the business—'

'To amalgamate it,' corrected Mr Gibson.

'To amalgamate it, then – need we, must we—?'

He pressed her closer, but she knew what the answer was. Indeed, she almost at once felt ashamed of her question. Mr Gibson's principles, or some of them, were high: certain of them rose like peaks from a low range – or rather like the mesas of a Mexican desert, that astonish travellers by their abruptness. He had never, for example, invited Dolores to assume his name, or even the married title, because he had such a respect for legal matrimony. 'We'll keep everything above-board,' said Mr Gibson. This did not prevent his concealing Miss Diver's existence from, for example again, his mother, under whose roof he continued to sleep five nights out of seven. Dolores was the romance in his life, its wonder and beauty for which he never ceased to be grateful; but the domestic gods still governed half his soul.

'I'm sorry,' apologised Dolores. 'I shouldn't have said that. I'm upset.'

Mr Gibson pressed her closer still. How wonderfully she understood! Just as wonderfully as she'd understood ten years earlier, when he brought her the lease of the little house. 'I don't like to think of you in the shop,' Mr Gibson explained, 'at any chappie's beck and call. I want you all to myself . . .' Dolores hadn't even hinted that there was another way of having her all to himself; she understood at once that important fur-merchants didn't marry girls from behind the counter. But though glad to get out of the shop on any terms (already troubled by fallen arches), basically she accepted the situation because she loved Mr Gibson. Romantically. Unlike her King Hal, who had lived unawakened to romance until he was forty, Miss Diver had been in search of it all her life. Why else had she rejected the pensionable post as telephonist, engineered for her

13

by her brother, to become an assistant in a West End haberdasher's? Why else (her heart and virtue, even in Piccadilly, so disappointingly unattacked) had she gone year after year to the Chelsea Arts Ball, until she was known as Old Madrid? She sought romance; and that she was thirty before she found it made it all the more wonderful when it came. To bloom in secret, the Spanish rose in King Hal's secret garden (actually number 5, Alcock Road, Paddington), had for ten years completely satisfied her.

Now all was over. She could exercise only one last right.

'You've told me so little, Harry, only about the business. Amalgamation—'

'It happens to be necessary,' said Mr Gibson heavily. 'I've never wanted to bother my little woman, but the fact is we're in a poor way. Amalgamating with Joyces' gets us out of the consommé.'

'Couldn't you amalgamate without marrying Miss Joyce?'

'It seems not,' said Mr Gibson – heavily.

There was a long pause. The declining sun, between the pink curtains, cast a sudden beam of brilliant light, making the stained-glass galleon sail in splendour. It was a moment the child Martha knew well.

'What's she like, Harry?'

'Cultured,' said Mr Gibson.

'How old?'

Mr Gibson hesitated. Miss Joyce's exact age was in fact unknown to him, and to say 'ripe' would have given a wrong impression. He answered obliquely.

'I'm not exactly a boy myself.'

'You are to me,' said Dolores. 'Will she make you happy?'

Again Mr Gibson hesitated.

'My mother says she will. Actually the mater is a cousin by marriage of her aunt.'

'So she must know all about her,' agreed Dolores, in a shaking voice. 'Or at least that she's cultured . . . Oh, Harry!'

It was no use, it was too soon to talk rationally, they had to break off and comfort each other.

'Dolores!' cried Mr Gibson – his voice shaking too.

'My Big Harry! My King Hal!' cried Miss Diver.

'My Spanish rose!' cried Mr Gibson.

They clung in genuine and ridiculous grief, collapsed together on the Rexine settee.

2

Martha was meanwhile out enjoying life.

She had been accorded periods of liberty before, but never so absolutely. She was used to getting her own supper, but always before seven. Now she simply made a mental note of cold sausages in the larder. (Martha never neglected her stomach. Though no longer fat, she was no more, at nine, the conventional skinny orphan. She was consolidating fat into muscle.) The cold sausages as it were an iron ration at base, Martha gently closed first the front door, then the front gate, on all adult embarrassingness.

She was wearing a navy-blue serge kilt, a navy-blue jersey, a brown straw hat and napper gloves. These last two items, picked up *en passant* in the hall, made her look very respectable. The time was about five o'clock.

The child Martha's only embarrassment now was that of riches. The nice shops in Queen's Road – the little house endowed by Mr Gibson stood on the confines of Bayswater and Paddington – competed for attention with shops scarcely nice at all in Praed Street, as did Paddington Station, all steam and bustle, with the rural peace of Kensington Gardens; and even so there were a couple of calls Martha meant to pay first. Actually it took her twenty minutes to reach the end of Alcock Road.

Immediately, there was the grating in the gutter. To anyone who troubled to squat on the curb and use their hands as blinkers, the iron bars of this gradually assumed the appearance of granite columns, ranged like the portico of a temple: a shift of focus advanced the strips of blackness in between, producing a prison-gate. Martha squatted here about ten minutes.

Directly across the road was a letter-box still bearing the monogram VR. To follow the raised curly letters with one's finger, covering every inch without jumping, was an exercise not to be resisted; it also, successfully accomplished, brought good luck for the rest of the day.

Beyond the letter-box beckoned a gate with a brass plate, carelessly cleaned. The smears of metal-polish all round dried white on the green paint in a different pattern each morning. To-day's was rather simple, just a flight of gulls, but Martha hadn't seen it. (As a rule she nipped across as soon as the careless maid went in.)

Three houses from Miss Taylor, chiropodist, if the front door happened to open, one could glimpse within a really remarkable umbrella-stand shaped like an enormous frog; worth hanging about quite a while for.

Martha's time of twenty minutes to the corner was in fact very good going, she could easily make Alcock Road last a whole afternoon. Now she was in a hurry.

Her first object was the Public Library, to which she had no official right of entry. (Children under twelve admitted only in company of an adult.) But her mild and serious contemplation of certain Chinese paintings, bequest of a nineteenth-century missionary, had so endeared her to the Librarian that he never found heart to apply the rules. Martha stumped in with justified confidence and had a good look.

Here was the real thing.

Reluctantly, Martha admitted it. Try as she would, she had never fixed, even among the unlimited possibilities offered by nine square feet of lawn, so satisfactory a balance between height, lesser height, and flat. (She didn't even know that this was what she attempted; she just wanted to get things right.) The bamboo brushed in ink swayed more lightly than the growing bents. The red of the painted azalea was more vivid than the red of the pimpernel – as the tiger on the next scroll was more lifelike than the living cat. . . .

'Tell me what they say to you,' prompted the kind, interested Librarian.

Martha didn't bother to reply. Having seen what she'd come to see, she turned and stumped out again without wasting energy. It was quite a long walk to Mr Punshon's.

Mr Punshon, who mended her own stout shoes and occasionally Dolores' pumps, was like all cobblers a politician: the walls of his narrow establishment were lined with cartoons from Rowlandson to Spy. Martha walked in and had a good look.

'No trade to-night?' enquired her friend humorously.

Martha stood politely on one leg to display a solid heel.

'Good leather,' said Mr Punshon, in self-approval. 'Want a dekko at my album?'

Martha hesitated. Mr Punshon's album, into which he pasted all the cartoons he hadn't room for on his walls, was very tempting. (It was bodily an old Burke's Peerage; Mr Punshon greatly enjoyed grangerising it with rude cartoons about the House of Lords.) But though Martha was tempted, her instinct told her she'd already looked at enough; even the contemplation of Mr Punshon's wall-display, after the Chinese paintings, had put a slight overload on eye and memory. . . .

'Thank you very much,' she said, 'but I'd rather come back.'

'Any time you like,' said Mr Punshon.

'Good night,' said Martha.

On the pavement outside she paused to consider her next move. What she now needed was relaxation, which to Martha meant using her ears instead of her eyes. Even looking in shop-windows wouldn't have relaxed her. Most fortunately, the little chapel neighbouring her friend's shop advertised a service of Help and Repentance for Hardened Sinners. Martha stumped in, and got a very good place up front.

3

Between the pink curtains no more sunlight penetrated. The sun had set. Exhausted by emotion, Dolores and Mr Gibson still sought to comfort each other.

'I shall be all right, Harry. You mustn't worry about me.'

'How can I help worrying about you?'

'I can easily go back to the shop.'

'Anywhere but that!' cried Mr Gibson.

Amazing, extraordinary power of love! Considering the state of the labour-market, anywhere else indeed, no West End haberdasher was going to look twice at Old Madrid: Mr Gibson was moved by jealousy. He saw his Spanish rose plucked across the counter by another's hand.

'I couldn't stand it, you're too attractive,' said Mr Gibson. He paused, fighting against fate. 'There's still half a year of the lease to run . . .'

'It can be sub-let.'

'Six months would give you time to look about.'

'No,' said Dolores. It was now she who took the high-minded lead, and though too delicate to put the argument into words she had also no need to – so used they were to reading each other's thoughts. Mr Gibson at once knew what she was reminding him of: any money he could lay hands on, for the coming year at least, would be Joyce money: in fact, a dowry.

'If we say toodle-oo, I think it makes a difference,' pleaded Mr Gibson. 'I believe anyone would think so.'

'No,' repeated Dolores.

'I always knew I wasn't worthy of you,' groaned Mr Gibson.

'But if my King Hal doesn't want me to go into a shop again, I promise him I won't.'

'You should have been a Queen,' groaned Mr Gibson. 'I wouldn't mind a Ladies' Department so much.'

'Just trust me, Harry, that's all I ask.'

'Or a Children's Wear. At least you'll have Martha to be a comfort to you,' cried Mr Gibson.

This was the first time, in some three hours, that either he or Miss Diver had remembered the child Martha; and as though there was now no comfort to be found anywhere, no sooner were the words out of Mr Gibson's mouth than he regretted them. Companionable as she might be in Dolores' sorrow, the child Martha would need to be fed and clothed; and Mr Gibson knew his beloved's resources almost to a shilling. She had a hundred pounds in the Post Office (chiefly because a horse called April the Fifth had won the Derby), ten one-pound notes he'd just put under the pierrot, and in her purse probably some loose change. He'd never been able to give her jewels – only a garnet brooch shaped like a heart, and it was a stroke of luck that garnets were her birth-stone. Together, recklessly, in the first days of their romance, they'd bought the bronze lady, as the most beautiful object they'd either of them ever seen; but even at the time Mr Gibson knew it wasn't a good investment. Now his one consolation was that he'd paid the gas-bill. He had the receipt in his breast-pocket.

As usual following his thought –

'Don't worry, Big Harry,' whispered Dolores. 'We'll manage.'

'I'm leaving you too much for any little woman to shoulder.'

'Just don't worry, my darling.'

'How can I help worrying!' cried Mr Gibson uncontrollably.

'How can I help worrying about *you*!' cried Miss Diver.

The settee creaked again under their embrace, Martha was forgotten, everything was forgotten, except love and despair.

4

All children enjoy charades. Martha, in the little chapel beside the cobbler's, naturally presented herself as a Hardened Sinner. The penitents' bench in any case needed patronage; after a really moving address only Mr Johnson, besides herself, advanced to be saved. Martha happened to know Mr Johnson quite well; he sold matches on the curb in Queen's Road, and when Martha could spare a penny she often patronised him, as a tribute to his extraordinary profile. (No gargoyle was uglier: he had a broken nose that under apish brows twisted east-west-east, and practically no chin. What broke Mr Johnson's nose was a blow with a knuckle-duster in his palmy days as bookie's tout, but on the tray of matches it said 'Old Contemptible, Wounded At Mons'.) Martha, unlike most people, enjoyed looking at him, and Mr Johnson appreciated it; kneeling side by side in their prominent positions they exchanged friendly glances.

'Wotcher think *you*'re doing 'ere?' muttered Mr Johnson, out of the side of his mouth.

'Repenting,' said Martha rather loudly.

'That's no tone o' voice to repent in,' said Mr Johnson snobbishly. 'Pipe down a bit . . .'

5

Hours passed, evening passed to night, and Miss Diver and Mr Gibson still hadn't stirred: as though to move at all was to initiate the act of parting. Mostly they were silent; only now and again some specially poignant memory was too precious not to voice.

'Do you remember the first time you gave me oysters, Harry?'

'You looked like a little girl taking medicine.'

'You said, "Now I know why they call the world an oyster. At last I've found my pearl."'

'You made a poet of me,' said Mr Gibson.

Fortunately it was quite a warm night. They weren't unbearably cold.

'Remember the first time we went to the Derby?' breathed Mr Gibson. 'When you wouldn't take the gypsy's warning?'

'Against a tall handsome stranger? When there you *were*? What I'd have lost if I had!' breathed back Dolores. 'My Big Harry, my King Hal!'

It wasn't too uncomfortable, on the settee. Presently indeed, shortly after midnight, Miss Diver fell asleep; and then at last Mr Gibson gently extricated himself, and took her in his arms, and carried her upstairs, and laid her on the big double couch that had witnessed first their inexpert embraces, and latterly (what in fact suited both much better) their calm connubial repose. It wasn't difficult, physically, for Mr Gibson to pull the coverlet over his love and leave her to sleep alone: it only broke his heart. One final weakness he permitted himself; when he drew the comb from her hair he put it, still warm, into his pocket. Then he pulled the curtains across the window, and went quietly downstairs, and walked home to his mother's flat in Kensington.

Martha had long before entered by the kitchen-window, and stuffed a pound of cold sausages into her hardy stomach, and gone to bed. She'd had a fine time.

CHAPTER THREE

I

Good morning, Mater,' said Harry Gibson. 'Have you come to watch me drink my tea?'

'It won't be I much longer,' said old Mrs Gibson. Her bright shrewd eye, round and brown as a berry, glanced swiftly over the table; she was sixty-nine, and had been up to set it herself. 'Eat your good eggs, Harry, and your toast and butter and marmalade. I like to see you!'

'I know you do,' said Mr Gibson glumly. 'It's why I'm overweight.'

'Who wants to see a big man like a scarecrow? Thank God your father put on some flesh before the end!' cried Mrs Gibson dramatically. 'That his last breath didn't smell of starvation!'

'It smelt of port.'

'I thank God for that too,' agreed Mrs Gibson resourcefully. 'What an end for my Peter after all, to die with the smell of wine on his mouth! – Those eggs are double-yolked.'

Harry Gibson regarded them inimically. He had no appetite. But he wasn't certain whether or not his mother had heard him come in, and the best way to avoid questioning was to behave as normally as possible. As he cracked one of the double-yolked eggs, and began to eat it, it crossed his mind that he would at least have to explain his future non-absences on two nights of the week. They were officially spent in Leeds, where he had invented a tie-up with a department-store.

Whether or not because he managed to swallow, his mother didn't question him. Nor did she continue, for which he was thankful, in the vein of dramatic reminiscence. Quite apart from the fact that it was too early, Mr Gibson had been trying all his life to shut his ears to just such recitals: the tale of his father's heroic flight from Moscow (1880) in search of political freedom and wider opportunities in the cheap-fur line, was something he strictly didn't want to hear. For Harry Gibson was British to the core. He was British-born, and proud of it, and did everything he could think of to make himself a true son of Empire. By a really remarkable feat of will, he couldn't remember any other surname than Gibson. In 1914, at the age of thirty-two, he volunteered for Kitchener's Army (they wouldn't take him until three years later), and it was the greatest satisfaction of his life to have held the King's Commission. (He'd have given a leg to be decorated, and could probably have summoned up the necessary valour; but Service Corps rarely engage an enemy.) He could even recognise the slight un-Englishness of his relation with his mother: calling her Mater was an attempt to bring it into line. In short, Mr Gibson had all his life devoted himself to becoming a true-blue Britisher – solid, humdrum, unemotional; and succeeded so well, that in middle-age his rejection of a genuinely exotic background took revenge, and he fell for a pseudo-Spanish rose.

'Dolores!' thought Mr Gibson, in silent anguish. 'What will become of you, O my Dolores, without your King Hal?'

The human countenance affording but a limited range of expressions, even a mother cannot always read her child's mind. What old Mrs Gibson saw in Harry's face was a justified regret that he hadn't been left a sounder business. She therefore made haste to direct a bright if oblique light upon his immediate prospects.

'When you see Miranda this evening, I shall not come with you, you will just give her my best love. How glad I am you have always liked her!'

Mr Gibson remained silent. The thought of the interview ahead of him, the proposal-in-form, was pure nightmare.

'As she has always liked you,' added Mrs Gibson, 'which of course is natural. Such a fine figure of a man my Harry is – not a scarecrow!

Do you know what we said to each other yesterday, her Aunt Beatrice and I? We said, "Why ever didn't it happen before!"'

Harry Gibson pushed away his plate.

'For goodness' sake, Mater,' he said heavily, 'let you and I at least be frank with each other. Whom else have I to be frank with?'

The old berry-eyes flickered. Mrs Gibson did not look unhappy.

'I agree there have been greater beauties,' she admitted companionably. 'But what an education! What piano-playing! You will be able to give musical evenings. How well I remember at your grandfather's house in Moscow—'

'Please, Mater!'

'Very well, then, forget Moscow! You are quite right, with such a future before you! My dear Harry, you are going to be so happy!'

'I agree that it's something not to go bankrupt,' said Harry Gibson.

With a sudden incautious gesture Mrs Gibson flung up her hands.

'And I suppose it's something not to leave our nice flat! I suppose it's something not to sell my nice furniture, to buy bread! I suppose it's something your old mother won't have to go out as a scrubwoman! Aren't all these somethings too?'

'At last you're being frank with me,' said Harry Gibson. 'And of course you are quite right.'

He got up and went to wash his hands, as he'd always trained himself to do, after any meal, and got his bowler hat and his umbrella, and came back to kiss the mater, before he went off. What pleasure these simple actions had given him year after year! Now he performed them as slowly as possible, not to savour them, but to hold back the day's events.

2

A mile away in Knightsbridge, Mr Joyce also was leaving for the day's work. He was a small, spare man, half the bulk of Harry Gibson, and so much shorter than his daughter that she had to stoop to kiss his cheek as Aunt Beatrice pecked at him from the other side. Mr Joyce stood passive between them, as he'd learnt to do, in his good custom-built suit and his neat spring overcoat –

Miranda always had him tailored in Savile Row – and waited for her to pat down, as she always did, the neat pearl pin in his neat grey tie.

'What time do you want me back?' asked Mr Joyce.

'Any time you like, Dadda!' said Miranda gaily. 'So long as you don't come into the drawing-room until you're fetched!'

Mr Joyce nodded intelligently, and with a spry step departed for Bond Street. This spryness was something of a trial to Miranda, who worked hard to make her parent look distinguished; even wearing the best Savile Row suit, once in motion Mr Joyce looked chiefly spry. (Miranda had her eye on Harry Gibson's apparel also: she meant to tone him first down, then up.) To-day, however, she was in no mood to regard anyone with discontent – not even old Beatrice, despite an overnight quarrel about the housekeeping.

'Auntie Bee, why don't you make us your special goulash? For dinner?'

'Does Harry like it?' enquired the old woman anxiously.

'Of course he likes it! Make us your *mont blanc* as well!'

There was nothing old Beatrice enjoyed more than a field-day in the kitchen. She began her preparations at once, while Miranda kept an appointment at the hairdresser's.

3

The child Martha was just waking up. She had naturally slept late. When at last her appetite roused her, she was pleased to find the little house so still. It gave her a free run of the kitchen, and there were eggs. Breaking three or four into the frying-pan she produced a sort of omelette, unorthodox but satisfying; and finding a pair of kippers set them tails up in a jug of boiling water as a second course. An hour later she felt very comfortable.

It was only then that she remembered saying good-bye to Mr Gibson. She logically presumed him gone for good. His departure didn't trouble her, however (she could take Mr Gibson or leave him), except in its effect on Dolores: the aura of adult grief, on the verge of which she had stood the previous night, affected the child Martha as the aura of sickness affects an animal. But though the herd may shun the stricken deer, Martha couldn't altogether shun Miss Diver, and she hoped extremely that Dolores would soon cheer up.

In Martha's experience, what cheered adult females was tea. (Ma Battleaxe in Brixton had been used to brew a dozen cups a day, so cheerless she and her cronies: Martha remembered them huddled round the pot like a coven of witches – Miss Fish and Mrs Hopkinson and Miss Jones – capping tales of wicked lodgers.) Dolores obviously hadn't breakfasted; Martha therefore, and it must be admitted chiefly out of self-regardfulness, made a nice cup of tea and carried it upstairs.

The door stood ajar; she padded in – and almost, because the curtains were still pulled, back into pre-dawn. The light had also an odd watery quality; Martha couldn't help pausing a moment to observe Dolores' bedroom transformed into a marine landscape. The big double divan loomed like a low rock, still half-awash under the tides of night: beyond, between the windows, the dressing-table rose baroque and pinnacled as the pavilion-end of a pier. – But the tea was cooling; Martha paddled on in, kicking aside a shawl as she might have kicked aside a jelly-fish, and gained the bed-side table as she might have gained a buoy.

Dolores lay very flat – as though drowned. Beneath the coverlet her narrow shape thrust up only two small peaks of feet. Even her head was down flat, the pillow at some point in her sleep having been thrust away. She was in fact sound asleep still; but Martha wasn't going to waste pains.

'Wake up!' said Martha loudly.

Miss Diver stirred; reached out a groping hand, uttered a little unhappy cry, and slept again. There was nothing for it but to shake her, and Martha had no hesitation in doing so.

'Wake up!' repeated Martha impatiently. 'I've brought you a nice cup of tea!'

With interest, but without surprise, she saw the cantrip work. Miss Diver opened her eyes and lifted herself a little. (Also, in the same movement, pulled the quilt higher – because she was fully dressed. So paradoxically do the conventions operate.)

'You've brought me a cup of tea?' repeated Miss Diver, wonderingly.

'To cheer you up,' explained Martha. 'I'm sorry I've eaten everything else, but if you'd like some bread and jam I could get you that too. . . .'

By this incident was the immediate pattern of their lives decided. For all her brave words to Mr Gibson, Miss Diver had reserved somewhere at the back of her mind the linked images of Martha and a nice orphanage. Miss Diver, with her closer experience, wasn't nearly so certain as Mr Gibson that Martha was going to be a comfort. They got on together very well, but never once in three years had a childish hand slipped confidingly into her own, nor a childish kiss spontaneously rewarded her care. In fact, had Miss Diver ever been able to pierce the clouds of self-induced romanticism, she'd have described her niece Martha as perfectly heartless. Before the chilling wind of Mr Gibson's dreadful news, those clouds momentarily parted. Miss Diver's unconscious mind, while she slept, had consolidated a new image of Martha altogether, and one almost unfairly realistic. Waking alone, Miss Diver would certainly have re-examined the advantages, to both of them, of a nice orphanage . . .

Now Martha brought her a cup of tea – to cheer her up. What more could a child of nine do? The clouds re-formed instantaneously. Swallowing tea and tears together, Miss Diver smiled gratefully at the kind little soul beside her bed.

'You're my little comfort,' affirmed Miss Diver.

Martha, again pleased to see the cantrip work, was far from realising what made it so efficacious. That very afternoon, however, Miss Diver set out in search of some employment that would support them both.

4

Mr Gibson's place of business was in Kensington; a very nice premises, taken when his father so rashly decided to launch out. It was over a high-class tailor's: there was a spacious show-room, with two private fitting-cabinets, a good work-room above, and a handsomely furnished office. The plate by the entrance still announced Gibson and Son: Mr Gibson glanced at it without piety.

In the show-room Miss Molyneux, vendeuse and model, and

Miss Harris, who fitted, were as usual discussing the private lives of film-stars. 'Why not?' thought Mr Gibson. They couldn't discuss the customers, because there weren't any; indeed it was only the endemic slackness of trade that made such pals of them at all. They broke off politely to bid their employer good morning, and Miss Molyneux had a message as well.

'Mrs Whittingtall phoned, Mr Gibson. The lady who looked at the nutria.'

'The one we offered to re-model at cost,' supplied Miss Harris.

'Well?' said Mr Gibson.

'She's decided against it, Mr Gibson.'

'Thank you,' said Mr Gibson. 'Come up to my office, both of you, in half an hour.'

'*Both* of us?' repeated Miss Molyneux, raising her plucked eye-brows. 'Suppose there's a customer?'

'There won't be,' said Miss Harris. But she was a good sort. 'Not at nine-thirty, dear,' she added tactfully. 'Luxury goods, I've often noticed, ladies rarely shop for much before lunch. . . .'

Mr Gibson went on upstairs. He didn't go into the work-room, because there was no one there. (In his father's rash hey-day it housed three girls and a cutter. Old Mr Gibson's downfall had been a passion for auctions; he bought up any quantity of second-hand goods, expecting to re-model and sell them at a handsome profit. Harry Gibson was presently over-loaded with such eccentric items as monkey-fur evening-capes.) Now there was no one at all, in the work-room, and Mr Gibson was momentarily glad of it.

There was naturally no one in the office. This also suited him: he needed the strictest privacy for his next act, which was to open the safe and place therein a Spanish comb. Recognising even as he per-formed it, its futility: how much longer would that safe remain inviolate? Joyce's accountants had been through the books a month before, and almost cynically returned them to Gibson custody; they could still at any moment re-enter. In a week, in two weeks, he'd have to find another monstrance. But so brittle a treasure couldn't be carried in the pocket, and he was perfectly aware that at home his mother went through his drawers.

The tortoiseshell was still warm. Mr Gibson's heart, if not his mind, refused to recognise that warmth as deriving from his own person. He shut Dolores' comb into the safe, first making a sort of nest for it with his handkerchief, as tenderly as if it had been a tress of her hair, newly-shorn.

There wasn't anything much to take out, beyond the ledgers. Mr Gibson studied them for some time – trying as so often before to spot where things had definitely begun to go wrong. Essentially it all boiled down to the auctions: a chinchilla coat, for instance, property of a Russian princess, his father had paid six hundred pounds for; it was still knocking about in store, no yellower than when bought, and now definitely unsaleable. A couple of bearskin rugs – 'My God, who wants bearskins?' thought Mr Gibson bitterly. 'Are we in the stuffed-animal line?' – had cost the firm two-fifty. 'They sent their equerries to bid against him,' thought Mr Gibson, full of hate for the entire Muscovite aristocracy, 'and he fell for it every time. But it's I who am left holding the cub – and now in the Depression!'

It was the Depression that had finished him off. 1932 was the year of the Depression, the year when even people who could afford new furs wouldn't buy them, because it was the thing to go shabby. 'All right, kill all trade together!' thought Mr Gibson violently. 'Where will taxes come from then?' But in his heart he knew the Depression only a final blow, that even if women started buying like mad again, Gibsons would never be able to unload a yellowing chinchilla coat . . .

The half-hour he'd allowed himself passed all too soon. All too soon – on the tick, in fact – Miss Molyneux and Miss Harris presented themselves in the doorway. There was nothing for it but to tell them.

'Come in, Miss Molyneux, come in, Miss Harris!' invited Mr Gibson – he hoped heartily. He hoped also that his heartiness would last out. Moderating it a little, he nonetheless achieved a fairly easy tone as he explained how a new era for them all was about to open. 'For all of us,' insisted Mr Gibson. 'You girls can come along too.' He was right to insist: he had made the retention of Miss Harris and Miss Molyneux a point of honour, and carried it with difficulty.

'Couldn't leave my girls behind, could I?' insisted Mr Gibson. 'Couldn't let down the old Regiment! So if you want to come along you can – even though it's toodle-oo to G. and S. . . .'

They weren't so distressed as he'd expected. He hadn't exactly looked for tears; but they evinced even a certain pleasure – especially Miss Molyneux. Joyces had such lovely *salons*, and in Bond Street! positively rejoiced Miss Molyneux: a girl showing furs at Joyces was really, if Mr Gibson understood, being really *looked* at, by ladies who knew musquash from lapin. 'And who *buy*,' added Miss Molyneux. 'Because depression or no depression, in Bond Street, Mr Gibson, you get all the foreign visitors. I believe I could sell *sables* there, Mr Gibson, just give me the chance!' 'Myself, I'm only too glad of any job, with this depression on,' said the more realistic Miss Harris; but she too looked pleased. 'Mr Gibson, I'll bring back monkey-fur!' declared Miss Molyneux earnestly. 'With Joyces' décor, I'll bring back monkey-fur. *Then* who's got the only skins in London?' 'We have,' said Mr Gibson grimly. 'No one else is such fools.' He didn't ask, he hadn't the heart to, why monkey-fur shouldn't have been brought back in his own show-room. He knew Miss Molyneux was right. It needed a décor like Joyces', to put monkey-fur across; and even if she succeeded in her mad project, the Gibson skins were by now half-bald . . .

The girls went off in high spirits, and Mr Gibson should have been glad. He tried to be glad, but the evening's engagement projected too heavy a shadow. It was all he could do to keep a stiff upper lip.

He had to fight hard not to telephone Miss Diver; and went without lunch in case Miss Diver should telephone him. But she too wasn't letting down the Regiment.

The few visitors to the show-room were such obviously poor prospects that Miss Molyneux didn't bother to summon him. Or else Miss Molyneux, her spirit already in Bond Street, wasn't bothering with *them*. Whenever Mr Gibson passed the door on his way downstairs (in case Dolores stood hesitant without), he heard nothing but heartless chatter about the beauties of the Joyce décor.

About four o'clock there arrived an immense bouquet of pink carnations. '*For Miranda, in case my busy boy forgets!*' his mother had scrawled on the card. Harry Gibson certainly hadn't forgotten Miss Joyce, but it was true he hadn't thought of flowers. Fortunately he met the messenger on the pavement, and so didn't have to explain them, or avoid explaining them, to Miss Harris and Miss Molyneux. Even the former seemed by this time to have lost her head a little: if she could once style a genuine skunk, Mr Gibson heard her declare, she'd show all Bond Street where it got off. . . .

Essentially he spent the day alone; yet felt it pass all too quickly.

5

Dolores knew her comb in Mr Gibson's keeping. When she had looked for it in the bedroom, and in the sitting-room, and in the hall and on the stairs, she knew he'd taken it. She wished it could have been – and for once the violence of romantic imagery was but plain-speaking – the ashes of her heart.

CHAPTER FOUR

I

Time, however slowly, passes. No one has yet found a way to hold it back. At six o'clock that evening a maid ushered Mr Gibson into the Joyce drawing-room – first floor, very good apartment in Knightsbridge – there to await his betrothed-to-be.

It was an excellent apartment. Considering that it housed only Miranda and her widowered father and her Aunt Beatrice, it was vast. The drawing-room alone, which Harry already knew fairly well, was at least four times the size of Dolores' sitting-room. Even a grand-piano didn't encumber it. From many points of view it was an ideal room for any confident suitor to be waiting in.

Seated in a handsome arm-chair, Mr Gibson waited. Seated in the stocks, he'd have been less ill-at-ease. Even physically he was uncomfortable, the great sheaf of carnations drooped awkwardly between his thighs and he didn't know where to put it down. But at least they were carnations, not roses . . . 'My Spanish rose!' thought Mr Gibson uncontrollably – and to his horror saw the bouquet, apparently of its own volition, describe a parabola through the air. He retrieved it furtively and laid it on the carpet beside him.

It was a good carpet, as the furniture was good furniture.

Joyces was a good firm.

Mr Gibson fortified his mind with the memory of their audited profits over the last five years. He was on to a good thing, better than his situation deserved, and he knew it. He knew he would never have been considered as a son-in-law (and derivatively as an associate), save as a last resort. Mr Gibson dwelt on the point, leaned on it; in his present frame of mind he preferred to think Miss Joyce's advertised liking for him a myth got up among the women. He didn't want her to like him. He wanted her to want to be married, as he himself wanted not to be made a bankrupt; he had an idea that as between man and woman it came to much the same thing.

A quarter of an hour passed long as a century. To an impatient lover it would no doubt have seemed longer: Mr Gibson was impatient only as a man about to be shot might be impatient. (Why hadn't he been shot, in '17?) The bitter parenthesis, by the memories it evoked, nonetheless helped his courage: when at last the door opened, like an officer and a gentleman Mr Gibson clutched his carnations and stood bravely up to meet the firing-squad.

Curiously enough, Miranda Joyce bore a marked physical resemblance to Miss Diver. Both were tall, black-haired, and bony. They were about the same age. Miss Joyce had even certain advantages: her make-up was better, she hadn't Dolores' slight moustache, and she was far better dressed. But whereas Mr Gibson saw Dolores with the eye of love, he saw Miss Joyce as she was, and whereas the aspect of Old Madrid made his heart flutter with delicious emotion, the aspect of Miss Joyce sunk it to his boots.

'My dear Harry,' cried Miranda gaily, 'I've kept you waiting! Auntie Bee made me. Was she right or wrong?'

Doing violence to all his feelings, Mr Gibson made a shot at gallantry. It seemed at the moment the only possible line. Moreover the gallant answer, remembering his hideous quarter of an hour, happened also to be the true one.

'Wrong,' said Mr Gibson heavily. 'Wrong every time.'

She looked at him speculatively, but made no comment. Then she looked at the carnations.

'With the mater's best love,' said Mr Gibson, thrusting them into her hands.

'I don't think *that's* quite right,' said Miranda, 'though I must ask Auntie Bee. Give mine to your mother, of course.'

'I will,' said Mr Gibson.

– Ominous, direful words! Words to seal a promise, a covenant! In this case the covenant already made with his mater and with Fate, and now to be made, specifically, with Miranda … Mr Gibson wondered whether he turned as pale as he felt; but the fearsome object of his vows, now seating herself, appeared to notice nothing amiss. The dreadful moment passed. The one that succeeded it, as Miss Joyce sat obviously expectant, was merely, if intensely, awkward. To postpone the moment that must come after, Mr Gibson very nearly asked her to play something on the piano.

He pulled himself together, kept a stiff upper lip. He was aware that a proposal in form was so to speak part of the bond – also that the sooner he got it over the better. He was still on his feet; the great thing was not to sit down. He knew he wasn't expected, in that day and age, to fall on his knees, it wasn't for that the good carpet had been laid; but he felt nonetheless that he oughtn't to propose sitting. Drawing a deep breath—

'My dear Miranda,' began Mr Gibson, 'I expect you know why I'm here.'

'*Do* I?' said Miss Joyce.

She wasn't going to let him off with a word.

'Well, a chappie doesn't usually come calling with a bunch of flowers,' pointed out Mr Gibson, 'unless he has something pretty serious on his mind.'

'I dare say some chappies do,' said Miss Joyce, playfully. 'And aren't they from your mother?'

Mr Gibson was damned if he was going to start an argument. He plunged on – if not straight to the point at least in its general direction.

'Anyone who plays the piano like you do, I mean anyone so accomplished and cultured all round, I dare say finds anyone like me a pretty rough diamond.' (Did a spark of hope flicker in his bosom? If so, it was quenched at once. She didn't take him up.) 'In fact,' continued Mr Gibson doggedly, 'if it hadn't been for what your Aunt Beatrice told the mater—'

'What *did* she tell her?' asked Miss Joyce rather sharply.

'That you – well, that you didn't dislike me. I must say it came as a bit of a surprise.' Again Mr Gibson paused; again nothing came of it. There was no escape. 'It gave me' – he chewed on the bullet – 'hope. And in that hope,' continued Mr Gibson rapidly – as though the bullet had been a sort of hashish – 'I'm here this afternoon even though you've every right to turn me down to ask you to be my wife.'

It was out. He'd got it out. Just before his knees gave way he lowered himself into the chair opposite Miranda's and waited for her reply.

'Oh, Harry!' said Miss Joyce.

'Well, what about it?' asked Mr Gibson impatiently.

'I'm so surprised too! I can't possibly answer straight away! I must have time to think!'

An appalling suspicion dawned.

'How long?' demanded Mr Gibson.

'At least a week! Ask me again in a week's time—'

It was just as he'd suspected. He was to be put through the hoop again. And quite possibly again after that – once a week, in fact, something to be looked forward to once a week (thought Mr Gibson incoherently), like his mother's Friday visit to the cinema. . . . Well, he wouldn't stand it. By comparison with such torture bankruptcy positively smiled at him. 'I'm damned if I'll stand it!' said Harry Gibson loudly. 'It's more than flesh and blood can bear! Either you give me an answer now, or you never see me again!'

It did the trick: as he leapt to his feet – and his eye was obviously on the door – Miranda too sprang up in pretty terror. She couldn't turn pale, because of her rouge – but with fluttering hand and eyelid indicated pallor; and her breath was genuinely short.

'How masterful you are!' breathed Miranda, enchanted. 'Oh, Harry, you just make me say yes!'

As she moved impulsively to accept his embrace, she impulsively pressed a bell; the maid who brought in the champagne must have been very handy.

2

'This is just for *us*,' said Miranda, 'before we tell everyone. . . . To you and me!'

Kissing her had been like kissing a sea-horse. Mr Gibson knocked back his drink thankfully. ('I shall turn into a sozzler,' thought Mr Gibson – dispassionate as a physician diagnosing the course of a disease.) For the moment, however, and although he'd had no lunch, he wasn't intoxicated. He still had himself well in hand – which considering Miranda's next choice of topic was fortunate.

Champagne, it seemed, turned Miranda into a woman of the world. With humorous understanding—

'Of course you have a mistress? Obviously,' said Miranda Joyce.

It was fortunate that Mr Gibson had himself in hand. He still couldn't control his blood. A long-disused system of arteries and capillaries rushed blood to his cheeks, up to his forehead, up to the roots of his hair. He blushed like a boy.

'My dear Harry, *I* don't mind!' cried Miss Joyce. 'A passionate man like you – why not?'

'Who told you?' shouted Harry Gibson.

Miss Joyce looked pleasurably frightened.

'No one in so many words. But away two nights each week—! Your mother told Aunt Beatrice *that*. Of course you have a mistress. I'm sure I could find out all about her, or Dadda could, if I was inquisitive!'

Mr Gibson perceived a possible course of action at all costs to be prevented.

'Since you know so much already – yes,' said Mr Gibson. (Though how far from the truth the literal truth! How far from the truth of King Hal and his Spanish rose!) 'Since you know so much already – yes,' said Harry Gibson. 'Do I need to tell you also that it's all washed up?'

A bony sea-horse kiss rewarded him. Unfortunately the sea-horse was still being a woman of the world.

'Of course she's been provided for?'

Mr Gibson's control went. So did all his carefully-cultivated

35

British slang, giving place to an older habit of speech, the speech he'd heard between his parents when he was a young boy.

'And out of what, tell me please, would I provide for her?' shouted Mr Gibson. 'You know, or at least your father does, my situation! How could I provide for a dog even?'

'You *are* passionate,' confirmed Miss Joyce. 'She must be behaving very well. Would it be kind if I went to see her?'

'If you do,' cried Mr Gibson, 'if you try to, I will never, this I swear, look at you or speak to you again. Is that understood, woman?'

'Passionate *and* masterful,' murmured Miss Joyce. 'Oh, Harry, I feel I've never known you before!'

3

Of the rest of the evening, of the intimate family supper that followed, Mr Gibson retained little subsequent memory. He still wasn't intoxicated, but he was bushed. He told Miranda's Aunt Beatrice the same (unsuitable) funny story four separate times. The arrival on scene of his mother astonished him more than it should have done. He wanted to know why she'd changed her mind about not coming. That she'd come after all, he argued, made nonsense of sending her best love; he showed unexpected heat on the point. There was in fact a moment after supper when old Joyce, Miranda's father, led him away to a private sanctum – and then looked uneasily at the decanters there. 'I am perfectly sober,' stated Harry Gibson pugnaciously. 'That's what I thought,' agreed Mr Joyce. 'You'll find a chinchilla coat in stock worth two thousand!' shouted Harry Gibson. 'Don't I know it, son?' agreed Mr Joyce placatively. 'What did you call me?' asked Harry Gibson – and laughed like a drain.

He then returned to the drawing-room and demanded that Miranda should play the piano. As soon as the first piece was finished, he demanded another. He kept her at the piano for one hour and twenty minutes. In a happy lover, such conduct wasn't altogether inexcusable: old Mrs Gibson, and Aunt Beatrice, like a couple of inexperienced commères, with many a beck and smile pulled off the feat of presenting it as infatuation. 'So much my Harry admires her playing!' murmured Mrs Gibson. 'It was music brought them together!' declared Aunt Beatrice. They had no audience except old man Joyce, perhaps they were rehearsing for the engagement-party, but their efforts weren't wasted. The evening not only passed off without disaster, but could be accounted a positive success.

In the taxi going home old Mrs Gibson wasn't even sleepy. Champagne and brandy, and wearing her best dress, and seeing her Harry at last on the way out of his troubles – all combined to reju-venate her. In Moscow, she'd have been ready to dance till morning. . . . The slight bother of hauling Harry out, and then getting him upstairs, and after that getting him to bed, tarnished her happiness not a whit. So a boy should come home, on such an evening!

CHAPTER FIVE

I

Loyal to their sad vows, Mr Gibson and Miss Diver refrained from all communication. Mr Gibson's only solace, at this time, lay in remembering the hundred pounds put by April the Fifth into Dolores' Post Office savings account. He still wished he'd made her promise not to try her luck again; for it was inconceivable to him that the future held any more luck for either of them, in either great things or small.

Dolores, treading the round from agency to agency and from shop to shop, was of the same mind.

2

Alas that her romanticism wasn't more flexible, that she had seen herself too long as a Spanish rose to see herself now a Sleeping Beauty! It would have helped her, if only a little; the image more-over would have been a truer one – supposing Beauty waked not by the Prince, but by the vanishment of her enchanted palace. Essentially, for ten years, Miss Diver's life had been as sheltered as the sleeping princess's, and as cut off from all reality. When she needed money, Mr Gibson supplied it, and the common rubs of social life never bruised her, for she had none. She had sought no friends, because she didn't want any. (An early overture from Number 10, where there were so many rowdy parties, she'd snubbed at once. 'Quite right,' said Mr Gibson. 'I like my little woman to be particular . . .' Dolores basked in his approval, but in fact the gesture cost her nothing.) Even before the advent of Martha, the work of the little house, and a little small-talk in the local shops, and a novel borrowed from the library, easily filled each day until King Hal came at evening to his Spanish rose. Even when he didn't spend the night, he came each evening, for half-an-hour.

In their secret garden (5, Alcock Road, W.2), she'd dreamed away ten years; and woke ill prepared to face the world without.

She had lost, for example (dreaming in Mr Gibson's eye of love), all ideas of what she looked like to any other eye. The first time the girls in the queue laughed at her, she didn't even notice; the second time, she was panic-stricken.

There was always a queue, if any shop had a vacancy. One vacancy drew twenty or thirty applicants.

Dolores on this second occasion was well towards the front; and had dressed with particular care to make herself look as young as possible. Perhaps her skirt was on the short side – considering the boniness of her legs; perhaps her blouse too peek-a-boo, considering the salt-cellars at her collar-bones; but when the girls behind sniggered, she at first, again, didn't realise who was their butt. '*Skinny Lizzie*,' they'd been whispering; but no one behind, or indeed before (Dolores looked both ways), seemed to deserve the cruel jibe. Many of those queueing were certainly thin, but only with a thinness then regrettably commonplace; so that it needed a figure of fun indeed to attract ribald comment . . .

'*O Skinny Lizzie*,' breathed a wicked voice, '*how's Scraggy Sister Maggie?*'

'*Careful! You'll put Lizzie in a tizzy!*'

'*Careful! Sister Maggie'll come and scrag-you-all!*'

They squealed with laughter, four young girls enchanted by their own wit, while Miss Diver looked about in perplexity. It was the kindest among them who enlightened her, a little creature of sixteen or so, suddenly moved to compassion. 'Poor old thing, it's a shame!' Dolores heard her hiss rebukingly – and with astonishment felt a bag of peppermints pressed into her hand. 'Go on, have one!' adjured the Samaritan. 'And don't you take no notice – Skinny Lizzies themselves!'

After this Dolores was afraid to queue again. She had a valid excuse; even a week had taught her that there was no demand for shop-assistants over thirty – there was no demand for anyone, over thirty – and this saved her from examining her fear too closely, so that she was able to forget the incident quite soon. In fact, what had rightly terrified her was no less than a threat to her identity.

The queues of job-hunters found ways to keep their spirits up. Each familiar face – and how many grew familiar! – had its sobriquet; Miss Diver herself could already recognise Ginger, and Russian Boots, and Once-I-Had-My-Own-Shop; a hilarity in the circumstances admirable fixed them like characters in a comic strip. In such company there was a place ready-made for Skinny Lizzie; Dolores' instinct warned her to flee while she was still a Spanish rose.

Not to betray the past: not to shoddy (even though he would never know it) King Hal's image of his love, was now Dolores' only ambition; and not an ignoble one. That it led her to risk a more fatal metamorphosis still, by advertising for a lodger, was in the circumstances inevitable.

Originally it was a blow to Miss Diver to discover that she couldn't after all sub-let. The terms of the lease, of the little house in Alcock Road, she found didn't allow it. This now appeared a rare piece of fortune. Only behind those pink curtains could she find refuge from the unkind world; and luckily she hadn't, speaking to the agent, mentioned lodgers.

3

Martha lettered the card beautifully – the single word 'Apartments' in a fancy script copied out of a *Tatler*. It was her first encounter with Indian ink, and to employ its turgid blackness on smooth white pasteboard ravished her. That she made more cards than one was still due mainly to a search after perfection; when the fourth and last appeared in the dining-room window, it was a master-piece.

Miss Diver meanwhile arranged the empty bedroom opposite her own, under Martha's attic, as the hybrid known technically as a bed-sit. This involved the purchase of a bed, but the rest of the furnishings came from the dining-room – two oak chairs, one with arms, and the sideboard translated into a bureau-cum-dressing-table – and the hall, denuded of its coat-cupboard. Miss Diver wished to lay out as little cash as possible, and was prepared, so long as the sitting-room remained inviolate, to strip the rest of the house to the bone. Actually nothing was missed, in a practical way; only twice a week had the dining-room been put to its proper use, in honour of Mr Gibson, the hall-cupboard was always kept empty, sacred to Mr Gibson's big overcoat. Dolores and Martha ate commonly in the kitchen, and the lodger was to be fed from trays. . . .

'Put "With Service,"' instructed Dolores.

Martha willingly took down the card and made another more beautiful still. It looked practically irresistible.

'What happens if we get *two* lodgers?' asked Martha.

'Then we must let the dining-room as well,' said Dolores, looking brighter than she'd done for days.

'Suppose we get *three*?'

'Then we must let your room,' said Dolores, 'and you must come in with me.'

Martha liked this less. The lettering (and the furniture-shifting, as an unusual employment) she'd enjoyed; the prospect of surrendering her privacy she couldn't. But she was very anxious not to see Dolores relapse, and so raised no objection.

In fact the point remained academic. No lodger came at all.

4

As regarded his own fortunes, on the other hand, Mr Gibson had been over-pessimistic. In Kensington, things were looking up. The shop over the tailoring establishment was discovered to be not such a dead duck after all. In fact, Joyces decided to keep it going.

'For a year, maybe two, making a little experiment,' explained Mr Joyce. 'Why not?'

Mr Gibson's response to this reprieve was less welcoming than resentful. His spirit was so thoroughly attuned to self-immolation, he was so ready to throw up the sponge and bury himself in some subordinate post at Bond Street, he even entered into argument. What was the point, demanded Harry Gibson, of a show-room without a clientèle? Admittedly certain old customers used to return year after year for re-modelling, but even this trade had been killed by the depression. 'Why not show 'em something new?' suggested Mr Joyce. 'Could they buy even lapin?' countered Harry Gibson. 'With my label in it, they might,' said old man Joyce.

Which was of course the point; and as the scheme developed Miss Harris and Miss Molyneux began to back it. They saw the shop in Kensington a branch of Joyces in Bond Street, whereat ladies of more taste than means (but whose cheques didn't bounce) might befur themselves in guaranteed Bond Street style. 'Truly, Mr Gibson, I believe we could make a very nice thing of it,' said Miss Harris. 'I'd looked forward, I admit it, to working on skunk, but if musquash means bread-and-butter, I for one shan't quarrel.' 'There'll be skunk to show, dear,' said Miss Molyneux consolingly. 'Mr Joyce promised. . . .'

Already they quoted Mr Joyce as though they'd worked for him all their lives.

Harry Gibson saw the scheme's advantages himself. What the Kensington business lacked was prestige. Any woman with money to buy a fur naturally preferred a Bond Street label in it: the new sample tabs displayed by Miss Harris took care of just this idiosyncrasy. *Joyce of Bond Street and Kensington*, ran the silken legend – sinking Gibson and Son without trace. 'And as Mr Joyce says,' added Miss Harris encouragingly, 'the depression can't last for *ever*. Think how nice it will be, Mr Gibson, when we're all going strong again in the old home!'

She was a good sort. So was Miss Molyneux a good sort. Miss Molyneux had thoroughly looked forward to peacocking about the Joyce *salon*, but she swallowed her disappointment so as not to spoil things for Mr Gibson. '*I* can see where style's needed,' declared Miss Molyneux nobly, 'and it's *here*. You've been ever so thoughtful of *us*, Mr Gibson, and I'm sure I'm only too glad to repay . . .'

Harry Gibson, ungratefully, wished he could simply shoot himself. In addition to all emotional distress he now suffered from a feeling that he'd somehow been diddled. He couldn't put a finger on it: old Joyce, taking over Gibson's lock, stock and barrel, had obviously every right to handle his new acquisition as he pleased: but if there was life in the old firm yet, if it wasn't the dead loss it had been accounted, in the preliminary negotiations – Harry Gibson felt he'd been diddled.

5

In Paddington Miss Diver paid half-a-crown to put up a card in the local newsagent's. Martha again lettered it splendidly: among its fly-blown and faded companions – '*Gentleman interested in photography seeks congenial model*,' '*Young lady free evenings seeks congenial employment*,' besides a dozen other apartment-cards – it really stood out. Martha often stopped to look at it. But apparently no one else did.

It was now that Miss Diver's lack of social relations showed as such a serious handicap. She was on no grapevine. She had no one to recommend her. And it was too late to do anything about it, for as she had once been too happy to make friends, now she was too wretched. She hadn't even neighbours. Alcock Road, without being exactly raffish, was a rather secretive little street, as such little streets in London often are. Could its walls have talked they might have told many an interesting tale – one or two perhaps as romantic as Dolores' own; for whatever reasons its inhabitants (except for the party-giving extrovert long since vanished) kept themselves strictly to themselves. The single house Dolores ever entered was that of Miss Taylor, chiropodist – and there kept her distance, because everyone knew how that sort of person gossiped . . .

Dolores had in fact always been rather grand, at Miss Taylor's. Certainly she couldn't bring herself to appeal there for help in finding a lodger. Which was a pity, because Miss Taylor actually knew of one not a stone's-throw away – the dissatisfied occupant of a bed-sit in Praed Street – and thus through pride Dolores missed an excellent chance.

She had no luck.

Paradoxically, as lodgers continued absent, her face began to set more and more in the irritated, worried expression associated by Martha with landladies. It was as yet but a foreshadowing; Miss Diver would never be a Ma Battleaxe; but lodgers yet unborn (so to speak) might not impossibly (so that expression foreshadowed) come to know her as Old Madrid . . .

Of this second threat to her identity, Miss Diver was unaware.

CHAPTER SIX

I

The shop was taken over lock, stock and barrel; so was Harry Gibson.

No prospective 'groom had ever less to do: between them Miranda and his mother and Auntie Bee and Mr Joyce saw to everything. Even the engagement-ring, a handsome affair of diamonds, appeared as though by magic in his pocket – Mr Joyce bought it and old Mrs Gibson put it there; all Harry's part was to give it back to Miranda. (Almost to his admiration, she received it with surprise. 'Oh, *Harry!*' cried Miranda. 'It's beautiful!' Mr Gibson took a look himself: no doubt old Joyce had got it through the trade, but even so he must have put down a couple of hundred. 'Dadda, see my ring!' cried Miranda – slightly overdoing things. Mr Joyce merely made a note to have it insured.) Nor did the question of where they should live, so often a problem to young couples, present any more difficulty; there was plenty of room in the Knightsbridge flat. 'Naturally you and Miranda will have your own sitting-room,' explained Mrs Gibson. 'You will not have to be all the time in that old Beatrice's pocket!' Her encouragements were superfluous; the last thing Harry Gibson wanted was to be shut up alone with Miranda. If his mother had been coming along too, he'd have rejoiced – but the mater on this point was wiser. 'It will be nice for you to have somewhere to visit,' she said slyly. 'Even Miranda will not mind you visiting your old mother, boy!'

Mr Gibson surrendered all initiative willingly. Indeed, he felt it would have been beyond his powers to deal with any one of these matters himself, so poignant were the memories they stirred. The only jewel he ever gave Dolores was a garnet – but what pleasure he'd taken in choosing it! The leasing of the little house in Alcock Road – what a delicious, rash adventure! Mr Gibson did his best to set such memories aside; but only succeeded, he hoped, in not betraying them. 'So much my Harry relies on Miranda's taste!' cried old Mrs Gibson – faced by his stubborn refusal to look at wallpapers for the new sitting-room. 'Whatever Miranda chooses he will think perfect! She will have everything her own way!'

The single occasion of his expressing an opinion was the night Miranda produced a sample of curtain-stuff. It was rose-pink bro-cade. 'I don't like the colour,' said Harry Gibson. 'But what could be prettier!' protested Joyce. 'Blue,' said Harry, at random.

He spent as much time as possible at the shop. There at least he had the illusion of being still his own master, and it was to a certain extent the truth: Gibsons of Kensington (though as to name sunk without trace, even the door-plate had by now been changed) so benefited by having a Gibson on the premises to act as link between old and new, that old man Joyce left his prospective son-in-law pretty well alone. As the days and weeks passed, Harry began to recover confidence in the security of his office; gradually assembled there one or two objects of special value to him. As the mementos of a ten-year-long romance, they weren't much. He had no photo-graph of Dolores – (She had one of him: in uniform. It used to stand on the ermine-cabinet; now it stood beside her bed.) – and no *gages d'amour*, because for his birthday and at Christmas Dolores always gave him liqueur-chocolates. Since she gave them because he had a passion for them, they were naturally all eaten. Mr Gibson was in fact reduced to a couple of theatre-programmes, a Derby day race-card, marked by Dolores' hand, and a bottle of anti-rheumatism pills Dolores had merely recommended. He also, one morning, on the pretext that it needed cleaning, brought from home a rather loud checked tweed jacket and hung it on the hook behind the door. It was obviously no nest of erotica that Mr Gibson arranged for himself; but in the office above the show-room, beside his still inviolate safe, he passed the few tolerable hours of his life.

At least once a day he took out Dolores' comb, and warmed it back to life between his hands. He had to hang on hard to his Britishness, not to press it to his lips. A sad and ridiculous sight was Harry Gibson – large, stout, fifty years old – holding himself back from mumbling a wafer of tortoiseshell, as a child holds back from sucking a forbidden sweet.

2

Dolores, his Spanish rose, had a good deal more to cherish. She had her King Hal's pyjamas, also his dressing-gown and bedroom slippers. For several weeks she arranged them each Monday and Thursday night appropriately about the divan. But Martha, who helped make beds, directed too enquiring an eye, and presently Miss Diver laid all away together in her wardrobe drawer. (Sprinkled with pot-pourri; it being obviously impossible to sprinkle underwear with liqueur-chocolates. Again the spirit of the absurd like a poltergeist haunted King Hal and his Spanish rose.) Dolores had also her Harry's photograph – splendid with two stars on each shoulder-strap. It was the sole object she had moved from the sitting-room, where nothing else was changed by a hair's-breadth, where in her daily dustings she was careful to replace each object exactly as it stood when Mr Gibson's eye last fell on it. If Mr Gibson had suddenly walked in again, he would have found no more change than in its mistress's heart.

3

On one other point besides that of the curtains Harry Gibson stood firm. He insisted on a six-months' engagement. Considering how smooth was being made his path towards matrimony, the ensuing argument, sustained vicariously, on the bride's side, by Mrs Gibson and Auntie Bee, was only to be expected: Harry Gibson stood firm. Three months he wouldn't hear of. 'But so well you children know each other already!' protested Mrs Gibson. 'And the paper-hangers need only a week!' cried Auntie Bee. 'It is not as though people might think anything!' added Mrs Gibson – at the time a little flown with wine. Harry Gibson stuck to his guns and wouldn't hear of a September wedding.

Appropriately enough, the spring of his intransigence was now economic: the reverse of his suspicion that he'd been diddled was that he now felt the gift of Miranda's hand less inexplicably above his deserts. In fact he felt Joyces were doing pretty nicely out of him. A spouse for the unmarriageable daughter, besides the makings of a very sound little business – Harry Gibson belatedly recognised that there were no flies on old man Joyce; but as well felt himself less of a pauper, less entirely on the receiving end. When Mrs Gibson suggested that Miranda might take offence, Harry Gibson laughed quite coarsely – and stuck to his guns. He would have liked a year, but this he did know to be impossible; six months was the longest grace he could win for himself – accurately he calculated it out, to December the sixteenth – and he succeeded in winning it.

'Suppose Mr Joyce changes his mind?' asked old Mrs Gibson, at last coming down to brass tacks.

'He won't,' said Harry.

He knew Joyces too committed to their new enterprise to draw back. The little strips of woven silk, at first so hateful, now gave him courage.

'I consider six months a proper time,' said Harry Gibson, 'and I am surprised Miranda doesn't think so also.'

Once again, his masterfulness did the trick. This last exchange with his mother took place at breakfast; that evening before dinner, in the Knightsbridge drawing-room, Miranda fluttered gratefully into his arms.

'It was only your mother and Auntie Bee,' whispered Miranda, 'who wanted to hurry things so! *I* need six months at least, to get used to my big, fierce lover!'

What Mr Gibson gained by this delay he knew only too well:

simply delay. For what was there could happen in even six months, to restore King Hal to his Spanish rose? There was nothing; he was simply postponing the nightmare moment when he would indeed be shut up alone with Miranda Joyce. It was still, as his mother would have said, a something . . .

All that evening Miranda behaved even more vivaciously than usual – a pretty upsurge of spirits natural to a maiden reprieved from the Minotaur. She played and sang, and sang and played, and teased Harry for his indifference to wallpapers, then relented and showed him the new curtain-stuff, blue because it was his favourite colour. 'To match his eyes!' cried Miranda – swiftly the little tease again. 'I truly believe that the reason! Oh, how vain my Harry is!' Nothing could have been less like sulks; with some complacency, Mr Gibson sought his mother's eye – and was astonished to surprise her in the act of directing a soothing glance upon Auntie Bee. They were always exchanging glances of some kind, however, far too complex for any male to interpret, so he paid no attention. He asked Miranda to play another piece on the piano, and she played one. He didn't ask for an encore, and she stopped playing. It was altogether one of the least disagreeable evenings he'd ever spent, at Knightsbridge; and as a further proof of independence, the evening after that he didn't dine there at all.

Miranda took the opportunity to have a little talk with her father.

4

'Dadda,' said Miranda Joyce.

As a rule she followed Auntie Bee to the drawing-room, and Mr Joyce would have preferred her to do so now; for once unencumbered by guests he'd meant to have a good go at the port. But his look of surprise was ineffectual as Auntie Bee's beckonings; Miranda stayed.

'Dadda, there's something I want to talk to you about.'

Mr Joyce pulled out an evening paper. Again, she didn't take the hint.

'Because I do sometimes feel, Dadda, that before we're married, I ought to know more about Harry's past.'

'Has he got a past?' enquired Mr Joyce unco-operatively.

'He admitted it to me, Dadda, the night he proposed.'

'Then that should be enough,' said Mr Joyce. 'He hasn't got a present, has he?'

'No, I'm sure not,' said Miranda positively. 'From his mother I know how he spends every minute.'

'Poor devil,' said Mr Joyce. After knowing Harry Gibson off and on for years, on closer acquaintance he'd taken quite a liking to him. (He'd enjoyed, at the family engagement-party, hearing Harry tell unsuitable stories to old Beatrice, and looked forward to hearing him tell her a few more.) Miranda's probings into Harry's past, and even more the rapidly-organised supervision-system now revealed, had the effect of putting him on Harry's side. 'You leave well alone,' Mr Joyce adjured his daughter. 'I consider six months a very proper time myself. You leave well alone – and let sleeping dogs lie.'

Miranda hesitated a moment, then jumped up and kissed him affectionately.

'Wise old Dadda, who always knows best!'

'And don't go hiring detectives,' added old man Joyce.

5

It will thus be seen that Miranda too had her anxieties. She didn't exactly think her big fierce lover would get away – she trusted Dadda too well for that; but what she did fear was the additional three months' strain on Mr Gibson's moral character. Such a passionate man as he was – a man who'd had a mistress! When he told her that was all washed up, Miranda believed him; but would it *stay* washed up, for half a year? Wasn't some interim backsliding at least possible? Without, she assured herself, the least jealousy or curiosity, Miranda couldn't help feeling she ought to know more of the facts – just in case Harry ever needed her help.

She didn't hire detectives. It was a course she had indeed envis-aged – actually half-way through Chopin's *Nocturne in G Major*; at the very moment when Harry surprised a glance between the mater and Aunt Beatrice – but only with her father acting as principal, to bear if need be the brunt of Harry's wrath; and wise old Dadda had made his position lamentably clear. What other courses lay open? Pumping old Mrs Gibson was no use, the latter, with excellent sense, having contrived to know exactly as little about her son's private life as Harry hoped she did. 'Two nights from home every week? In Leeds,' said Mrs Gibson firmly. 'How glad he is too, now no more tiresome railway-travel!' Miranda was left anxious; her happiness in the possession of a big fierce lover was by no means unflawed.

Upon Dolores this postponement – for such she instinctively felt it to be – of the Gibson-Joyce nuptials worked almost as disquietingly. Dolores, daily searching the social columns of her newspaper, and finding at last the announcement she dreaded, read of a mid-December wedding with something like terror. For next month or in six months, what difference? – while to know her beloved for six months more still not irretrievably another's prolonged the worst of her anguish, which was to hope. There was nothing that could happen, in six months, to restore him to her; yet until those six months were run out, how could she find the graveyard-peace of hopelessness?

The one person completely happy at this time was old Mrs Gibson. Old Mrs Gibson was rejuvenated. Wearing her best dress so continually that she would soon need another – continually popping round to Knightsbridge, even though she dined there most evenings, for coffee and cakes with Auntie Bee – old Mrs Gibson bloomed. Her berry-brown eye gleamed bright; her small spare frame eagerly braced itself to meet every demand. It was she who tirelessly accompanied Miranda on shopping-expeditions, when fat old Beatrice flagged. Miranda's trousseau, promised Mrs Gibson, would be something in the old style – three dozen of each, also monogrammed! 'In the depression, does it look so good?' objected Harry censoriously. 'All is British, even to the brassières!' swore his mater. 'It is praised already, at all the stores, how we buy only British!'

From the smaller shops, especially where she knew the management, she often came away with a little something for herself. A pair of gloves, a pair of stockings, once a nice embroidered blouse – there was no refusing them, when the shop-people were so kind! Even a box of handkerchiefs she didn't turn up her nose at, but added complacently to the growing pile of loot. 'One would think I was starting a trousseau for myself!' cried old Mrs Gibson happily. 'One would think it was I going to be a bride!'

CHAPTER SEVEN

I

The child Martha also was happy, but she wasn't being much comfort to Dolores.

It was a failure of sympathy. June passed into July, July wore on to August, and never once did Martha forget Miss Diver's early cup of tea. She could easily fit in any piece of routine. But whereas to Dolores the little house, though still a refuge, without Mr Gibson's daily visits was also a desert, if anyone had asked Martha what difference his absence made, she would have replied, in the food.

More precisely – and food was one of the only two subjects Martha ever was precise about – kippers instead of chops. On bread and margarine and kippers, and other such low-priced comestibles, she and Dolores now largely subsisted. Martha didn't particularly mind. She liked kippers. She would simply have been giving a straight answer to a straight question – and arguing *post hoc ergo propter hoc*. Mr Gibson's rôle had never been clear to her economically, otherwise she would have missed him more.

'I don't believe you miss him at all!' cried Dolores bitterly.

'Miss who?' asked Martha. Another failure of sympathy. To Dolores the masculine pronoun had only one reference; to Martha it might mean anyone from Mr Punshon to the milkman.

She was also, at the moment of Miss Diver's outburst, occupied in

53

trying to draw a saucepan hanging on the kitchen wall. It was unexpectedly difficult. Martha had never tried to draw anything, before her encounter with Indian ink; now every old envelope bore her blots. She didn't draw landscapes. The hard outline Indian ink so satisfyingly produced had alerted her eye instead to small, hard-outlined objects – like saucepans. The trouble with Indian ink was that it was too final. Martha had in fact started off in the wrong medium. This naturally had to dawn on her at some point, and it happened to dawn on her then. 'Can I have the laundry-book pencil?' asked Martha. 'Miss who?'

If Dolores didn't tell her, how could she guess? But Miss Diver didn't even answer about the pencil, but instead, with extraordinary irrelevance, cried that Martha hadn't even been able to thread beads.

'I didn't want to. It was silly,' explained Martha, surprised but patient.

'And why shouldn't you sometimes do something you don't want to? If you'd looked sweet, if you . . . if you'd twined yourself about his heart,' reproached Dolores passionately, 'who knows?'

Martha suddenly perceived that the whole shape of the saucepan, foreshortened pan-part and straight handle, fitted into another, invisible shape: a long oval. It was a very happy moment.

'You're not even listening!' cried Miss Diver.

'Yes, I am. Who knows what?' asked Martha. 'Can I—?'

Miss Diver flung down pencil and laundry-book together and retreated to the sitting-room in tears.

More and more of their conversation ended thus unfortunately; Martha sensibly went on drawing. In pencil it was easier; she started all over again and drew the invisible oval first. She put Miss Diver's incomprehensible remarks out of her head at once. Indeed, a great many of Dolores' remarks, or ejaculations, were at this time incomprehensible to her: 'King Hal!' for instance, Dolores would cry – before the bronze lady: an obvious piece of nonsensicality. Or 'Big Harry!' ejaculated Miss Diver, caressing a stuffed ermine. Martha took as little notice as possible.

She was thus unsurprised (and took equally little notice) when

Miss Diver repeatedly described the situation of Mr Gibson's establishment.

'In Kensington High Street, over a tailor's,' explained Miss Diver. 'At the corner of Kensington High Street and Almaviva Place.' (She had never been there; but could have mapped like a surveyor Mr Gibson's daily route between home and shop.) 'Kensington Gardens is where you like to go and play, isn't it, dear? Well, the High Street is just the other side . . .'

Martha said yes, and you could also take a bus.

This was her greatest failure of all. For Miss Diver and Mr Gibson, though they had bound themselves not to communicate, hadn't bound the child Martha, and Miss Diver couldn't help dreaming dreams. Martha had only to run across the Gardens (or if she preferred it, go by bus), and then again who knew, who knew! *'Oh, Mr Gibson, can't I just take Dolores a message?'* Miss Diver imagined Martha pleading. *'I know it would make her so happy!'* Though Martha had quite egregiously failed to twine herself about his heart, a child's pleading who can resist? Dolores didn't see her King Hal resisting long; and it would be neither her doing nor his, that communication was re-established. . . .

It was weakness on Dolores' part, not treachery. She knew their future, divergent fates inevitable. If she hoped that perhaps Mr Gibson would follow his message in person, it was with no idea of trying to seduce him from the path of duty – just to see him once again, in the sitting-room, without exchanging a caress, or even a word, would have comforted her. Miss Joyce might still have been right to take alarm, as she undoubtedly would have done, had she heard Mr Gibson's address so perpetually drummed in Martha's ears. It was an oddity of the situation that Miranda now recognised Mr Gibson's passionate nature better than Dolores did; and wouldn't have trusted him in Alcock Road a moment.

Again the point remained academic, because as far as Martha was concerned Mr Gibson's shop might have been on the moon. She had no idea why Dolores (recapitulating familiar topography) bent such pressing looks on her. And after not very long Dolores herself lost heart. Something peculiarly stolid and self-contained about

Martha – as she squared her elbows on the kitchen-table to draw a saucepan, or a casserole, or a mustard-spoon soaking in an egg-cup – caused Miss Diver to lose heart.

2

'If a kiddie comes wanting to see me,' Mr Gibson instructed Miss Molyneux, 'send her up. She'll be from Jaspé's.'

To his surprise, Miss Molyneux at once looked intelligent.

'*We*'ve heard that too, Mr Gibson – how Jaspé's have been buying at auction. Miss Harris thinks there'll be some very nice bargains going indeed, and I'm sure I agree – for they certainly haven't anyone like *her*, to re-model! Not that I can think it right, however hard-pressed, sending a child with a great heavy box.'

'She won't have a box,' said Mr Gibson.

'Anyway, I'll give her a choc,' said kind Miss Molyneux.

Thus a warm welcome awaited Martha in Kensington. Miss Molyneux would have bustled her up to the office and fed her chocolates when she came down. Mr Gibson would have turned no deaf ear. (His train of thought paralleled Dolores' so closely, he cast Martha's plea in almost exactly the same form – '*Oh, Mr Gibson, mayn't I just take Dolores a message?*') But of course Martha never came. The idea never entered her head. She was too completely, happily busy trying to draw a saucepan, or a casserole, or a mustard-spoon in an egg-cup, to remember Mr Gibson at all. It was a genuine annoyance to her, a tiresome distraction, that she about this time remembered a Brixton bedroom.

Possibly as a delayed result of Dolores' early over-optimism, when she'd envisaged herself and Martha sharing a room in Alcock Road, Martha suddenly remembered the room in Brixton she'd for three years shared with Ma Battleaxe.

She began by simply remembering it; presently recalled in some detail a satisfactory arrangement of shapes; and was then bothered to the point of obsession because the shapes weren't right. She could visualise the window, and Ma Battleaxe's bed (her own box-ottoman at the foot); but there should have been a linking-shape in

56

between, high and narrow, of which the exact proportions eluded her. A wardrobe was too wide; but what else than a wardrobe could have stood there? After mulling over this problem for a week, one Monday towards the end of July Martha went to check up on site.

She had at this time less than her usual liberty, but half-a-crown. (Ungrateful Martha! It derived from the generosity of Mr Gibson.) Mr Punshon told her where she could pick up a bus – quite conveniently, at the other end of Church Street; and by setting out in mid-afternoon she not only avoided explanations with Dolores, who was lying down, but also secured a good place up front.

In point of fact, Miss Diver saw her leave. Too restless to sleep, as she now usually was, Miss Diver heard the click of the front gate and in an instant was at the window. No portly beloved figure, however, not the top of Mr Gibson's bowler hat, rewarded her hopeful eyes; but sad it is to relate that the sight of Martha stumping down the road fanned those hopes afresh. Martha had undeniably the air of being bound on some errand of importance. She wore her sailor-straw and napper gloves. A useful instinct always led Martha to look as respectable as possible; it was probably why no education-officer on the prowl ever spotted her. Dolores, used to seeing her grubby about the garden, was on this point at fault; Martha's important and business-like air deceived her equally. For what possible errand of importance could the child have (thought Miss Diver, her heart lifting), unless to Mr Gibson? As Martha stumped down Church Street to board a Brixton bus, Dolores visualised her stumping across Kensington Gardens towards Kensington High Street. As Martha waited stolidly at the bus-stop, Dolores visualised her scampering (the modulation inevitable) on towards Almaviva Place. . . .

It is the classic pathetic fallacy that man, observing Nature's storms or calms, engages either with his own current predicament. Dolores made a similar mistake about Martha.

CHAPTER EIGHT

I

Martha remembered the address perfectly: 11, Hasty Street. Three
full years had passed since she quitted Brixton in Miss Diver's taxi,
and she had never been back; but she remembered 11, Hasty Street
perfectly. Nor was it surprising; she'd carried the legend tied to her
buttonhole as soon as she could walk, and been able to pronounce
it before she could read. (Ma Battleaxe disliked children underfoot.)
Upon descending from the bus Martha needed only to take direction from the first passer-by, and from the corner of the road homed
like a pigeon.

She found she remembered quite a lot – up to about four feet
from ground-level. The pattern of the iron railings was familiar,
though not the yellow-brick housefronts behind; so was a scar in the
base of a lamp-post familiar – it looked like a dog's head – though
not the fluted column above. And though there were no front-
gardens in Hasty Street, Martha found herself instinctively looking
out for a patch of colour, something bright and full like nasturtiums . . .
and found it in a red-tiled gate-step still immaculately ruddled by
the Yorkshirewoman at Number 6.

At Number 11, however, neither memories nor nostalgia halted
her. Martha walked straight in (the door as always on the latch),
crossed a narrow hall smelling of cabbage and wet mackintoshes

(here memory did slightly stir), and down a flight of stone steps into Ma Battleaxe's kitchen and private stronghold.

It looked just like a witches' kitchen. There they all were – Ma Battleaxe and Mrs Hopkinson from next door, and Miss Fish and Miss Jones from further up – average age sixty, personal habits deplorable, whiskery of chin and malevolent of eye. Martha regarded them with pleasure. Grouped about the inevitable tea-pot, the solid bulk of Ma Battleaxe balanced the almost equally important bulk of Miss Jones: between them skinny Mrs Hopkinson and meagre Miss Fish sketched a contrasting arabesque. Then they saw Martha in the doorway, and broke the pattern to stare back.

'Well!' cried Miss Jones and Miss Fish in unison. 'Well!' cried Mrs Hopkinson. 'Well!' grunted Ma Battleaxe. 'If it isn't little Miss Martha, come back to visit us at last!'

Martha sensed a certain umbrage. It didn't trouble her. She was strictly on business.

'If you mean why haven't I come to see you before,' said Martha straightforwardly, 'it's because I never thought of it. Now I have. Can I go up and look at where I used to sleep?'

Ma Battleaxe needed a moment or two to take this in. Ponderous of mind as of body, she was still in the state (to use her own subsequent phrase) of knock-me-down-with-a-feather. Then her eye at once brightened, and moistened. So did the eyes of her cronies – ready each bleary orb to drop a crocodile tear.

'I suppose your fine Auntie's turning you out?' suggested Ma Battleaxe hopefully.

'No, she isn't,' said Martha, with dignity. 'I'm her greatest comfort. For instance, if that was her toast she'd give me a piece straight away.'

It was a shot that told. The eyes of Mrs Hopkinson and Miss Jones and Miss Fish now turned on their hostess with censure. Certain laws of hospitality are recognised even, or particularly, by savages, and Ma Battleaxe, in not offering Martha a bite, had committed a sad breach of etiquette. She hastily pushed across the plate. But Martha managed to swallow her saliva.

'Thank you, I've had so much dinner I'm quite stuffed.'

'Just the half,' pressed Ma Battleaxe. 'You can have bloater-paste on it.'

'My Aunt gives me bloater-paste every day,' said Martha. 'I'll just go upstairs, thank you, and then let myself out. I won't touch any of your things.'

'Not having a barge-pole, we presume,' said Miss Fish nastily.

Martha took no notice and stumped out – leaving, as a playwright said, her character behind her.

She knew her way. A flight of linoleum-covered stairs, a linoleum-covered landing, then the second door on the left. The landing was familiarly cluttered with suit-cases – there had always been a tenant either coming or going; Martha noted the signs indifferently. With equal indifference she passed the door of what was once her father's room; Richard Hogg, excellent though humble Civil Servant, had left extraordinarily little impression on his daughter; his second wife so to speak, had been the Post Office, with all its allied social activities. (He started the local Sketching Club single-handed.) Martha went straight on to the back bedroom she used to share with Ma Battleaxe.

It was just the same. The box-ottoman was still there, only dirtier. The slovenly bed mightn't have been made since she last saw it. From the hook behind the door still depended the old winter coat used by Ma Battleaxe as a dressing-gown, its colour a dingy puce Martha had particularly disliked. But all these offences her eye accurately omitted, and she saw simply what she'd come to see. The jutting-up piece that bothered her wasn't a wardrobe, it was a grandfather-clock. (How it came to be there, upstairs, in a bedroom, wasn't Martha's concern. The long tale of compounded debts and subsequent furniture-shiftings wouldn't have interested her in the least.) She noted carefully, however, the narrow shape of the clock in relation to the broader shape of the window, and to the low squat oblong of the bed, and found all three in conjunction as satisfactory as she hoped. Only then did she look at the box-ottoman, to remember how she'd slept on it for two years – and even as she did so remembered something else: the hippopotamus-hump of Ma Battleaxe a-bed. What a silhouette it had presented, as in lamplight or at dawn Martha

60

opened her infant eyes! A prize, a plum too good to lose, not even the sudden racket on the landing without could divert her from its recapture. . . .

In any case she knew what was going on, just suit-cases being hurled downstairs. Ma Battleaxe regularly so sped a parting guest, especially the high-and-mighty sort who gave notice of their own accord. Martha in frivolous youth (that is, before the age of six) had found these dramas pleasantly exciting, and in fact was once herself, hovering too near, bowled over by a Gladstone bag. Now she simply closed her ears like a hunting-dog's.

It was thus by no design that some fifteen minutes later she made contact with Mr Phillips.

2

Martha let herself out as she'd intended, without going back to the kitchen; if she was heard, Ma Battleaxe and Mrs Hopkinson and Miss Fish were all too busy holding ghoulish wake to bother with her. (The pot re-brewed black and strong, all the old corpses disinterred – of Mr Pyke who robbed the gas-meter, of Mr Comfrey who cooked in his room, of Mr Byers who brought in women. High-and-mighty Mr Phillips, now added to the grisly roll, had asked for a sheet changed every week . . .) Any listener who didn't know the ropes must have supposed lodgers a desperate race indeed, must have marvelled that defenceless females ever dared to harbour them: to Martha, however, the chorus of commination was simply the natural coda or amen to the suit-case-chucking, too familiar to interest, and she went straight out.

It was pleasant in the open air again, after the smells of the house. Martha strolled relaxed. Observing suit-cases in her path, she indulged herself with a game of jumping over them. They were by the gate with the red-tiled step; she naturally loitered a little; and so observed a dejected figure being turned from the Yorkshire woman's door.

Martha sized up the situation at a glance. It was obviously the lodger just ejected by Ma Battleaxe, the high-and-mighty Mr

Phillips, seeking fresh accommodation – and she could have spared him his pains. There were never any vacancies at Number 6, whose celebrated Regulars actually kept their rooms on while holidaying, so clean and comfortable the beds, so excellent the Yorkshire cooking. Mr Phillips, returning down the path, showed a familiar face of disappointment as the door behind him closed on a familiar face of pride.

'I could have told you that,' said Martha smugly.

'Told me what?' asked the frustrated lodger, angrily seizing his bags.

'That it's always full. She makes ginger puddings.'

'Can you tell me anywhere that isn't?' demanded Mr Phillips.

The question was actually a rhetorical one, but Martha took it literally, and it jerked her out of her own preoccupations. Until that moment she had in no way considered Ma Battleaxe's as a source of supply, indeed she had completely forgotten, among the battered landladies at Number 11, that Dolores was attempting the same dangerous trade. Now she considered Mr Phillips with interest. She was pretty certain who he was, and regretted that she hadn't listened longer at the kitchen-door to hear the worst. At sight, Martha judged him elderly but not likely to die on one (always an important point), and quite clean: and since he had his baggage with him, a High-and-Mighty, not a Bilking Tom.

'Did Ma throw you out, or did you give notice?' checked Martha in business-like tones.

'I gave notice. I don't remember seeing *you* about,' said Mr Phillips.

'I don't live there any more,' explained Martha. 'I just heard. Haven't you anywhere else to go?'

Mr Phillips looked injured.

'I gave a week's notice this morning, allowing myself time to glance around, and she throws me out as I set foot in to-night! I'm not sure it isn't illegal.'

Martha nodded intelligently. The phrase stirred memories again. (Richard Hogg, that exemplary public servant, would have been surprised to know what experience his infant daughter was accumulating. He alone, Number 11's solitary Regular, had never seen Ma in form.)

'It's her way,' quoted Martha, 'never to stand under notice. It's why she's so looked up to. And no one ever does have the law on her. – All right,' said Martha decisively, 'we'll take you. There's a bus at the end of the road.'

'Here, steady on!' said Mr Phillips – in not unnatural surprise.

It was however about six o'clock, and he was in a predicament. He was ready to catch at a straw. He also observed of Martha, as she had of him, that she was clean.

'You're certain there's a bed for me?' he asked warily.

'With clean sheets,' promised Martha. 'Both. But if you're only coming for just one night, perhaps it isn't worth the laundry.'

'I'd stay a week anyway,' offered Mr Phillips – thus unexpectedly put on the defensive, 'if comfortable. What's the weekly rate?'

'I don't know. I'm only a child,' pointed out Martha severely. 'Are you coming or aren't you?'

Mr Phillips deliberated no longer – his predicament was serious – but with a bag in each hand, and a parcel under his arm (which Martha didn't offer to carry), accepted her guidance to the bus-stop and on to the right bus. Only as he paid their fares did he realise how remote lay their destination; but he worked in central London, in an office almost equidistant from Brixton and Paddington, and did not now draw back.

'Is it your mother who lets rooms?' he asked, near Kennington.

Martha hesitated. 'Aunt' was tabu, and some instinct bade her reject 'Dolores'.

'It's Miss Diver,' she said repressively. 'I'm an orphan.'

Every now and again, during their long ride, Mr Phillips glanced at her curiously. At least she seemed a *silent* sort of child. Mr Phillips was a great one for peace and quiet – it was another reason why he'd been so uncomfortable in Hasty Street – and if there'd been too much chattering he'd still, he told himself, have cried off. In fact, after that single question and answer, there was dead silence. In fact, Mr Phillips wanted to put several questions more. The fact was, Martha didn't encourage him.

3

The little house in Alcock Road surprised Mr Phillips by its classy exterior; but for the card in the window he'd never have guessed lodgers taken there at all. As until that moment, of course, they hadn't been: Dolores, hurrying out to question Martha, found herself a landlady unawares.

'I've brought a lodger,' said Martha casually. 'I got him from Ma Battleaxe's.'

'The name is Phillips,' Mr Phillips said.

'I thought it was,' agreed Martha. 'He gave notice himself,' she added to Dolores. 'Shall I get my supper?' – and without waiting for a reply stumped through to the kitchen and there as a reward for her exertions opened the last three tins in the larder – a tin of salmon, a tin of pineapple, and a tin of baked beans. It was so long since she'd felt a little sick after a meal, the sensation was rather agreeable; and she easily settled herself down with a few plain biscuits.

Evidently the negotiations between Mr Phillips and Dolores came to a satisfactory issue, for he slept that night in the spare room.

CHAPTER NINE

I

Had Miss Diver's luck turned at last?

'Good morning, Mr Phillips,' said Miss Diver, every morning.

'Good morning, Miss Diver,' replied Mr Phillips; and raising his trilby hat (which he always put on in the hall), went off to work.

'Good evening, Mr Phillips,' said Miss Diver, every evening.

'Good evening, Miss Diver,' replied Mr Phillips, wiping his feet on the mat. Then he went upstairs to his room, and half-an-hour later Martha carried up his supper-tray (as she'd carried up his breakfast-tray in the morning), and that was the last seen of Mr Phillips.

As a member of the desperate race of lodgers he was indeed a shining exception. Tidy, quiet, and punctual in payment, he neither robbed the gas-meter, nor cooked in his room, nor brought in women. Nothing could have been more reassuring than his profession, which was that of clerk in an Insurance Company. Nor was he as old as Martha had thought, being about forty-five – and thus good, in landlady-calculations, for another fifteen years at least. The only point on which he gave the slightest anxiety was the cardinal one of whether he would stay.

It was difficult to put a finger on. Mr Phillips gave no overt sign of discontent. The week bargained for by Martha elapsed, and he entered on a second. Yet his manner, during the brief conversational exchanges reported above, became more, not less, reserved. They were so very brief, there was hardly room, so to speak, for much manner at all; but Dolores was already acquiring a professional sensitivity, and the first overtone a landlady learns to recognise is that of the concealed grievance.

'Good evening, Mr Phillips,' said Miss Diver. 'I hope you're quite comfortable?'

'A.1,' replied Mr Phillips – and Dolores was left with the impression that he might give notice at any moment.

Fortunately this nerve-racking period did not last long. In fact it lasted just about the same length of time as the uneasy period three years earlier following the introduction of Martha. Again, Miss Diver managed to avert calamity.

2

'I suppose he hasn't said anything to *you*?' Miss Diver asked Martha.

'I never talk to him at all,' said Martha.

There was something in the tone of this that caught Dolores' attention; disturbingly. Could it be Martha who was upsetting Mr Phillips? Yet how? To ask, Do you *tease* Mr Phillips, in the face of that flat statement, was obviously silly; moreover if there was one thing Martha wasn't, it was a tease. There was still something in her tone Dolores liked so little, she felt herself on a possible scent.

'Good morning, Mr Phillips,' said Miss Diver.

'Good morning, Miss Diver,' replied Mr Phillips.

'I hope Martha brings you your breakfast nicely?'

'Very punctual indeed, thank you,' said Mr Phillips.

Dolores didn't like the tone of this either. Also Mr Phillips, instead of going straight on out, for once paused.

'I hope she hasn't ever been . . . discourteous to you?'

It was now plain that Mr Phillips had something to say. His hat was half-way to his head; he lowered it and looked steadily into the lining, while Dolores waited with increasing apprehension. His next words took her by surprise.

'I'm always fully dressed,' stated Mr Phillips. 'I make a point of it.'

'I'm sure it's very thoughtful of you,' said Dolores – still at a loss. She had made a point of it herself: carrying up Mr Phillips' breakfast-tray was a service Martha could most usefully perform, especially since Miss Diver no longer felt able to afford chiropody; but the latter had made careful and immediate enquiry as to the state of Mr Phillips' attire. A dressing-gown she would have tolerated, even pyjamas (both halves); impeccable Mr Phillips! – Martha reported him complete to shoes and tie . . .

'So there's no reason why she shouldn't look at me,' continued Mr Phillips, still with restraint. 'I only mention it. I mean, she isn't exactly feeding a dog.'

After that Martha not only carried in Mr Phillips' breakfast-tray, but looked him in the eye, and said 'Good morning, Mr Phillips' every morning. As she tried to explain when Dolores scolded her, she hadn't looked at him before simply because he didn't look *like* anything. 'He looks like your bread-and-butter,' said Dolores sharply. 'Remember that!'

Had she reflected, she might have wondered whether Martha's steady dispassionate gaze, first thing in the morning, was really going to make Mr Phillips any happier. Yet he seemed satisfied.

3

Thus at last Dolores' luck turned. Mr Phillips stayed – the perfect Regular. Even his undiminished reserve, now that it no longer hinted at concealed grievances, became a virtue: an extrovert who cracked jokes or grew familiar Dolores would have found intoler-able, for though finally translated into a landlady she was still, she assured herself, no ordinary one, of the type that hob-nobs with the lodger. Mr Phillips, by keeping his distance, she felt acknowledged this. She felt his reserve a tribute to her unusualness. It didn't dis-please her to fancy that she seemed a little mysterious to him. There was no personal element involved; had Dolores' skein of thought been unravelled, the clue-thread would have proved not any regard for her day-by-day self, but regard for an image existing only in her own mind. (And in the mind of Harry Gibson.) It was to the image of King Hal's Spanish rose that Dolores required tribute; as it was the fragrance of that rose, she hoped, shed mystery. . . .

As an individual her lodger didn't exist for her. Even in rebuke to Martha, Dolores found nothing more to say for Mr Phillips' appearance than that he looked like their bread-and-butter; and after a month could hardly have described him much more accurately. He was of average height, and neither fat nor thin. He wore some sort of a moustache, and his overall coloration was greyish. This peculiar nebulousness in the impression Mr Phillips left on Dolores was indeed chiefly due to her preoccupation with another masculine image altogether – bluff, florid and stalwart; but the fact remained that any description was difficult, of a man so peculiarly featureless.

He didn't so much live in the house as haunt it. He was like a ghost that appears at a regular time and place – in Mr Phillips' case, twice a day on the stairs. Otherwise he was invisible. Neither Miss Diver nor Martha ever saw him enter, for example, the bathroom; it was as though he materialised, when necessary, inside. What he did with himself at the week-end, on Saturday afternoons and on Sundays, might have been a mystery to Dolores in turn, had she ever speculated on it (as an ordinary landlady would have done). Was he a great reader, a student of commercial Spanish, a follower of racing-form? (A caster of horoscopes, a composer of minor poetry? Was he in the house at all?) Miss Diver didn't even speculate. Whatever Mr Phillips' week-end occupations, they kept him typically and satisfactorily unobtrusive. His unobtrusiveness was in fact one of his greatest virtues. Apart from the mechanical provision of his lodgerly requirements, Miss Diver could ignore him.

4

'Good morning, Martha,' said Mr Phillips, every morning.

'Good morning, Mr Phillips,' replied Martha; and by deliberately unfocusing her eyes reduced him to a shapeless blur.

68

It was a trick she had known ever since she could remember, and which she now regularly employed to his, and Dolores' deception. She still had to say 'Good morning,' and though always more jealous of her eyes than of her tongue, disliked saying it because she was made to.

CHAPTER TEN

I

As though they were two buckets over a well, as soon as Dolores'
fortunes rose a little, so Mr Gibson's sank.

Miranda Joyce, naturally interested in all that concerned her
betrothed, found her way into the shop.

How could Mr Gibson keep her out? 'You must remember it's
going to be my bread-and-butter too!' cried Miranda gaily. 'If I see
you working very very hard, I shall make Dadda raise your salary!'
Of course Mr Gibson couldn't keep her out. Soon she was popping
in every day, to gossip with the girls in the show-room, and then to
run up for a word with her Harry. To the latter's annoyance, the
show-room made her welcome. 'If you see what I mean, Mr Gibson,
she does *dress* the place a bit,' said Miss Harris practically. 'Many
ladies don't like to find a shop quite empty.' 'And she's ever so
friendly,' added Miss Molyneux. 'Really you'd scream, Mr Gibson, to
hear some of her jokes about our old stock!' It was unreasonable of
Mr Gibson to be annoyed: besides dressing the show-room and
keeping Miss Molyneux in stitches, Miranda more usefully still
brought in some of her own friends, one or two of whom actually
made purchases. They naturally got special terms; but in their wake,
as though this little trickle of business acted as a sort of pump-
priming, appeared one or two genuine new clients to be impressed

by the new Joyce of Bond Street labels. In Mr Gibson's opinion, these labels were the best of their money's worth. In Mr Gibson's private opinion, Joyces were unloading *their* old stock on Kensington. Apart from the promised skunk for Miss Molyneux to display, there was nothing, in Mr Gibson's opinion, so very much out of the ordinary. 'I could make a joke or two myself,' thought Harry Gibson.

All the same, it was unreasonable of him to object to Miranda's activities in the show-room. Possibly he mightn't have done, if they hadn't involved the running-upstairs afterwards. But his whole scheme of existence, at this time, was designed to avoid being alone with her – he was assiduous at Knightsbridge, he dined willingly in Knightsbridge most evenings of the week, because there would be Mr Joyce and Auntie Bee, also the mater, and he could always ask Miranda to play the piano, or if the women's manœuvres looked like being too much for him, demand to talk business with old man Joyce. The tête-à-têtes in his office filled him with dismay.

He kissed Miranda twice a day as it was. (Upon arriving at the Knightsbridge flat, and upon leaving it.) It was still like kissing a sea-horse, but he had trained himself not to flinch. She expected also to be kissed in the office – with less formality. If he didn't take care, she was on his knee. The first time Miranda so impetuously showed her affection, Mr Gibson had no other resource than to seize the E to K telephone directory and look up the Hudson Bay Company. The act dislodged without discouraging her. Upon hearing the engaged signal (in one way not unwelcome, Mr Gibson telephoned simply because he'd looked up the number, he had nothing to say to Hudson Bay), Miranda was back on his knee in two shakes.

She wasn't any bonier than Dolores. Her good face-cloth jacket was better padding than a Spanish shawl. But Mr Gibson felt no fragile rose upon his bosom: he felt a skeleton.

Her ungloved forearms were no leaner than Dolores' – in fact a slight *duvet* of black hair by comparison softened them: Mr Gibson, whose dislike for dogs had often troubled him as being un-British, felt a greyhound's paws about his neck.

In a way it was as much for Miss Joyce's sake as for his own – the die being cast, the inescapable accepted – that he issued a doubly roundabout ultimatum.

'Will you please explain to your chum Beatrice,' Harry Gibson instructed his mother, 'that a man would rather run his business by himself? Also that if he comes up to scratch every single damned night of the week, his days at least should be his own?'

Old Mrs Gibson giggled. If Miranda was at this time behaving like a girl of seventeen, Mrs Gibson was behaving like a frivolous sixty. All she lacked was a knee to sit on herself.

'So Miranda comes to the shop too often? Then throw her out, boy!' advised old Mrs Gibson. 'Show yourself masterful!'

Of course the women had got together. Harry's masterful wooing was now a family legend.

'Throw her downstairs!' cried old Mrs Gibson. 'There is nothing dear Miranda would like better!'

This was in fact precisely what Harry Gibson feared might happen. When he remembered the parabola described by a bunch of pink carnations, he felt he could hardly trust himself with Miranda at the top of the steep office flight. Whether or not something of this showed in his face, Mrs Gibson sobered.

'All joking apart, of course you are quite right,' she agreed. 'The whole pleasure of marriage is that a man should have a wife to come home to; even in the pleasure of being engaged, the girl should not over-do things.'

For a rare moment, she looked at her son anxiously. They were sitting at breakfast together: for all her new pleasures and excitements it was still the best hour of the day to her. Mrs Gibson had deceived herself with wonderful success: the fundamental satisfaction, the knowledge that her son wasn't marrying a wife who would take him away from her, was buried so deep that when she exclaimed how much Harry admired Miranda's piano-playing, how completely he relied on her taste, how well the two children suited each other, for ninety-nine per cent of the time Mrs Gibson believed every word. Now, in a hundredth moment, she looked at him anxiously.

'Is all well, Harry boy?'

Undoubtedly Mr Gibson would have been decorated, had war as waged by Service Corps offered more opportunity. It was reserved to civilian life to show his mettle. His personal future stretched before him like a desert – or rather like war itself: a perpetuity of discomfort diversified by moments of terror. When he thought of Dolores, of how Dolores might be faring, he often had to loosen his collar. He suffered constantly from hallucinations – thinking he saw her in the street, or in a restaurant, or on a passing bus. But out of his deep tenderness for his mother, and out of a dogged resolve to play the game like a true Britisher, he drew strength to clear his brow and smile.

'Do I know when I'm on velvet, or don't I? – Toodle-oo,' said Harry Gibson.

At least, after this conversation, Miranda didn't visit the shop quite so often, and when she did she stayed below. Whatever old Mrs Gibson said, to Auntie Bee, or to Miranda herself, or, possibly, to Mr Joyce, her words took effect. It was again a minor victory; but at least Harry Gibson did Miranda no physical injury.

2

Dolores too suffered from hallucinations.

She was still unluckier than Mr Gibson in that she had less to occupy her mind. It was the obverse of her luck in getting Mr Phillips: in the job-hunting queues, what with anxiety and aching feet, she had often forgotten her King Hal for whole hours at a time; those days over, and as Mr Phillips settled, no mere domestic routine could pull her thoughts from their North, and they dwelt on the happy past without intermission. Admittedly Miss Diver made no attempt to discipline them, on the contrary. Her ritual dusting of the sitting-room has been described; in time her nonsensical ejaculations before pieces of bric-à-brac, so unsympathised with by Martha, became a ritual preface to each solitary evening – *Big Harry* (the stuffed ermines), *King Hal* (the bronze lady), *King Hal* (the china pierrot), *Big Hally* (the pierrette). It was foolish, even reprehensible, so to play on her own feelings – as it was foolish to lie, later, staring at a photograph by the bed and willing it to utter; but so foolishly, reprehensibly, did Miss Diver behave. And when she went out into the streets, she saw Mr Gibson at every turn.

Gargoyle-faced Mr Johnson, selling matches on the curb of Queen's Road, to Dolores momentarily assumed the likeness of Harry Gibson. A man in front of her at the butcher's, before he turned his head, looked like Harry Gibson. A passenger descending from a bus looked like Harry Gibson. Each likeness naturally dissolved into reality before Dolores had time to pluck a sleeve, or cry a name, or run after – supposing she could have brought herself so to pluck, to cry, or run. The disillusion was nonetheless bitter.

All separated lovers know this particular anguish. Such hallucinations are a common phenomenon, when lovers are separated.

Lovers of the more obviously romantic sort have the world's sympathy to sustain them. Runaways to Gretna Green still find witnesses; film-stars not quite thrice-divorced are sustained by the sympathy of their fans, as they battle on to a fourth exchange of life-long vows. Mr Gibson and Miss Diver enjoyed no such moral support. Only they themselves could preserve their romantic vision: and that each held in mind an image to all but one another unrecognisable, must be accounted a remarkable proof of their true love.

Even to herself, Dolores was finding it difficult to retain the character of a Spanish rose. As she soon discovered, even the most perfect lodger has one inevitable disadvantage: that of postulating a landlady. However quiet his step, however unobtrusive his demeanour, a man going in and out twice a day is bound to be observed; and as the card in the window, so long as it remained an empty show, had not, the coming of Mr Phillips universally declared her new status.

Miss Taylor the chiropodist stopped her familiarly in the street.

'So you've got a lodger at last!' cried Miss Taylor, in congratulatory tones. (This was actually a little disingenuous of Miss Taylor, who it may be remembered could have sent along a bed-sit, as soon as Dolores put her card up; but she had merely been returning snub for snub, as she was now – another sign of Dolores' declension –

willing to let bygones be bygones.) 'I hope he suits?' asked Miss Taylor, quite anxiously.

Dolores, her head high, replied that she seemed to have been very fortunate.

'Then treat him like a basket of eggs, my dear,' exclaimed Miss Taylor, 'for they're scarce as hens' teeth! The liberties *some* expect to take – though I'm sure *you'd* never allow – passes belief. How are the tootsies?'

Dolores, moving on, replied that they gave her no trouble at all.

'Well, don't let them go too long,' advised Miss Taylor shrewdly, 'now that you can treat yourself again . . .'

Which was bitterer to Miss Diver, a chiropodist's familiarity, or the discovery that her own financial straits had been common knowledge? By comparison with either, the ache of a fallen arch was nothing.

In the shops, where even during the leanest period, when her purchases dwindled to a minimum, the tradesmen's manner exhibited an awareness, so to speak, of her social superiority, the same sansculotte wind blew. As a lady of independent means (however small, derived from whatever source), Miss Diver was a cut above. Now all knew how she got her living—

'Chops again? Funny how all lodgers cry out for chops,' observed the butcher sociably.

Dolores, who always used to acknowledge his remarks about the weather, remained silent.

'Though they don't all, if I may say so, get 'em as regular as your chap,' added the butcher – helpful and good-natured. 'What about a nice pound o' mince?'

'I'll take chops, thank you.'

'Feeds separate,' noted the butcher intelligently. 'Very nice too. My sister-in-law once tried it.'

Bracketed with a butcher's sister-in-law, Dolores was nonetheless forced to wait while he cut her order. Of course she didn't ask the expected questions; but butchers, unlike lady-chiropodists, are so little used to being snubbed that they do not know it when they are.

'It didn't answer. In fact, it ate up all the profits,' continued this self-appointed mentor, 'her buying chops just the same as you. To *which* the answer, as I told her, is rissoles. Take a nice pound o' mince—'

'Thank you. Good morning,' said Dolores.

Every such encounter a little abraded, each day, her power to retain the character of a Spanish rose. She knew it. She would have stayed entirely within-doors, and sent Martha to shop, had it not been for the perennial, perennially-betrayed, hallucinating hope that drew her out. What would she have said, if she'd truly encountered her King Hal at the butcher's? She didn't know. No more than when she'd envisaged Martha at Kensington had she any really treacherous thought. She simply wanted to see him again – longed with all her heart. In any case, she never did. It was always an hallucination.

3

Martha saw him.

As Miss Diver, before she lost heart, reminded her, she liked playing in Kensington Gardens. The phrase wasn't strictly accurate, but rather one of Miss Diver's customary prettifications: it was convenient to let Martha go walks by herself, and a curious back-wash of the Edwardian Barrie-and-Nanny myth – Peter Pan, all those nice children – led Miss Diver to dispatch her trustfully to the Gardens. Martha never actually played there. She had no one to play with – and never loitered on the outskirts of a game, of tag or French cricket or cowboys, in the hope of being co-opted. Nor did she particularly appreciate the Gardens themselves – preferring for interest Alcock Road, where to Martha's mind there was more to look at. Large-scale natural beauty never said much, to Martha. In fact, her walks took her to the Gardens far less often than they were supposed to; and when Miss Diver supposed her ring-o'-rosing round Peter Pan, she was far more likely to be earthed with Mr Punshon.

On this particular morning, however, some three weeks after Mr Phillips' arrival, Martha might have been acting on instructions.

It was fine mid-August weather, pleasanter in the Gardens than between houses; Martha nonetheless sauntered straight across, casually emerged into Kensington High Street, casually – but as though she were obeying instructions, or being Guided; Dolores would undoubtedly have plumped for Guidance – bore right, and presently found herself at the corner of the High Street and Almaviva Place, where she halted to contemplate a tree.

This in itself was abnormal. (The beauties of nature saying so little to her.) But the tree in question stood alone, a great chestnut spared for its antiquity by Borough Council after Borough Council. It wasn't cluttered up with a lot of other trees: Martha could see it. She thought she could draw it all inside two triangles. Lacking paper and pencil, she was forced to memorise. This was such hard work that when Mr Gibson, emerging from the shop, crossed her line of vision, Martha instinctively shut her eyes.

Because Mr Gibson's shape was vaguely familiar, and therefore eye-catching. Her eye caught, and distracted, by a familiar ovoid silhouette, what else could Martha do but screw down her lids? When she opened them again, Mr Gibson was gone.

He for his part didn't see Martha. His vision was as narrow as hers. The shape perpetually sought by Mr Gibson's eye was long and narrow – or tall and slender; a dumpy silhouette under the chestnut his eye as automatically abolished, as the eye of Martha abolished him.

This was the only chance Chance offered, to bring Miss Diver and Mr Gibson once more into contact. Their stars had at last pulled it off, all the necessary factors were assembled in conjunction. But the vigorous star that ruled the child Martha wasn't interested.

4

Martha's star at this period had actually its own battle to fight. Mr Phillips entering on his fourth week in Alcock Road, allowing for the first few days off Martha had said 'Good morning' to him seventeen times.

'Anything on your mind?' asked Mr Punshon.

Martha shook her head. She was drawing the big china beer-mug he kept his tobacco in. It had a flat metal lid which when cocked up added interest: cylinder and disc.

'Well, anyone been treating you rough?' persisted Mr Punshon.

Martha shook her head again.

'Myself, I'd as soon try getting rough with a young Pachyderm,' said Mr Punshon reflectively. 'All right, I can take a hint.'

He pushed across a paper of fish-and-chips, as he always did if Martha dropped in while he was eating fish-and-chips, and Martha took the largest chip. It was delicious – so soused in vinegar that even licking the fingers afterwards made one cough. 'Thank you very much,' said Martha. Then Mr Punshon got on with his work, and she got on with hers.

. . . 'You bin robbin' a till and got the dicks after you?' enquired Mr Johnson.

'No,' said Martha.

'You might as well 'ave. You ain't bin back to that Chapel an' got a sense o' sin, I hope?'

'No,' said Martha, walking round on the pavement to look at Mr Johnson's face from the other side. It was part of his charm for her that he had two quite different profiles; yet somewhere in the middle they obviously joined. . . .

'Any time you want, come and take my likeness,' offered Mr Johnson generously.

'Thank you very much,' said Martha.

Not even to these two friends could she unburden herself. To say she didn't like the new lodger would have been an over-simplification: and the true root of her malaise lay so deeply entwined with her inmost feelings, she couldn't bring it to light. Put briefly, while Martha didn't mind carrying up Mr Phillips' tray, to have to look at him and say Good morning represented the imposition of an alien will.

When Mr Gibson desired Martha to cease threading beads, Martha co-operated gladly – because she didn't want to thread beads. Mr Gibson preferring her out of sight, that suited Martha too. To a most unusual degree she had escaped the common fate of childhood, which is subjection. Now, however triflingly, she was subject to Mr Phillips.

It was unexpected. When Mr Punshon called Martha a young Pachyderm, the phrase was as apt as picturesque. Her thick-skinned stolidity impressed even acquaintances. (The kind Librarian called it unmistakable force of character.) Mr Phillips was by comparison a nonentity. Even his virtues were negative – he didn't rob the gas-meter, et cetera. He had of course economics on his side, the economy of the little house in Alcock Road was now based on his weekly payments; but no one, seeing Mr Phillips tread so doucely in and out, would have guessed him the victor in any brush with a really strong, pachydermous character.

CHAPTER ELEVEN

I

The day of the missed chance, when Martha failed to see Mr Gibson, and Mr Gibson failed to see Martha, in Almaviva Place, happened also to be the date of the big official party to celebrate, and publicise, Mr Gibson's engagement to Miranda Joyce. There had been several smaller affairs before – little dinners for Harry to get to know people – but this was the gala. It was an evening entertainment of the highest class.

All the guests were very nice people indeed, many of them quite big names in the fur-trade. No poor relations of any sort had been invited. All the men were in evening-dress, and their ladies décolletées. Miranda sparkled in pale blue (her fiancé's favourite colour), pink carnations at the shoulder. There was a buffet-supper, with champagne.

Among all this splendour and festivity Harry Gibson moved, as his mother pointed out, like a man in a dream. His eye was a little glazed, his smile fixed like that of a man who has died smiling in the snow; he did not seem always to take in what was being said to him. When one of the biggest names of all, a man connected with the Hudson Bay Company, told him he remembered Mr Gibson senior, Harry said something quite obscure about Grand Duchesses; as to a lady who complimented Miranda's dress he said something about sea-horses; in each case however with such glazed politeness – matching his glazed eye – as to cause surprise rather than offence. It was still wise of old Mrs Gibson to keep close on his heels. 'Like a man in a dream!' she repeated gaily. 'My boy Harry is like a man in a dream! Do you know what he said to *me*, Mrs Conrad, Madame Grandjean, as he was dressing? When I brought him his white waistcoat, he said, "In Japan and India they too wear white!" My boy Harry, and why not, is completely in a dream!'

Fortunately neither Mrs Conrad nor Madame Grandjean had any more knowledge of the East than Mrs Gibson. A Mr Demetrios who had, and who knew white there to be the colour of mourning, fortunately didn't overhear. With his mother at his heels Harry Gibson circulated acceptably – a man in a dream.

Every now and again he found himself standing arm-in-arm with Miranda. They were generally in a circle of her unaffianced girl-friends. 'You make my big Harry shy!' cried Miranda – adroit as his mother. 'See how he loses his tongue! But Marion and Rachel and Denise I went to school with, Harry – there is no need to be frightened of them!'

They all gazed at him, Denise and Marion and Rachel, envyingly. Only a plump brunette with a bigger engagement-ring than Miranda's enquired, a trifle maliciously, why shouldn't he be frightened of them? Her Bobby was. Her Bobby had made her promise on a wet finger never to let a school-friend into their house. . . . Mr Gibson shot this unknown sympathiser a grateful look; but it was his only indiscretion of the evening.

Admittedly he kept Miranda, after supper, rather long at the piano. ('So what?' demanded Harry Gibson of his mother, when she suggested a pause. 'Are we to have musical evenings or aren't we?') Old Mrs Gibson and Auntie Bee, swinging into their well-rehearsed routine, handled this too acceptably. (It was music first brought the children together, et cetera.) In short, the evening, like the evening two months earlier, might have passed off far worse. In the circles frequented by Miranda Joyce, it was generally agreed that she'd got hold of a bit of a stick-in-the-mud; she was also, generally, envied.

Old Mrs Gibson wore at this party a brand-new French grey velvet; draped skirt, passementerie about the bodice. It came from the dressmaker entrusted with Miranda's trousseau. So did Auntie Bee's charmeuse.

PART II

CHAPTER TWELVE

I

The first time Mr Phillips saw the sitting-room was on a Thursday night five weeks after his arrival in Alcock Road.

Dolores had never invited him in before. Why should she have? She had every reason not to: apart from her policy of keeping him at arm's length, the sitting-room was sacred ground, which even Martha was now discouraged from frequenting. Dolores spent every evening there alone, sipping tea, looking through old *Tatlers*, and thinking long rambling thoughts about Mr Gibson. Whatever object her eyes rested on set her off; every object was precious for that reason; and that Mr Gibson's eye had once so rested too, lent to each an added patina of almost unendurable beauty.

No wonder Mr Phillips had never seen the sitting-room. It was no ground to be profaned by a lodger's foot.

Dolores didn't precisely invite him, that Thursday. The whole episode was an accident. Mr Phillips notifying himself out to supper (also for the first time), to so excellent a tenant how could his land-lady refuse the key? She could not; and upon his return at the moderate hour of ten Mr Phillips notified himself in again by tapping at the sitting-room door.

Dolores, on the settee, had kicked her shoes off. Before she could recover them, Mr Phillips tapped again. Sooner than pad to

encounter him in her stockings – 'Come in!' called Dolores; and so
Mr Phillips entered.

2

He had not only never seen the sitting-room before, he had never
seen anything like it.

A penurious youth in Manchester, a wide experience of third-
rate London lodgings hadn't prepared him for the bowl of glass fruit
lit up from inside. The social evening he'd just spent, with a married
friend in a two-room flat, hadn't prepared him for the black cushions on the settee, or for the china pierrot with matches; still less for
the bronze-and-ivory statuette. Wherever he looked, his eye rested
on evidences of a luxury as astonishing as unexpected. If he'd found
himself in the Throne Room of Buckingham Palace, Mr Phillips
couldn't have been more startled.

'Is that the key? Thank you,' said Dolores – sitting up straighter,
but otherwise without moving.

'I've slipped the latch,' muttered Mr Phillips.

His dazzled eye took in more and more: the high-class Rexine
upholstery, the stuffed ermines in the gilt cabinet, the pierrette to
match the pierrot. . . . He still held the key in his hand.

'Thank you, you may put it down,' said Dolores.

Mr Phillips advanced an awkward pace towards the mother-o'-
pearl table. Upon it stood Dolores' tea-things. But she didn't offer a
cup to Mr Phillips – as an ordinary landlady might have done; she
simply waited for him to go.

Mr Phillips took a last look round. His eye, as it catalogued each
treasure, wasn't Martha's, still less Dolores'; it was nonetheless avid.
He'd have particularly liked a closer look at the statuette. . . .

'Good night,' said Dolores, dismissively.

3

That was all. Mr Phillips was in the sitting-room perhaps two minutes. It took him however nearly two hours to get to sleep. He heard

eleven strike, and twelve; and even so shortly before dawn woke again and lit a cigarette.

It was his first lodgerly misdemeanour. All landladies hate their lodgers to smoke in bed, because of the risk to sheets, also a lodger frizzled alive (should the whole bed catch) means an inquest. Mr Phillips, hitherto of all lodgers the pearl, now reached for matches and cigarettes without a second thought, so confused in mind was he still.

The luxury of Miss Diver's private apartment had more than startled, it had staggered him. For all his wide experience of lodgings, he'd never before lodged in a house with such a room as that in it. In a house that let lodgings, it seemed . . . unnatural. To take the ornaments alone – what was that statue doing there? A bunch of dried grass would have been more the mark. Searching his memory, Mr Phillips recalled a couple of stuffed bullfinches: never a whole pack of stuffed ermines. (Ermine, good lord! The most expensive animal there was!) As for the bowl of glass fruit casting its multi-coloured glow, it struck Mr Phillips as almost improper.

In fact the whole room struck him as a bit improper.

But this wasn't what struck him most. Summing his whole impression, he returned to his first thought of all, the thought that crossed his mind actually as he first contemplated (not with Martha's eye, not with Dolores') the sitting-room's astounding contents.

'There's been money spent,' thought Mr Phillips.

As he lay smoking and thinking this over, another point occurred to him, of which he'd been hitherto aware only subconsciously. All the curtains, in the house in Alcock Road, matched. They were all (he checked them over in his mind) pink. They were pink, he was pretty sure, even at the back. To an experienced lodger, this again was very striking.

'There's been money spent,' thought Mr Phillips.

His cigarette was only two-thirds smoked; but realising that at the moment he couldn't get much further, he economically cut off the end with his nail-scissors, blew down the butt, and once again composed himself for sleep.

4

The first time Mr Phillips assisted with the garbage-pail was on the Sunday morning following. Dolores, caught beside the dust-bin, wasn't altogether pleased. She knew her apron soiled and her make-up rudimentary; as a Spanish rose, she felt taken at a disadvantage. 'Aren't you down very early?' she asked sharply. 'By chance, I felt like a walk before dinner. That's too heavy for you,' returned Mr Phillips, seizing the pail with one hand and the dust-bin lid with the other. 'Allow me!' Dolores recovered her poise – it was obviously impossible to start a tug-of-war – and replied more affably that he was very kind. To her relief, he didn't appear to notice her undress. . . .

Soon he was emptying the garbage quite regularly. Dolores left it outside the back door for him last thing at night, and he disposed of it before leaving each morning; and was allowed to wash his hands afterwards at the kitchen sink.

The only immediate result of this was that Martha, who was usually laying her own and Dolores' breakfast, at last noticed something about Mr Phillips' appearance. The back of his neck was grooved by two extraordinarily long, deep hollows, beginning behind the ears and disappearing into his collar: which by throwing his spinal column into unnatural prominence, made his head from behind look like a can stuck on a pole.

Dolores didn't mind Mr Phillips in the kitchen. It wasn't sacred ground; she had no feeling for it. She cooked and ate meals there, but never lingered – preferring her bed-chamber in the afternoon and at evening the sitting-room; and this suited Martha very well, because it gave her the kitchen-table to draw on undisturbed.

5

She drew regularly every afternoon, from about two till half-past five. She found she drew better, regularly. She got on.

This happy spell of intensive work nonetheless brought its problems. Martha was now using up a great deal of paper, and even had the supply of old envelopes been unlimited, which it was not, they were inconveniently small. No sort of paper abounded, in the house in Alcock Road, and she knew better than to ask Dolores to buy any specially. Martha would soon have been in serious straits, had she not fortunately discovered an important, and free, source of supply.

There was half-way along Praed Street a large and popular drapery establishment, whither Miss Diver occasionally sent her for a reel of cotton or a packet of needles. A more interesting department than the haberdashery offered nets, veilings and lace, which came wrapped around large sheets of thin white cardboard; and as these were emptied, they were thrown away.

Martha saw them being thrown away – a whole heap, kicked together on the floor behind a counter by a sales-lady's foot. It seemed impossible, but so it was.

'Don't you *want* those?' asked Martha incredulously.

'What, this rubbish? I should say not,' replied the sales-lady, looking amused.

Martha didn't hesitate an instant.

'Can I have them?'

'Well!' said the sales-lady. 'Whatever for?'

'To draw on.'

The sales-lady wavered; and as she had been taught to do whenever out of her depth, called a shop-walker.

'Mr Connaught! Can this little girl have our old cardboards to draw on?'

Mr Connaught, approaching, appeared equally surprised. But shop-walkers are compact of *savoir faire*. He regarded Martha quizzically, showing off his easy mastery of any situation.

'And what does she want to draw?'

Some instinct led Martha to reply, 'Pussies.'

Actually both the term and the subject were equally repugnant to her; if there was one thing that hadn't a hard outline, it was a cat, and if there was one thing Martha despised it was baby-talk. But her instinct was sound; both adults at once smiled benevolently on her, and at each other with understanding. A little girl who wanted to draw pussies – what a rare note of sweetness in the long commercial day! They let her have the cardboards at once. And Martha, stifling her distaste for such puerilities, as soon as she got home slapped off a couple of big fluffy cats with bows round their necks, to carry back next morning as presents.

After that she had as much cardboard as she needed. She collected it in a business-like way once a week.

Where had she seen a lot of pencils?

6

'Dear me, you're quite a stranger!' said the kind Librarian.

Martha stared at his desk. Five or six pencils at least lay in the tray, and some were easily short enough to be given to a little girl.

'I forgot,' said Martha vaguely.

'Have you come to look at our landscapes again?'

Martha followed his prompting glance and recognised with surprise a bamboo swaying in the wind, a tiger crouched upon a rock. She *had* forgotten . . . and even now wasn't interested. They were right, but they hadn't any hard outlines. The kind Librarian watched her face and sighed. 'How soon it passes,' he was thinking, 'the gift of natural, instinctive appreciation! I wonder' – for he was a very conscientious man – 'if I could have done more?'

Martha turned back to the desk and fixed her gaze on the pen-tray. She wasn't there to hang about.

'Perhaps you're tired of them,' said the Librarian. 'One day, if you like, I could take you to see some really beautiful pictures – hundreds and hundreds of them. They're in a place called the National Gallery. Would you like that?'

'Thank you very much,' said Martha, in rather final tones. 'Do you use *all* those pencils?'

The Librarian sighed again. She was after all just a child like any other – and all children always wanted pencils.

'Do you need one for noughts-and-crosses?'

Martha didn't want to draw any more cats for anyone, so she said yes. It was unfortunate, and came of putting all adults in the same box. Pussies would have left Mr Agnew cold; but if she'd told him of her involvement with shapes, he'd have given her all the pencils on his desk. As it was, she got just the stubbiest.

'Thank you very much,' repeated Martha glumly.

It wasn't nearly so successful a foray as she had hoped for; moreover something in the Librarian's manner frightened her off, so that she never went back to try again. (Interferingness: the adult vice.) In the end she turned to cadging odd stumps from Mr Punshon, who always had one or two lying about his bench. She rubbed out with bread.

7

'How soon it passes!' mourned the Librarian, that same evening, to his gentle, artistic fiancée.

'How soon what passes, darling?' asked she.

'The natural, instinctive appreciation of beauty. You remember that little girl I told you about?'

'Who came to look at the landscapes? Of course I do, darling. Has she been again?'

'To beg a pencil to play noughts-and-crosses,' said the Librarian sadly. 'She doesn't even *see* them now. I offered to take her to the National Gallery—'

'Darling, I think you're the kindest man in the world!' cried his fiancée impulsively.

Mr Agnew looked round, and gave her a quick kiss. They were pacing beside the Serpentine, in the blue dusk. Pale amber streamers, reflected lamp-light, floated on the surface of the water as pennons float in air: the upper branches of the trees, to the west melting into the sky, to the east showed still in detail against the up-thrown glow of London. As he finally put Martha from his mind—

'If I showed her *this*,' said the Librarian, 'I don't believe she'd have eyes for it. . . .'

Which was perfectly true. Martha's eyes were at that very moment glued to a pair of kippers, tails up (the tails formed a double bow-shape), in a cylindrical jug.

CHAPTER THIRTEEN

I

Leaving home in the morning, kissing his daughter and allowing himself to be pecked at by old Beatrice—

'Toodle-oo,' said Mr Joyce.

The door shut behind him – on Mr Joyce wearing his new winter overcoat, a loud fawn and brown check, very hairy, and his new silk scarf, striped in loud and probably regimental colours. Old Beatrice turned nervously to Miranda.

'Such a nice idea I have for our lunch! Why don't I make us my special goulash?'

'In the middle of the day it's too heavy,' said Miranda crossly.

Both knew what they were to eat at night; roast beef. Both knew what Mr Joyce would say, as it came to the table, as he sharpened the carving-knife and caught Harry Gibson's eye.

'Good British grub!' Mr Joyce would say.

2

Mr Joyce had found a friend.

A wholly unexpected result of Harry Gibson's domestication at Knightsbridge was the formation there of what could only be called a masculine front.

Passive as he was, Harry by his mere presence had from the first, and inevitably, changed the numerical proportions between the sexes: what no one could have foreseen was Mr Joyce's rapid organisation of an offensive alliance.

Miranda placed the blame squarely on her father. The overtures hadn't come from Harry, whatever Mr Joyce learnt from him Harry hadn't wilfully taught; it was again, apparently, the result of his mere presence – as though daily contact with anyone so big and bluff and British spurred Mr Joyce to emulation. Spontaneously he picked up Harry's British slang, spontaneously discarded the tastes of a lifetime to prefer good British grub to Beatrice's goulash; but the result, of course, was that he ... *encouraged* Harry; until Harry was now encouraging him back.

Miranda had no wish to see her lover brow-beaten. His masculinity was precious to her. But she'd certainly expected the Joyce ethos (so much the more refined) to work upon the Gibson, and not the other way about. She certainly hadn't expected her father to behave like an only child who suddenly makes a friend.

He supported Harry on every point, great or small – and with particular pleasure, it seemed, if the result in any way irritated Miranda or old Beatrice. (Miranda was too obtuse to recognise this pleasure's spring; but the whole of Mr Joyce's domestic life had been dominated by females he provided for.) On the point of a six-months engagement, he'd taken Harry's part; now after roast beef, or liver-and-bacon, or steak-and-kidney pie, the Knightsbridge table offered steamed pudding every night. And as though that wasn't sufficient offence to old Beatrice's *monts blancs*, Mr Joyce deliberately – there could be no other word for it – began to put on weight. 'He wants to be a big man like my Harry!' chuckled Mrs Gibson, much amused; and indeed in his new winter overcoat, which he was wearing long before the weather warranted it, Mr Joyce managed to look several sizes larger.

Harry went with him to choose it – and not in Savile Row. ('Half the price as well!' reported Mr Joyce delightedly.) It almost exactly duplicated the one Harry had.

Miranda might have been right in putting the first blame on her parent, but her fiancé's influence was certainly no longer passive. Mr Joyce had encouraged him so much, they now encouraged each other. . . .

How strangely, beautifully (from Mr Joyce's point of view), things had turned out! Harry Gibson was by no means the son-in-law he'd have put his money on given a choice. Most rarely, among the natural money-makers, old Joyce thought little of money for its own sake. To scrap over three or four pounds was instinctive, but in thousands he thought like a Maecenas; and it had been the secret dream of his life to wed Miranda to some violinist, or painter, or composer, whose early struggles, by himself financed, would in time gloriously flower. (Not too late: while he was still alive: every patron has his limitations, and Mr Joyce wanted to shine in reflected glory.) Like the practical man that he was, he took positive steps to this end – had Miranda's portrait painted, frequented private views, cultivated an acquaintance who ran a concert agency; to acquire only a taste for modern art and a dislike of modern music. All the painters seemed to be married already, and the musicians not to care for Miranda.

No embryo genius coming on the market in the course of so many years, Mr Joyce at last accepted Fate's rebuff and settled for Harry Gibson – even as a business prospect poor, but a necessary husband for Miranda. And how had Fate rewarded him? By finding him a friend.

The lot of Harry Gibson, by this circumstance, was also ameliorated. He wasn't, like Mr Joyce, happy. He was far from happy. But he felt a friendliness towards the old man on his own account, he grew fond of the old boy, and the knowledge that Mr Joyce valued his company – more than valued it, thirsted for it – made his attendance at Knightsbridge less unendurable. Harry Gibson was never for a moment happy, in the Knightsbridge flat; but he had become domesticated there.

CHAPTER FOURTEEN

I

The first time Mr Phillips took Dolores and Martha to the pictures was on a Saturday afternoon early in September.

The leap, from Good morning and Good evening, to such an invitation, was hardy indeed; even though his garbage-emptying and subsequent hand-washing had slightly extended their conversational terrain. To do him justice, Mr Phillips appeared aware of this. Encountering Miss Diver in the hall – where he had obviously been waiting for her to emerge from the kitchen – he put it very properly, as a favour.

'It would be doing me a favour,' stated Mr Phillips, 'to give me the pleasure of your company.'

Dolores' first impulse was to refuse. It was such a – how to put it? – such a *lodgerly* thing of Mr Phillips to do! But she hadn't been to a cinema for months; the piled-up monotony of her solitary evenings was sometimes almost crushing; and the refusal meant to be so prompt and firm weakened to hesitation.

'I really don't think I can, Mr Phillips . . . leave Martha in the house alone.'

Mr Phillips hesitated in turn – but only for a moment.

'Bring Martha too.'

'How very kind! But thank you, I think not.'

'It's just the sort of picture you'd like,' persuaded Mr Phillips.

If he baited the hook with intent, it was skilfully done. What sort of picture *did* Mr Phillips think she liked? No woman could have failed to feel a little stir of curiosity, even of vanity, and Dolores was doubly engaged – for was it a landlady's taste Mr Phillips believed himself to have divined, or that of the mysterious Other she felt he sometimes glimpsed? A Western or a war picture or a comedy would have answered the first; far narrower the range acceptable to a Spanish rose.

'Romantic,' added Mr Phillips.

How could Dolores not give way?

They might have passed a very pleasant evening, if they hadn't taken Martha.

2

Martha was comfortably settled at the kitchen-table, drawing the gas-oven. It was the most complicated subject she'd yet tackled, and to make things more difficult she had opened the door half-way – the gas-rings on top looking somehow rounder when one could see the straight parallel lines of the bars inside. She reckoned she had three good hours before it was time to put the oven to its ordinary use.

Thus when Miss Diver returned and asked if she wouldn't like to go to the pictures, Martha naturally said no.

'But Mr Phillips is taking us!' cried Dolores. He was actually, which made Martha's attitude all the more unfortunate, in the kitchen with them, having followed on Miss Diver's heels.

'I'd rather stay here and draw,' said Martha stubbornly.

'Don't be silly, you draw all the time,' rebuked Miss Diver. 'Say thank you to Mr Phillips and get your coat.'

With an impatient exclamation she crossed to shut the oven door. Mr Phillips however kept his eyes on Martha. He'd been looking at her ever since he entered, and Martha knew it, though she wouldn't look back.

'Perhaps she wants to show me her picture first?' suggested Mr Phillips blandly.

Martha answered by deliberately laying her forearms across the sheet. The drawing was on such a scale, however – filling a whole cardboard – that quite a lot still showed. Mr Phillips came up close behind and looked over her shoulder.

'What's it meant to be?' he asked. 'A bird-cage?'

'I don't know,' muttered Martha, scowling.

'Just scribbling, eh?'

'There, Martha!' cried Miss Diver brightly. 'Scribbling's nothing to stay in for! Besides, you'll strain your eyes. Look at them now!'

'I'd strain them worse at the pictures,' said stubborn Martha.

Dolores glanced at Mr Phillips apologetically. He was still standing behind Martha's chair (in such a kind, interested attitude!) and Martha was still crouched over her drawing like a lion-cub over a piece of meat, and somehow the impression was produced that neither meant to give way an inch. It was a most painful contest between sulkiness and benevolence.

'I feel sick,' added Martha.

By this time Dolores at least was weakening. Indeed, it quite astonished her that Mr Phillips was still prepared to take Martha out at all: no child could have looked less grateful. No child, to put it plainlier, could have looked more stubborn, surly and thoroughly bad-tempered. A concentrated spell of work always sent Martha's temperature up and made her cheeks red, but she had now the appearance of being scarlet with rage.

'If she really doesn't want to come—' began Dolores doubtfully.

'She's coming,' said Mr Phillips.

Benevolence won. It is almost impossible for a child to disobey a direct order, at least after the reckless age of 'Shan't' and 'Won't'. Upon Miss Diver's now directly ordering her to go and get her coat, Martha at last sulkily gathered up her work, and stumped out into the hall.

3

It was thus no very festive party that set forth from Alcock Road. Their disunion was apparent from the start – Martha walking not

97

alongside her elders and betters, but a little behind. She also dragged her feet in the way all children know to be irritating.

'Martha, pick up your feet.'

'My shoe-lace is undone.'

'Then stop and tie it up.'

They all stopped, while Martha knelt on the curb. (Well past the Greek-temple-prison-gate gutter-grating: not for worlds would she have risked drawing attention to its loveliness.) The business took her rather long, because she broke the lace and had to knot it. Then they all went on again, Martha now lifting each foot in turn about six inches from the ground, as though plodding through snow. This naturally slowed her down still more, so that she acted like a drogue on Miss Diver's and Mr Phillips' progress, but in time they reached the Locarno, where Mr Phillips took seats in the one-and-threes.

As he had promised, the film was a romantic one – and how sudden, how beautiful, how complete, the transition to Old Vienna! How *familiar*, that enchanting city! Not one of the population was missing – neither the hero in the Hussars, nor the heroine selling posies, nor the fiddlers playing the Blue Danube Waltz to the boatmen on the Blue Danube. It was indeed just the film Miss Diver would have enjoyed, if she hadn't had Martha beside her.

'Martha, stop sighing.'

'I'm hot.'

'Then take your coat off.'

Mr Phillips, on Dolores' other side, behaved impeccably. It must be revealed that Dolores' hesitance before her lodger's invitation was due not only to its essential lodgerishness, but also to certain more general apprehensions. Sheltered as she'd been for the past ten years, Miss Diver was thirty when she met Mr Gibson. She knew what went on, in cinemas. She'd had her hand held (however briefly, disappointingly, she preferred not to think of it) in the darkness of a cinema. Couples in front of her, in the darkness of a cinema, she'd beheld going much, much farther. Dolores certainly apprehended no such outrageousness on the part of Mr Phillips – but what *did* a lodger expect, taking his landlady to the pictures? Even a mild pressure of the hand Miss Diver would have felt bound to refuse. Perhaps she exaggerated her own charms; she still welcomed Martha as chaperone. It was now with genuine relief that she found every apprehension groundless.

Mr Phillips sat so narrowly in his seat, only occasionally their elbows brushed, and when they did, he said 'Pardon.' He kept his knees and feet strictly to himself, and his hands in his lap. If it hadn't been for Martha snapping her hat-elastic during the love-scenes, Miss Diver could have lost herself completely in the beautiful story unfolding.

'Martha, take your hat off.'

'I don't know where to put it.'

'Put it under the seat.'

Beautifully, romantically the story unfolded. Extraordinarily: for it bore a striking resemblance to the story of King Hal and his Spanish rose. To the Hussar also duty called, in the person – it really *was* extraordinary! – of an heiress chosen for him by his Emperor, and the flower-girl sacrificed herself. They parted by moonlight on a rose-strewn terrace, the fiddlers now playing La Paloma . . . Miss Diver had still to look aside from the screen.

'Martha! What are you eating?'

'I found a toffee on the floor.'

'*Martha!* Take it out at once!'

It was almost a relief when the film ended. Dolores would have left immediately, only Mr Phillips said they might as well get their money's-worth and see the news. Of course he hadn't been *next* to Martha – but his forebearance was still striking: when at last they got home, and Dolores could scold Martha properly, it was exhibited in the highest form.

'I'm sure Mr Phillips will never take you out again!' finished Dolores angrily.

Mr Phillips looked at Martha, and for once Martha looked back at Mr Phillips – without unfocusing her eyes. It wasn't a look one would have thought to induce any further display of benevolence; yet it did.

'We'll see,' said Mr Phillips kindly. 'Eh, Martha?'

4

As Dolores in the course of her scolding complained, Martha had never behaved so badly before. It was true. Her bad behaviour was in fact a rare burst of juvenility; and after keeping her nose to the grindstone for so long, she felt all the better for it. She drew better and more easily next day. But Dolores was angry with her.

'How you could *be* so rude!' reiterated Dolores. 'When Mr Phillips was so kind!'

Martha was so bored with being scolded, she for once made an effort at explanation.

'It wasn't kind, when I didn't want to go. It was just to make me.'

'Nonsense, of course it was kind!' snapped Dolores. 'Taking a cross little girl to the pictures—! Can't you think of anything *nice* to do for him, to show you're sorry?'

Martha gave up. She felt (as adults often do with children) as though she was talking to a brick wall . . .

'No,' said Martha comprehensively.

It thus fell to Miss Diver to do something nice for Mr Phillips. Quite apart from the danger of offending him, she really felt he deserved it; and an evening or two later invited him into the sitting-room for a cup of tea.

CHAPTER FIFTEEN

I

'D'you know what I've been thinking, Dadda?' said Miranda Joyce. 'I've been thinking that after we're married, perhaps it mayn't be such a good plan after all, Harry and me living at the flat.'

Mr Joyce in his surprise trod with one foot off the curb and was brushed by a passing car. They were walking down Bond Street, Miranda having called for her parent at the shop; and that she chose so unlikely a moment to open her mind was because she'd just heard him say toodle-oo to the door-man.

—'Really, Dadda!' said Miranda coldly. 'Is that quite suitable?'

'If it suits *me*,' returned old man Joyce brashly, 'why not? I learnt it from your Harry.'

Miranda frowned.

'I still don't think it sounds right to a commissionaire, Dadda. I know he's been with us for years—'

'Also he was in Harry's old Regiment,' said Mr Joyce. 'All sorts of things I learn from that boy!'

It was the last straw on the load of grievance Miranda had been accumulating for weeks. What didn't he learn from Harry! What didn't he *teach* Harry – the one as bad as the other? For weeks now Miranda had begun to feel that her marriage would be a thing of far greater beauty if it didn't embrace Harry and her Dadda under the same roof. . . .

'After all,' pursued Miranda (in Bond Street, her parent just brushed by a passing car), 'most married people do start in their own homes, don't they, Dadda?'

'I never heard such craziness in my life,' returned Mr Joyce promptly – and turning to shake a fist at the receding traffic. His uninhibited manners out of doors often distressed his daughter. 'Did your mamma and I start in our own home?'

'That was a long time ago, Dadda. We should only need a flat—'

'What is wrong with our flat?' demanded Mr Joyce, stepping out again. It was a muggy September evening, but he always returned home on foot when he could spare the time, because he enjoyed the life of the street; at least part of his annoyance with Miranda was because she was spoiling his walk. 'What is wrong with our good-address flat in Knightsbridge, four hundred a year besides rates?' demanded Mr Joyce. 'Tell me what is wrong with that?'

'Nothing at all, Dadda,' agreed Miranda hastily. 'It's only—'

'Also am I made of money?' enquired Mr Joyce, proceeding to irony. 'Do I look in my pockets each morning and find a bag of gold? What about the new curtains, twelve-and-six a yard, also blue for Harry's favourite colour?'

'Of course we'd take them with us. . . .'

'What about the new wallpaper, then, five-and-nine a piece? Will you take that with you? Scrape it off the wall?'

'It makes a room very nice for Auntie Bee . . .'

Mr Joyce suddenly stopped before a lighted window. It was another of his street-arab habits – staring into shops. Except at certain jewellers, he had the money to buy almost anything that caught his fancy; he remained content with staring. It irritated Miranda that he now stopped to examine a straight-grain briar pipe with every appearance of attention. There was an irritating *insouciance* even in the way he stood: his hat on the back of his head, his loud check overcoat flapping open – this indeed because it was really too close to wear it – and his new regimental scarf sticking up round the collar . . .

'Dadda!' said Miranda sharply. 'This is an important conversation! Will you please think about Harry and me?'

'Harry I am thinking about this moment,' returned Mr Joyce benevolently. 'I am going to buy that boy a pipe. I notice you don't tell me how Harry is so crazy to leave the old man.'

Miranda hesitated. Actually she hadn't yet broached the subject to Harry at all, she meant to present him with a *fait accompli*, a new arrangement cut and dried.

'Harry will think as I do. . . .'

'Ah ha!'

'Naturally I consult you first, Dadda. For goodness' sake, first you argue about the curtains—'

'A nice argument I like,' admitted Mr Joyce cheerfully.

'—then you call it all just craziness! What *is* crazy is to pretend you can't afford it – a little flat for Harry and me! You have plenty of money!'

'So I can buy two pipes,' agreed Mr Joyce. 'For the heart, at my age, Harry says, a pipe is better than so many cigars.'

Miranda was forced to recognise that her parent was thoroughly out of hand. She was too angry to speak; she would have walked on alone, but at that moment he finally tore himself away (with many a loving backward glance at the most expensive straight-grain briars in London) and set gaily off again. Miranda still kept silence, merely emanating, with some ability, waves of alternate anger and reproach.

Mr Joyce seemed to enjoy the rest of the walk very much. His spirits were high. Pausing to buy a newspaper, he cracked jokes with the vendor in what he believed to be Cockney. By Hyde Park Corner they encountered a one-man-band: Mr Joyce contributed sixpence, also – because it wasn't in his nature to give sixpence and be done with it – halted to form a critical one-man-audience. (Miranda halted further on.) The band in question was actually rather an ingenious one, including cymbals (strapped to the knees), a mouth-organ and a couple of spoons. Mr Joyce thought it would be improved by a few bells. 'Round the chest, as on a child's harness,' he explained helpfully. 'So you would be four-piece instead of three.

Also Swiss effects,' added Mr Joyce, giving his imagination rein. 'Any visitor from Switzerland, the money would jump out of his pocket! Take my advice, remember what I say! Toodle-oo!'

When at last they reached the flat, Harry Gibson was there on the doorstep. He too wore a loud check overcoat, flapping open, and a regimental scarf. He too had an evening paper under his arm. It wasn't the same as Mr Joyce's; they had arranged always to buy different ones, so that they could swap, but though Mr Joyce was confident of this, he carolled his ritual greeting.

'*Star, News* or *Stan-dard?*' carolled Mr Joyce – imitating a paper-boy.

'*Star!*' replied Harry Gibson smartly.

'I've got the *News*. Let's hope it's good!' punned in Joyce, reverting to his own personality with a happy grin.

Harry Gibson grinned back. It was rather, he thought sadly, like the gag he used to have with Martha about Martha and Mary; but he played up to the old boy, not disappointing him. . . . They all entered together, and in the lobby Harry rang for the lift, and up in the flat hung his coat on its accustomed peg, and hung Mr Joyce's coat up too, and kissed first Miranda and then his mother, who was already in the drawing-room, and let himself be pecked at by Auntie Bee. He never knew a moment's happiness, in the Knightsbridge flat; but he was undoubtedly domesticated there.

CHAPTER SIXTEEN

I

A parallel domestication had taken place in Alcock Road, where on most evenings of the week Mr Phillips was now to be found accepting a cup of tea in Miss Diver's sitting-room.

This, too, was unexpected; yet it came about very naturally, and owing to Mr Phillips' new habit of taking a last-thing-at-night stroll. A breath of air, last thing at night, he found cleared his lungs; and though he now possessed a key of his own, his unfailing consideration led him always to notify himself returned. Dolores had always tea brewed; the habit of not entertaining her lodger once broken (to make up for Martha's rudeness at the cinema), a new habit inevitably formed; by the time Aunt Bee in Knightsbridge was regularly ordering sirloin, Dolores, in Alcock Road, as regularly set out an extra cup.

Indeed, she had begun to find Mr Phillips' company not unwelcome; his deferential presence a relief from so much solitude. His occasional remarks (for Dolores still leafed through her *Tatlers*, and Mr Phillips through his evening paper) were flat and undemanding – a mere human noise. After so much silence, Dolores rather welcomed it. It was a pain at first to see him stare about – obliterating, so to speak, the last traces of a beloved eye – but even this his admiration soothed. 'My word, that must be valuable!' marvelled Mr

Phillips, beside the bronze lady. 'I believe it is,' said Dolores carelessly. 'And those china orna-ments?' suggested Mr Phillips. 'French,' said Dolores.

If questions unspoken hovered in the air, she didn't answer them. Mr Phillips could see that there'd been money spent, but he got no further. He still couldn't fathom a house with such a room in it, and a lodger in it as well. He couldn't make out what was what.

It was Martha who eventually, and unwittingly, gave him the clue; though not for some time.

2

Martha's own internal state, at this period of Mr Phillips' domestication, resembled an armed fortress – sentries posted, guns manned, boiling lead ready on the battlements; yet at the citadel calm. Behind her defences she was working well, and so long as she wasn't attacked intended no sortie; but if anyone, for instance, took her to the cinema again, she was prepared – dropping the dignity of metaphor – to be sick. In pursuance of her sensible policy, she gave fair warning. 'I nearly *was*,' Martha informed Miss Diver gloomily, 'last time. I told you before we went.'

There are certain possibilities before which every adult recoils. Miss Diver said something to Mr Phillips. 'She doesn't *look* like a child with a weak stomach,' objected Mr Phillips suspiciously. It was very true; Martha didn't; still, there are certain possibilities et cetera. The point was in a sense shelved, since Mr Phillips didn't take Dolores to the pictures again either, the first visit turned out to be also the last; but Martha here undeniably won.

Her drawings, also, she withdrew as it were to the citadel – that is, whenever Mr Phillips was in the house she hid them in her attic. He had no second opportunity to look over her shoulder. This denied her the use of the kitchen-table at the week-end, but fortunately Mr Punshon kept his shop open all Saturday, and there on Saturday afternoons Martha regularly installed herself.

It was no hardship. Martha liked Mr Punshon's shop very well. There wasn't much room, she had to stuff herself between the end of the work-bench and a shutter hung with bunches of shoe-laces that tickled the back of her neck, but she enjoyed the craftsmanly atmosphere and worked well there; and Mr Punshon made no objection, so long as she didn't glare at the customers.

—'I didn't know I did,' said Martha, genuinely surprised.

'When they get in your light you do. Like a young Pachyderm,' said Mr Punshon, employing his favourite simile. 'I won't say trade's suffered as yet; but any more females in the family way such as we just rubber-heeled may well get nervous how their basketful's going to turn out. . . .'

Martha took the warning to heart. Thenceforward her amiable expression, in Mr Punshon's shop, occasionally covered exceedingly black thoughts, but rarely failed altogether. It was a useful piece of discipline such as she was all too unaccustomed to; for as Mr Phillips rightly pointed out, she had never really been disciplined at all.

'You must remember she's an orphan,' pleaded Dolores.

'I do,' said Mr Phillips.

For at least he had fathomed Martha. King Hal's Spanish rose, already declined into a landlady, had submitted also to decline into an aunt.

Mr Phillips' surprise at hearing Martha address her as Dolores hadn't been unmannerly – when was he unmannerly? – but it had been apparent. Miss Diver glimpsed a danger, however absurd, that he might jump to some wrong conclusion. She therefore casually referred, one evening, to her deceased brother (in the Civil Service), to her poor sister-in-law who had died so young (this was actually all Miss Diver knew about her late sister-in-law), and of course to Martha in so many words as her niece. Mr Phillips' attention was rewarding. The few questions he asked – 'In what branch of the Civil Service?' enquired Mr Phillips. 'The Post Office,' Dolores told him, rather shortly – but underlined a sympathetic interest. Dolores had no doubt but that she was believed; nonetheless, just to fix the relationship firmly in his mind, she bade Martha in future address her as Aunt.

'I think you'd better call me Aunt,' instructed Miss Diver.

Martha didn't protest. A little burst of protestation Miss Diver couldn't help feeling would have been in order – '*But Dolores suits you so much better!*' Martha might have wailed: even a flat refusal – '*I can't call you Aunt! I won't!*' Miss Diver would have forgiven. She was ready to comfort and persuade. But just as four years earlier, in the taxi going home from the funeral, Martha's reaction was unbecomingly placid.

'Aunt Dolores, or just Aunt?'

'Whichever you like,' snapped Miss Diver.

It struck her how little, in four years, Martha had developed. Even physically she looked much the same, she'd grown simply from a fat child into a stocky little girl, with no upshooting into grace, and her disposition had flowered no more. Admittedly she was useful in the house; admittedly, and importantly, she'd found Mr Phillips; but where was the harvest of affection her aunt so richly deserved to reap? – It was a point on which Mr Phillips was truly sympathetic.

'I only hope she appreciates all you've done for her,' said Mr Phillips gravely.

Dolores hoped so too; but there were few signs of it. It would be wrong to say that she had begun to dislike Martha, but she began to be discontented with her – perhaps unfairly, the child's affection never having been important to her so long as she possessed King Hal's, yet understandably, now that a kiss or a caress, spontaneously offered, would have a little warmed the chill about her heart. Miss Diver, living on the husks of love alone, found them but a Lenten diet.

She definitely, though it was her own doing, disliked her new title. Like the chattiness of the shop-people, like Miss Taylor's familiarity, the unromantic appellation was sadly abrading to the image of a Spanish rose.

3

With so much on her mind – remembering to call Dolores Aunt, also not to glare at Mr Punshon's clientèle, besides keeping guns trained in readiness on Mr Phillips – what wonder that Martha, setting down the latter's breakfast-tray, one morning made a slip of the tongue? She herself didn't notice it; but Mr Phillips did; and a few evenings later used it to his advantage.

In the meantime, Martha had been back to Almaviva Place.

CHAPTER SEVENTEEN

I

When Martha, in Almaviva Place, stood memorising the chestnut-tree, she had confidently expected to be able to put it on paper as soon as she got home; but this was not so. She couldn't get the two triangles, into which the whole tree should fit, in the right proportions. She put the attempt aside, but now and then took it out to look at; it bothered her to leave any piece of work unfinished. In the end, as she'd done with Ma Battleaxe's bedroom, she returned for a check on site.—

This time her methods were more professional; she took her equipment with her. A single sheet of cardboard obviously wasn't rigid enough to draw on (and rub out on), standing up: but Martha laid five or six together, used ones, and so made a very satisfactory block. She took also her best pencil, a knife to sharpen it, and a good-sized hunk of bread. This last turned out to be a slight nuisance, since the crumbs attracted pigeons; otherwise, in the quiet cul-de-sac of Almaviva Place, she was undisturbed.

Martha propped her back against a convenient lamp-post, emptied her pockets, and set to work. It was a brilliant October morning, but the first cold snap; her hands were awkwardly cold. This difficulty Martha overcame by pulling down the wrists of her jersey inside her reefer-jacket and cutting slits to push her fingers through. Thus mittened, her hands warmed; only her feet froze. She looked about for something to stand on. In Alcock Road there would almost certainly have been an old newspaper about, perhaps even an old sack: Almaviva Place was unusefully well-kept. Martha considered; she knew her temperature would rise as soon as she started drawing, and her jersey was thick; so she removed her jacket and stood on that. It took her ten minutes or so to get comfortable, then she settled down for a good long spell.

It looked almost as though Fate was offering a second chance. If Mr Gibson had glanced from his office window, he might have seen her. But he didn't. He was too deeply engaged with old man Joyce, completing a survey of the first quarter's trading under the new régime.

2

Mr Joyce occupied, naturally, the chair behind the desk. Harry Gibson didn't mind. His welcome had been genuine – based not only on friendship but on gratitude to his friend for not dropping in more often. The illusion that he was still his own master might be an illusion and no more, but Harry Gibson had at least been allowed to cultivate it, and find what comfort he could in it, without the daily interference circumstances would have warranted.

He didn't mind seeing Mr Joyce go through the balance-sheets; as always, Harry Gibson felt the force of the old man's sympathy – a sympathy which naturally hadn't prevented the sinking of Gibson and Son without trace, nor the diddling of Son in the way of business, but which humanly speaking amounted almost to love. They were fond of each other! 'What a damned queer turn-out it's been!' thought Harry Gibson.

Also, as far as the business went, he felt himself in good, if rapacious, hands. Rapacity in the way of business was something he understood; even appreciated. Harry Gibson sat content enough.

'Not so bad,' summed Mr Joyce at last. 'For a beginning, not so bad!'

He got up, shaking himself like an old dog – also with the off-hand air of a knowing old dog who has just buried a bone. Harry Gibson read the signs and smiled.

'Also not such a bad bargain?'

'When do I ever make a bad bargain?' countered Mr Joyce. 'A man like me cannot afford bad bargains.' He was at the moment putting on his overcoat bought because it was like Harry's; because he was so fond of Harry he wanted to look like Harry; he still wasn't giving anything away, in the way of business, to Harry. 'But you know what?' added Mr Joyce. 'Such a place as this I'd like to have myself. Not too big, not too small; just right. But for me it's back to Bond Street.'

On his way downstairs he dropped into the show-room for a word with Miss Harris and Miss Molyneux. They received him enthusiastically, and what he heard there pleased him: the little trickle of business was swelling to a little stream. Miss Harris indeed shouldn't have been there at all, she should have been in the work-room tacking up a canvas. 'Which is the first, Mr Joyce, I really do believe, since old Mr Gibson's time,' marked Miss Harris – her excuses benevolently accepted. 'How I wish he could see it!' 'Perhaps he can, dear,' said Miss Molyneux, looking spiritual. 'He'd get a shock if he saw the label,' said Mr Joyce; and left in a very good humour.

Outside he paused. It was always his habit to look over any piece of property with thoroughness; having noted the new brass plate properly cleaned, he stepped back and looked up to note the show-room blinds properly aligned, then walked round the corner to check the fitting-room windows at the side. (Properly curtained, nice clean net.) It was also in his mind to wave to Harry if Harry happened to be looking out of the office; but he wasn't. Mr Joyce paused a moment, quite disappointed, on the pavement of Almaviva Place; and thus chanced to observe, on the other side of the road, backed against a lamp-post, a stocky little girl making a drawing.

It was a sight to attract him at once. Friendly, inquisitive, fond of children, also fond of giving advice – how often in trouble with Miranda for stopping at a Guy or a one-man-band! – if the child had been merely skipping, Mr Joyce would have stepped across to count for her a bit. That she was drawing struck him (and it was the first time Martha so struck anyone) as a sweetly pretty sight. 'A little artist!' thought old man Joyce benevolently; and unlike Mr Gibson three months earlier, crossed the road.

3

'By Gum!' said Mr Joyce.

It wasn't what he'd intended to say. He wasn't even addressing the child at all – upon whom he'd intended to bestow a few kind words and perhaps sixpence. Approaching from the rear, his eye fell on the drawing first; and what he saw so startled him, he simply pushed his nose over Martha's shoulder and stared as though the drawing under her fist had been hanging in a gallery.

His long haunting of art-galleries had given Mr Joyce an eye. He had a couple of Modiglianis, bought at a gallery in the Tottenham Court Road, that he was holding on to while the price went up and up. He stared. Only when Martha turned and scowled did his attention shift – it being impossible to ignore Martha scowling at close quarters.

'Did *you* do that?' demanded Mr Joyce – foolishly enough.

'I'm trying to do it *now*,' growled Martha.

With her usual defensive movement she pushed a forearm lion-cubbishly across the sheet. But she was holding six or seven sheets at once, and the cardboard was slippery; the motion fanning them out, they cascaded to the pavement – kippers in jugs, saucepans and casseroles (for they were all covered on both sides) and the kitchen-stove.

'By Gum!' repeated Mr Joyce; and again oblivious of the artist instantly squatted down on his heels to see better.

—There was always a touch of the street-arab about Mr Joyce. His ancestors had been used to trade on pavements. He squatted down, in his new check overcoat and his good custom-built suit, with as little self-consciousness as Martha would have done. A lady just then passing by he noticed as little as Martha did.

'You drew all of these?'

Martha nodded. She was still wary, but no longer savage. That spontaneous unselfconscious squat, so unexpected in an adult (and so like one of her own motions), roused hopes that this was a person of good sense. Martha was beginning to be rather hungry for criticism and appreciation – from a person of good sense. To put her hopes to the test, she pointed with one stubbily-shod toe at the drawing Mr Phillips had called a bird-cage.

'What's that?' demanded Martha sternly.

'Gas-oven,' replied Mr Joyce at once.

Admittedly Mr Phillips had seen only the edges, but the unhesitating answer warmed Martha's heart. She had been a little doubtful about the gas-oven herself. She warmed.

'I opened the door because of the lines across inside.'

'Had to have 'em,' agreed Mr Joyce. 'D'you know why?'

Martha thought.

'They make the rings on top look rounder.'

'By Gum, you know what you're doing,' marvelled Mr Joyce. 'Where d'you go? I mean, who's teaching you?'

'No one,' said Martha.

'Mozart and holy angels!' ejaculated Mr Joyce. 'You mean you found all this out for yourself?'

'Yes,' said Martha. 'And I don't want to be taught.' There was here a slight confusion, Martha equating being taught with going to school; she already regretted letting out, as she thought she'd done, that she didn't. But to her relief this extraordinarily sensible adult merely nodded reflectively.

'Just now perhaps you're right,' agreed Mr Joyce. 'Not later, but just now you may be right. Might be like training a voice too young. D'you always draw on this shiny stuff?'

'It's all I've got,' said Martha.

Mr Joyce rose to his feet and considered her with active benevolence. From her respectable but unprosperous aspect he divined a decent home but no spare cash; from the peculiar ferocity of her manner, that her talent was unencouraged. Filing both these larger points for future reference – and with a sensation almost of joy – he

114

took in the details of her equipment. The bending, slippery card-boards were used on both sides. Looking at the drawing in his hand (while Martha carefully gathered up the rest), he saw the pencil-lines doubled and tripled to achieve substance.

'Ever tried charcoal?'

'No,' said Martha. 'I don't know what it is.'

'Come with me,' said Mr Joyce.

4

It would be hard to say which of them had the better time, in the big artists' colourmen's shop in Kensington High Street. Martha was nearly sick.

It was indeed fortunate for her that Mr Joyce didn't let her have her head. He nearly did; in an exuberance of generosity he nearly lost his own. Easels, canvases, paints – his money almost jumped out of his pocket at the sight of them; a quarter-size lay-figure (boxwood, articulated, eleven-pounds-ten) practically hypnotised him. But he was too wise to throw such strong meat even before a lion-cub, and held himself in. Also wisely, he let Martha choose nothing for herself. He kept her away from the oils-section altogether; and finally bought her four drawing-blocks, two large and two small, four packets of charcoal-sticks, of varying thicknesses, and two boxes of sanguin chalk.

'Anything else?' asked Mr Joyce.

'Rubbers,' gasped Martha.

He bought her rubbers.

'Anything else?'

'Could I have a pencil-sharpener?'

He bought her a pencil-sharpener. Martha gazed at him reverently. It was a pity that her eyes were small and grey, rather than big and blue, even looking reverent Martha still looked uncommonly stolid; but Mr Joyce's notion of her character was now fixed to his complete satisfaction, and he felt no disappointment. The egoism of the artist was by both hearsay and experience familiar to him; gratitude he knew to need prompting.

Mr Joyce accordingly prompted it. A patron – and no one more eager than he to shoulder a patron's rôle – has still certain admitted rights.

'Now don't you want to give me one of your drawings?'

How true to type as an artist! – Martha, her arms encumbered with his bounty, hesitated.

'Which one do you want?' she asked uneasily.

'If you let me choose – this,' said Mr Joyce, flicking out the gas-oven. Martha didn't actually snatch it back. 'I suppose you wouldn't want to give me the lot?' prompted Mr Joyce.

Again Martha obviously wrestled with her better feelings; and this time won.

'No, because I might want to look at them. Anyway, you've got the best.'

'Fair enough,' agreed Mr Joyce. 'I see I should have made a bargain first. Now then: you take this card, it's got my name on it and where I'm to be found, and when you get home tell your mother to come and see me, because I want to have a talk with her. What's her name?'

At this point, Martha lied.

It was inexplicable. She liked Mr Joyce, she felt confidence in him, she had every cause for gratitude. Yet she lied. She didn't even say 'Hogg,' which would have been true, if not the truth as Mr Joyce meant it. She said, 'Brown.'

For some reason, Mr Joyce grinned.

'Why not?' said Mr Joyce, grinning. 'No fancy names, for the real thing! Now you cut along home; I'm an hour late already.'

5

With so much to carry, Martha would have been glad to take a bus; but she couldn't, because she had no money. The tramp back across the Gardens was arduous; twice she had to stop and sit down; and the second time tore Mr Joyce's card into very small pieces and dropped them under the bench.

She didn't know why, any more than she knew why she'd lied. It just seemed wisest.

It also seemed wisest, when she got home, to go round by the back and conceal her burden behind the coal-shed, until she could smuggle it up to her attic.

6

Mr Joyce was equally secretive. He knew better than to display Martha's drawing to his womenfolk, whose taste was strictly Royal Academy, and he didn't think Harry would appreciate it either. (From the latter, indeed, Mr Joyce concealed his artistic leanings altogether, in case Harry should find them un-British.) He stowed Martha's drawing in excellent company, in the special portfolio that housed his two Modiglianis, now and again took it out to admire, and waited for the arrival of Mrs Brown in Bond Street.

Mr Joyce intended to treat this parent very tactfully, in a manner unalarming to any possessive maternal jealousy. All he wanted to ensure was that the child shouldn't now be forced from her natural bent, or, later, be taken too early from school and set to earn. (It was a grief to Mr Joyce to reflect how many years must elapse before Martha's first one-woman show, before he could even send her for proper teaching; but he was prepared to wait.) What he intended to offer was to supply all the child's drawing-materials for the present, in the future make himself responsible for her artistic education, and if necessary subsidise her as a non-earner from the age of twelve, in return for the pick of her output year by year.

In return, also, of course, for a share of fame. He didn't mean to say anything of this to Mrs Brown, however; he foresaw that he would seem eccentric enough to her in the first place. But he had great faith in his powers of persuasion, and looked forward to the interview with confidence.

'A Mrs Brown coming to see me,' Mr Joyce instructed the commissionaire, 'get one of the girls to bring her to my office straight away. Maybe she won't look like regular clientèle, but I'm expecting her.'

It occurring to him that a woman of the type he anticipated would be reassured by a cup of tea, he also instructed one of the girls to get him some tea-things and a tray with a doily on it. 'Attention to detail!' thought Mr Joyce, grinning. 'The homey touch! I am eccentric, but homey!'

No intending patron could have been more acute, or better-intentioned. It was a pity Mrs Brown never came.

CHAPTER EIGHTEEN

1

At ease in Miss Diver's sitting-room, drinking his now ritual cup of tea—

'Didn't you tell me,' asked Mr Phillips, 'you'd never taken lodgers before?'

'No, never,' said Miss Diver readily.

'Then who,' enquired Mr Phillips, 'is Mr Gibson?'

2

Dolores had been lighting a cigarette: her hand trembled so violently that the match-flame shuddered out. Mr Phillips noticed, and waited.

'Just a friend,' said Dolores. 'Has – has Martha been talking to you about him?'

'No,' said Mr Phillips. 'But a day or two back, when she brought me my breakfast, she said, "Good morning, Mr Gibson."'

There was too long a silence. Dolores' riposte, when it came, wasn't a bad one; but there had been too long a silence . . .

'I can assure you,' said Dolores, with a smile, 'she has never said anything to Mr Gibson except good afternoon.'

There had been too long a silence.

'She must have said it pretty often,' observed Mr Phillips, 'the way it slipped off her tongue.'

'As I say, he was a friend.'

'A close friend?'

Dolores nodded. The great sob checked by her first surprise was rising in her throat.

'Who doesn't visit here any more?' suggested Mr Phillips.

There are times when every woman has the right to lie.

'His business took him abroad. . . .'

'For good?'

At all times one has the right to refuse answers, that the questioner has no right to ask. Dolores summoned unexpected resources of dignity.

'My dear Mr Phillips,' she said coolly, 'my private affairs can hardly concern you. If you weren't such an excellent tenant – which is the *only* reason, I assure you, why I occasionally invite you into my private sitting-room – I should tell you to mind your own business.'

It was bravely spoken. Mr Phillips was silenced. But he had learnt what he wanted to learn. He withdrew silenced – but leaving Miss Diver for the first time in months to sob all night on the Rexine settee; he himself now knowing what was what.

3

Carefully, slowly, as he did all things, Mr Phillips made up his mind. He was a very careful, prudent man. His decision to make Miss Diver Mrs Phillips was nonetheless based on a misconception.

He thought the house was hers. He put two and two together and made not four but a dozen. He thought the vanished Mr Gibson had either given her, or been blackmailed into giving her, the house.

The point was a cardinal one; since she didn't attract him personally. Indeed, there were several things about his landlady Mr Phillips positively disliked. He didn't care for her appearance; her hair with its coronet of braids struck him as too outlandishly arranged, he thought it made her look foreign, and that it would look better in a bun. This of course was something that could be seen to after marriage; but her scarecrow thinness was probably for keeps, and she was a proper Skinny Lizzie. What Mr Phillips chiefly disliked, however, was that she evidently had some sort of opinion of herself.

He wasn't unjust. A woman owning a house he allowed entitled to think something of herself – not so much as a woman who owned a whole row, of course, but still something; and had Miss Diver's uppishness derived from a sense of property he could have pardoned it. But he had an irritated feeling that it did not. She never mentioned the house, with any reference to ownership. In fact, it seemed as though it was actually herself, her own feminine person, she had an opinion of: which in a woman of that age and appearance struck Mr Phillips as downright silly.

It will be seen that he was far from sharing Dolores' own conception of herself as a Spanish rose, even while perceiving in her its effects. They would have put him off altogether, he would have found her altogether too lah-di-dah, if it hadn't been for the house. As it was, he resolved to wait until after they were married, and then take her down a peg.

It will be seen also that Mr Phillips had no idea of a refusal – for all that he'd been sent off with a flea in his ear. And naturally: what Miss Diver stood to gain was nothing less than being made an honest woman of. ('Just a friend, eh?' thought Mr Phillips sardonically. 'I'm none so green as that, my lass!') Her house-property notwithstanding, Mr Phillips was confident that his landlady would jump at him. He still wasn't in any particular hurry. He had plenty of time, he feared no rival; moreover the knowledge that with four words he could transform the whole set-up in Alcock Road, gave him a sense of secret power too enjoyable not to savour while he might . . .

'Should I have placed a word amiss,' offered Mr Phillips, at their next encounter, 'I tend my sincere apologies.'

Dolores, who certainly didn't want him to leave, and whose mind in the interval had been apprehensive on this account, inclined her head forgivingly.

'I suppose we all speak thoughtlessly at times, Mr Phillips.'

'When carried away by our own interest,' said Mr Phillips gravely.

They were soon on their old terms again. Mr Phillips continued to empty the garbage; after a week Miss Diver resumed her habit of inviting him into the sitting-room for an evening cup of tea. On the surface their relation remained that of lodger and landlady: a very considerate lodger, a landlady wonderfully fortunate. The person to whose life this new undercurrent first gave a fresh direction was, unexpectedly, Martha.

4

'What's that stuff on your hand?' asked Mr Phillips kindly. 'All that red stuff?'

'Blood,' said Martha.

It was in fact a smear of sanguin chalk. Naturally she said, Blood.

'Dear me! We must tie it up for you,' said Mr Phillips – with all-too-ready credulousness.

Martha put her hands behind her back.

'I don't want it tied up. . . .'

'If it's not clean it may turn nasty,' warned Mr Phillips. 'You'd better let me see you wash it.'

'I don't want it washed,' said Martha.

'I'm afraid you're a dirty little girl,' said Mr Phillips.

'No, I'm not,' said Martha.

'I say you are.'

'Then it's not true,' said rude Martha.

Rude, and resentful. Martha didn't want to be rude: acceptable manners, like a respectable appearance, she had long found one of her best defences in a world of interfering adults. But it now happened continually – and even when she had less excuse, for in this particular instance Martha was pretty sure Mr Phillips didn't believe in her cut hand a moment, he was just being nosy – it happened continually that his each kindly attempt at conversation ended in

Martha's being rude. Without appreciating his dialectic skill, Martha felt she was being made to be rude, that the character of a rude child was somehow being imposed upon her, by Mr Phillips for his own ends.

What these were, she had to guess. But not only friends, or lovers, without a plain word spoken, divine the underlying trend of each other's thoughts: so also do enemies. Martha guessed, and guessed rightly, that Mr Phillips no longer aimed merely at bridling her will, but wished to be rid of her altogether; and feared that by turning her into a rude child, he might make Dolores want to be rid of her too.

It was indeed the truth. Mr Phillips' design for wedded bliss didn't include Martha. In the first place – being a man whose hatred of all qualities above the mediocre, especially in a female, almost put him off Dolores with her house-property – Mr Phillips disliked Martha even more than she did him. Confronted by any superior temper (especially in a female), his instinct was to thwart it, and Martha had successfully held her own. In the second place, her attic would be needed for a lodger – for Mr Phillips had no idea of wasting space, himself moved up to the position of husband; another lodger in his old bed-sit., and yet another in Martha's attic, were essential factors in his thrifty plan. (It was no mad dream, like poor Dolores'; a large Insurance Company, with a large intake from the provinces, offers exceptional supplies of lodger-timber.) Martha's attic could be let with ease; and with her Civil Service connections in mind, and having taken pains to inform himself on the subject, Mr Phillips knew of two orphanages already where she could hardly be refused.

At such details Martha's powers of telepathy naturally broke down. She was nonetheless apprehensive; and so took what measures she could to consolidate her position.

They were economic. Children are frequently more interested in making money than their elders think quite nice, only the little girl gathering sticks to support an aged grandmother has passed into sentimental legend. Martha, who was not sentimental, had never contemplated supporting Miss Diver; but once her egoism took alarm, she was more than ready to turn to.

'How much do I eat a week?' asked Martha.

'Good heavens, you should know that!' exclaimed Miss Diver sharply. (Her voice was sharpening like her profile.)

'I mean in money?' persisted Martha.

'I'm sure I don't know. Perhaps a pound. . . .'

Dolores really didn't know. In her muddled housekeeping Mr Phillips' payments, with an occasional dip into her own savings account, just kept them all going. Martha however took the figure as accurate, and cogitated. If she could earn a pound a week she wouldn't be costing anything, and she carried all the trays. Earning a pound a week she would be not only a self-supporting child, but a profitable child. It undoubtedly showed a flaw in Martha's character that she so completely discounted her aunt's affection for her. Dolores was still prepared to go on being fond of Martha, as she used to be fond, in the overflow of her love for King Hal, if Martha had shown the least sign of reciprocal tenderness. But Martha, herself unaffectionate, put no reliance on affection; she relied on economics. If she could earn a pound a week, she thought, she would be in a really strong position.

Spurred by this ambition, as splendid in conception as hopeless of execution, Martha embarked on her professional career.

5

She began by making out a beautifully lettered card announcing REPAIRS DONE WHILE YOU WAIT, with a drawing of a boot in one corner and a shoe in the other, which she carried round to her friend Mr Punshon. 'What's this, a present?' asked Mr Punshon, agreeably surprised. 'No, it's a shilling,' said Martha. 'If you want it, of course.' At this Mr Punshon scrutinised the card more narrowly. (It was a moment Martha found intensely exciting. Her knees actually stiffened – and not with financial anxiety alone. She was meeting her first public.) 'A boot all that heavy wants a thicker sole,' pronounced Mr Punshon at last. Martha looked for herself and acknowledged him to be right. She also realised how the mistake had come about – through shaving down the original boot-sole, because the boot-corner over-balanced the shoe-corner, without altering the upper to match.

'I'm sorry,' she apologised. 'Thank you for telling me.'

'Business is business,' said Mr Punshon. 'Seeing you're in the business way.'

'I want to be,' said Martha. 'If I make a new one, properly, will you order it?'

Mr Punshon agreed. Out of this first commission, because she had to buy a fresh bottle of ink, Martha made eightpence.

The criticism offered by her other friend Mr Johnson, off whom she took sixpence for a fresh WOUNDED AT MONS card, was equally professional. 'Just tread it in the gutter a bit, will you?' said Mr Johnson. 'It won't suit me too posh. You got to meet your market, see?' elaborated this professional hero. 'What's my market? The charitable human 'eart. The downer-and-outer I look, the more it beats for me. I took one-and-six this very afternoon.'

'I wish I had,' said Martha.

Mr Johnson looked at her thoughtfully. He wasn't wondering why. Martha was fortunate in having such sensible friends, neither Mr Punshon nor Mr Johnson saw anything odd, or not very nice, in her wishing to make money; they'd each of them been earning themselves, at Martha's age. Mr Johnson wasn't now unco-operative: on the contrary.

'In the good old days gone by,' he mused, 'I'd ha' taken you on. Dressed up proper in rags, you could ha' bin my pore little child. I've no doubt we could ha' made a very nice thing of it, 'specially if I acted 'arsh towards you. But what'ud happen to-day?' asked Mr Johnson regretfully. 'They'd whip you off for care-an'-protection before you could say knife. But I'm good for a tanner now and then, if it's any help.'

It was Martha's turn to look at Mr Johnson. As Mr Punshon had said, business was business. To go into the ragged-child line was something she wouldn't have objected to at all, but she wasn't in it yet; and her professional conscience stirred.

'Did you give me that sixpence just to *give* it me?'

'Why not?' said Mr Johnson. 'I get 'em give *me*.'

The card was still in Martha's hand. She hadn't yet dirtied it. She hadn't wanted to, even to meet a market. (The bayonets decorating each side had red-ink blood on them.) She said slowly,

'If you like to give it me because I'm a friend, thank you very much. But I'd rather you didn't take the card, because I don't think you really want it.'

'You go on being so sharp, one day you'll cut yourself,' agreed Mr Johnson amiably.

This second episode was important chiefly because it taught Martha where she stood. She had stumbled, in fact, on a cardinal point of professional ethics, and obscurely recognised it. The taking of Mr Johnson's sixpence as a pseudo-payment, instead of as a gift, would have stamped her an amateur; and the gulf between amateur and professional opening at her feet, she instinctively chose the professional side.

She never approached a friend again. (Mr Punshon was different; Mr Punshon had criticised with genuine authority. When in due course Martha made him a couple of cards more, at a shilling apiece, she in each case had to do the work twice – once on a point of bootlaces, once on a point of tongues. She was glad to.) Fortunately for her financial prospects, however, she lived in a district uncommonly rich in the sort of newsagent and sweet-shop that add to their income by displaying local advertisements – one actually adorned already by her handiwork. Martha went back to look at her Apartments card, and found it still markedly superior to the rest. Some were almost illegible. ('Ain't that gent found 'is congenial model yet?' derided Mr Johnson, who happened to be by. 'No wonder, the way they're writ!') Martha stood and stared for half an hour, and so perfect was her visual memory that a day later she returned with the whole display neatly and accurately duplicated in Indian ink.

The newsagent gave her two bob for the lot, any more that came in to rate twopence apiece.

At two other newsagents, and three sweet-shops, Martha made

the same terms. After a first capital gain of nine shillings, her tak-
ings naturally fell off; but she usually made about one-and-eight a
week.

6

One-and-eight is a far cry from twenty shillings.

Martha was sometimes uneasily aware of this; yet it couldn't
dim the pleasure of entering each consecutive twopence in the
shiny black note-book she bought specially for the purpose.
(Buying the note-book a pleasure in itself; having money in her
pocket.) She added the total once or twice a day, making it
sometimes more, sometimes less; and since her subtraction was
equally uncertain, commonly ignored the occasional pennies
she spent on sweets. (It was too much to expect of a regular visitor to three sweet-shops never to buy cocoanut-ice; which
indeed a more sophisticated accountant might have laid off as
good-will.) Martha's long-term project was in fact rather lost
sight of; however threatening the future she had immediately
money in her pocket, the constant interest of seeing if any fresh
cards had come in for her, cocoanut-ice, and appreciation for
her skill. She also enjoyed, as most children do, getting to grips
with life.

Mr Johnson pointed out that if she used ordinary ink, instead of
Indian, the new cards would fade as fast as the originals had done,
thus reviving the demand. Mr Johnson knew of an ink made with
powder that faded even faster. But Martha wouldn't.

7

Miss Diver had no note-book for such daily consultation; but she
had a calendar. Through the two mid-weeks of December was drawn
a thick black line, covering the date, as yet precisely unknown to
her, upon which Mr Gibson would make Miss Joyce his bride.
Dolores turned to it almost as often as Martha – but with how
different emotions! – turned to her note-book. Whether the twelfth

or the eleventh, the fourteenth or fifteenth, the day was drawing very near.

It was actually to be the sixteenth. Harry Gibson too in his diary had drawn a thick black line, only with more precision.

CHAPTER NINETEEN

I

Whether Miranda would still have insisted on six bridesmaids, if Mr Joyce hadn't turned down her plea for a separate establishment, must remain in doubt. She did insist. Strong in Harry's moral support – intoxicated with the new-found pleasures of friendship – Mr Joyce had been obdurate. So was Miranda now obdurate. She got her way. The result was to bring the wedding as it were much closer, and consequently again to reanimate Harry Gibson in his original, proper character of Miranda's fiancé, not her father's sidekick.

No longer, after dinner, were the two allowed to sit peacefully swapping their papers while Miranda played the piano. Reinforcements of femininity invaded the Knightsbridge flat. Bridesmaids dropped in almost every evening, often bringing their mothers, to finger patterns and discuss styles, debate coronals against Dutch bonnets, nosegays against flower-baskets. (All flowers, for a December wedding, Miranda reminded her Dadda pointedly, would have to be *grown*. Specially, under glass. Or perhaps flown in from somewhere. What an expense! – but he and Harry would have December. . . .) Marion and Rachel and Denise turned up, whom Mr Gibson could never tell apart, also three other maidens less identifiable still – but not the plump brunette with the big diamond, she being already united to her Bobby. (Harry Gibson vaguely regretted her. He remembered her sympathetic glance as a drop of dew in the furnace of the engagement-party.) They were all, moreover, the daughters, and their mothers the wives, of Mr Joyce's business associates, which made it difficult for him to turn his back on them; only rarely could he and Harry shut themselves up in the study, with the port. . . .

'Chin-chin,' said Mr Joyce gloomily.

'Have they even settled on a colour yet?' groaned Harry Gibson.

'Six young ladies, and six mammas, choosing one dress to suit all six, how should they settle on anything? – Fill your glass, Harry boy,' said Mr Joyce.

It was perhaps fortunate they were never long uninterrupted: the study had begun to take on rather the character of a speakeasy – one drank up while one could. But sooner rather than later Miranda always ferreted them out, to look at a new pattern of lace brought in by Denise or Marion, or because Mrs Conrad was there, or Madame Grandjean. (They spread over the week with diabolical punctuality, as though on a roster.) And how they chattered! All at once, like a cage of starlings. Even old Mrs Gibson complained at last, asking were they never to have a quiet evening again; and openly encouraged Harry to rebel.

'What a thing to say, but Miranda will make us all sick of her wedding!' cried Mrs Gibson. 'If you do not go so often no one will blame you at all! I have a good mind not to go so often myself!'

A month or two earlier Harry would have jumped at the absolution; it astonished his mother that he didn't now. Indeed he longed to. Only loyalty took him back, night after night, into the millinery inferno. But there was a silent appeal in his friend's eye, a touching gratitude in Mr Joyce's nightly welcome, which he couldn't find it in his heart to disappoint.

'It has to be,' said Mr Joyce, trying for philosophy. 'All women are like this before a wedding. Fill your glass, Harry boy.'

'Would you mind,' asked Martha of Mr Punshon, 'if I kept these here?'

She had her arms full – of drawing-blocks, of boxes of charcoal and boxes of sanguin chalks. Martha had begun to be anxious lest this hoard should be discovered: Dolores rarely entered the attic, which Martha was supposed to keep tidy herself, and when she did wasn't likely to look under the bed (not being that sort of house-keeper); but someone else, Martha fancied, someone more inquisitive, had been in behind her back. Returning after a Sunday morning in the Gardens, she found her three-legged stool a little displaced: the row of jam-pots on her window-sill, from which last summer's brew of nasturtium-tonic had long evaporated, just out of alignment – the largest perhaps no more than picked up and set down again; but Martha had a very accurate eye. Mr Phillips, taking a look round the accommodation, believed himself to have left no trace; Martha's only uncertainty was how to safeguard her supplies in case he came noseying again. After some deliberation, she tore off a sheet or two from each block for current use, hid them under the lining-paper of a drawer, and smuggled the rest round to Mr Punshon's.

'They won't take up much room,' added Martha, unloading, 'and if you give me a newspaper I'll wrap them up out of your way.'

Mr Punshon examined the pile on his bench with more interest than she welcomed. He appeared quite struck.

'Good quality,' said Mr Punshon, running his waxy thumb over the topmost block. 'That's worth a bit, that paper is. Chalks in boxes, too. You never bought this little lot out of my two bobs.'

Martha couldn't think what explanation to offer, so she offered none, and her silence gave rise to a slight misunderstanding.

'And you don't want to keep 'em at home,' mused Mr Punshon. He looked at Martha thoughtfully. 'You've not been in for a bit of shop-lifting, have you?'

Martha didn't tell him the truth, of course, but she managed to convince him, by the extreme earnestness of her denials, that he wasn't being put in the position of a receiver of stolen goods. (Mr Punshon was ready to do much for Martha, but there he drew the line.) 'All right, stow 'em under the Readies,' agreed Mr Punshon at last – and to make amends for his suspicion offered her a dekko at his album of cartoons.

Martha accepted from reciprocal courtesy. Her friend's collection, like the Chinese landscapes at the Free Library, had lost their attraction for her. They had hard outlines, but they were too bitty . . . Even as she turned the pages, Martha's free hand reached desirously to a stick of charcoal, a stick of sanguin. She had just learnt not to snap them, and as the thick black or red line marched firmly over the paper, experienced such ecstasy that sometimes she forgot to breathe and nearly burst.

She also forgot to wash.

'Dirty hands again!' noted Mr Phillips regretfully. '*What* a dirty little girl!'

'I'm not,' said Martha.

'I seem to have heard that before,' said Mr Phillips, with his patient smile. 'Your thumb's quite black.'

'It's my skin,' lied Martha wildly.

'I wonder your Auntie doesn't give you a smack,' said Mr Phillips. 'Telling stories as well!'

It was said in Miss Diver's presence, in the kitchen, where Mr Phillips now often came himself to fetch his supper-tray – so anxious he was to spare trouble. Dolores looked from her niece to her lodger unhappily.

'Martha, don't be rude.'

'I'm not,' repeated Martha.

'At least don't be rude to your kind Auntie,' admonished Mr Phillips. 'After all she's done for you.'

3

Whether Miranda would still have insisted on a honeymoon in the South of France, if Mr Joyce hadn't insisted on a common establishment, must also remain doubtful. She did insist. There were two good arguments against her – the expense beyond the bridegroom's means, and that it was unpatriotic to go abroad in the Depression; both she overrode. 'Of course it's Dadda who'll be paying!' cried Miranda – gaily indeed, but without bothering to wrap the matter up. 'I'm not going to let Dadda be stingy! And as for staying at home, everyone knows honeymoons don't count!'

Mr Joyce suggested Bournemouth. His reasons were partly selfish, but he saw also that the South of France roused no enthusiasm in Harry, and as usual prepared to back his friend. 'On the Riviera, at this time of year, doesn't it often snow like hell? If you would rather Bournemouth, only say,' urged Mr Joyce. 'To Bournemouth I might come myself, for the week-end, to see how you get on. Why not? We could have a nice time,' said Mr Joyce wistfully. He was prepared to back Harry to the limit, and it was he who held the purse-strings. 'Or if you would like Scotland, why not Scotland?' prompted Mr Joyce. 'There are hotels there cost the earth, and you could teach me to play golf. . . .'

Harry remained mute. It wasn't that the Riviera was any less repugnant to him than Gleneagles – or Gleneagles more repugnant than Bournemouth, or Bournemouth than the Riviera again. The fact was that he couldn't bring himself to contemplate, he was mentally unable to contemplate, any moment of time beyond the actual wedding-ceremony. A mental shutter slammed down at the holy portal. He could visualise himself (sometimes in nightmare detail, as when his sock-suspenders came undone), up to that very last moment, but no further. He saw himself going *in*, that is, but not coming out. Sometimes he wondered whether this meant he was going to drop dead on the pavement. The notion was so far from distressing him that he examined the life-line in his palm for confirmation – hoping to see it cut short at fifty. But no, it ploughed on deep and straight as a furrow to what looked like seventy-five at least . . .

Evidently someone was going to come out on his feet: Miranda's husband. As soon as Harry Gibson recognised this, the shutter slammed down.

He was thus not only indifferent to what lay beyond, he couldn't even contemplate it; and by no possible means could be brought to side with either Miranda or Mr Joyce. His neutrality was all Miranda needed. She sent for an enormous number of brochures, one from every expensive hotel between Monte Carlo and the Pyrenees, and told all her friends Harry was carrying her south to the sun.

4

'Anything the matter with your hand, boy?' asked Mr Joyce.

Harry had been looking at his palm again. It was becoming a habit. He shook his head.

'A splinter, I took it out . . .'

'My mother could read the hand,' remarked Mr Joyce unexpectedly. 'We used to tell her, when we were teasing her, she should go to tell fortunes like an old gypsy-woman, have her palm crossed with silver. How angry she got!' chuckled Mr Joyce – inviting Harry to join in; he often tried to amuse Harry with such humorous little anecdotes. '"A journey across the ocean!"' mimicked Mr Joyce, pretending to be an old gypsy-woman. '"Beware a tall handsome stranger!"'

—Instantly, appallingly, a terrible thing happened. The study dissolved, Mr Joyce vanished, Harry Gibson was back with Dolores on Epsom Downs. More agonisingly still, the vision doubled: the sitting-room in Alcock Road superimposed itself upon, mingled with, the gypsy booth; at one and the same moment Mr Gibson saw Dolores laughing in the sun and felt her sobbing against his shoulder. 'When you were there!' he heard her cry. 'My Big Harry, my King Hal!' He shut his eyes; but the vision under his lids was clearer than before. He could see every detail of the little tent, the worn red-and-white canvas and straining guy-ropes, also every detail of the sitting-room from the ermines in the cabinet to the gilt-and-bronze lady. Only the two Doloreses merged into one, she who laughed and she who wept; and again with the greatest precision he saw the separate streaks of hair divided by her comb, the slight down on her upper lip, the knotted fringe of her Spanish shawl. 'My Spanish Rose!' cried Mr Gibson's heart. 'I am still your King Hal!' With all his will he tried to project the message to Paddington; with all his being, even more ridiculously, harked for some message in return. All that reached his ears, naturally, was the voice of Mr Joyce.

To his astonishment, it was no more than kind.

'Harry boy, you work too hard,' said Mr Joyce. 'Just now a minute, you turned quite white. Perhaps the Riviera will do you good after all, in the south, in the sun. Unless it snows there,' added Mr Joyce, still wistful.

CHAPTER TWENTY

I

Mr Phillips was no impatient lover. A month, two or three months more might have elapsed before he declared himself, but for an exterior circumstance. It began to be bruited about the office that a position slightly more responsible than his own, at a slightly increased salary, would soon fall vacant in the Midlands; and he was aware that he stood a good chance of being offered it. He would still be better off, however, commanding a house and two lodgers in Alcock Road. Actually Mr Phillips rather regretted this, he didn't much like London any more than he much liked Miss Diver; but financial considerations, as always with so prudent a man, prevailed. His answer was ready, and it was a refusal. On second thoughts, it struck him as the part of wisdom to be equally ready, if needful, with an acceptance. He didn't think it would be needful, the last thing he expected was a refusal from Miss Diver; the habit of prudence still led him to register (so to speak) his holding in Alcock Road before dropping out of the running for Brum.

The tender interview took place in Miss Diver's sitting-room.

By this time Mr Phillips was quite at home there. (He had already, for example, a fair notion what everything would fetch, when it was cleared out and made to look respectable.) He didn't take any special pains with his appearance, he always washed before supper and had cleaned his nails with a bus-ticket on the way home. He relied on his natural advantages.

Dolores, on the other hand, as always now that Mr Phillips regularly took tea with her, was in evening beauty – hair assiduously arranged, make-up immaculate; for she felt she owed it to King Hal's rose to appear thus distinguished in a lodger's eye. In point of fact, Mr Phillips preferred her looking as he'd once seen her beside the dust-bin. Dolores had been wrong in thinking her appearance then unremarked: Mr Phillips had remarked it in detail, from the smears on her apron to the smudges on her cheek, and far from being put off was heartened. Most women, in Mr Phillips' experience, looked like that first thing, and he was far more at ease with the dishevelled than with the lah-di-dah. Dolores' impulse to hide herself was still correct: it was the memory of her dishevelment by the dust-bin that made her approachable to him now.

'Another cup, Mr Phillips?' offered Dolores.

'Thank you, as it comes,' replied Mr Phillips; and added, 'I don't know whether it's struck you, as it has me, that we get along very nicely.'

2

It has been said that every woman, for however fleeting a moment, considers every man she encounters in the light of a possible husband. This wasn't true of Dolores and Mr Phillips. Even during the last period of something approaching intimacy, her emotions were too fully preoccupied with the past. But now in a single flash of intuition she made up for lost time, and knew at once that Mr Phillips was about to propose. She was startled, but positive. Naturally she didn't show it.

'In fact, in many ways,' proceeded Mr Phillips methodically, 'we suit. Neither of us, for instance, is as young as we once were. I may say I am forty-seven.'

He paused a moment.

'I don't suppose *you'll* ever see – well, thirty – again?'

Dolores shook her head. She was unaware that Mr Phillips had offered a compliment. Indeed, she was altogether *unaware*: her emotions included surprise, a slight uneasiness, a slight expectancy; but no gratification. The notion that Mr Phillips was conferring any sort of favour, had it entered her head, would have struck Miss Diver as simply fantastic. She hadn't yet uttered a word; but her silence didn't appear to embarrass him; he expected at this stage, it appeared, only attention.

'My position in the Insurance world may not be showy,' continued Mr Phillips, 'but it's safe; and I qualify regularly for a bonus. As to my general character and habits, you know all about them. You can take my word for it I've no encumbrances, but ask any questions you like. I,' said Mr Phillips pointedly, 'shall not.'

At last Dolores stirred. The deliberate flow of his speech (as from an agenda) had almost mesmerised her, but those last words pricked.

'I don't think either of us need ask any questions, Mr Phillips!' she said sharply.

'As I say, I don't,' agreed Mr Phillips, 'though some men would.'

'Because I don't care to continue this conversation, Mr Phillips!'

He regarded her with slight impatience – only slight.

'That's daft,' he pointed out. 'I can see you're a bit overcome. It's only natural. But I may as well finish now I'm started. For instance,' continued Mr Phillips, before Dolores could speak again, 'naturally you wouldn't want to leave this house of yours. Well, neither should I. With another lodger or two we could be very snug. Which brings me to another point. Martha. I don't say she isn't your niece—'

'Stop,' ordered Dolores.

She had been sitting motionless so long, she was too stiff to spring to her feet; but she rose not without dignity, and to Mr Phillips' surprise in anger. What had he said to offend her? To make her stalk to the door like a tragedy-queen? Mr Phillips hastily checked over his proposals – and saw at least an omission.

'Here, wait a bit!' cried Mr Phillips. 'I'm ready to marry you!'

3

Miss Diver paused. However ill-put, however undesired, a proposal in form is something no woman can entirely ignore. Even a refusal must be put into words – however cold.

'Then you had better forget the idea, Mr Phillips,' said Dolores coldly.

'Perhaps I started off on the wrong foot,' admitted Mr Phillips, 'cutting out the frills. I took you for a reasonable woman.'

'I *am* a reasonable woman, Mr Phillips.'

'Then think it over,' urged Mr Phillips, 'and you'll see you'd be far better off with a man like me to look after you.'

At last, at the eleventh hour, he had said something that touched her.

To be looked after again! It was the one thing above all others Dolores now yearned for. Half the continuing power of Mr Gibson's image over her mind and heart derived from its aura of protectiveness: all the tarnished clichés – a strong arm against the world, a sheltering wing, a safe harbour from the storm – were minted anew each time she thought of her King Hal. Life without his love was hard enough; but also he not only paid the gas-bills, he remembered to pay them. Continually, in the running of the little house, Dolores stumbled on some such familiar-unfamiliar problem: the ordering of coal, for instance – when, and who from? Mr Gibson always had it sent. It had pleased him to keep an eye on such trifles as electric-light bulbs; Dolores watched them gradually dim, and was taken by surprise when they failed. (The one in the bowl of glass fruits was dead already.) She was inefficient to begin with, and Mr Gibson had encouraged his little woman's helplessness; now even when she felt most like a Spanish rose, Dolores' thoughts frequently turned not to Mr Gibson's person, but to the masterly way he renewed washers. . . .

'I'd see to everything,' said Mr Phillips, watching her face. 'I'd count it a privilege.'

'You didn't sound as though you'd count it a privilege!' retorted Dolores.

'That's because I don't know how to express myself. I don't know how,' said Mr Phillips humbly, 'to talk lovey-dovey. You have to take it as read. But I'd look after you all right.'

How badly Dolores needed someone to look after her! She couldn't help softening a little. Though she still shook her head, and still withdrew (leaving Mr Phillips for the first time in possession of the sitting-room), she bade him good night less unkindly than might have been expected.

4

At the Office, the Birmingham appointment seemed to be hanging fire. All October passed, the calendars were turned to November, and still neither Mr Phillips nor anyone else was summoned for promotion. Mr Phillips at least was perfectly indifferent.

CHAPTER TWENTY-ONE

I

In Knightsbridge, November was pleasurably marked by the arrival of the first wedding-gifts.

'I wonder who does old Demetrios know in the Burlington Arcade?' mused Mr Joyce.

The object of his contemplation was a splendid bronze-and-ivory statuette, the bronze here and there gilded, representing possibly Joan of Arc. As each tribute arrived Miranda unpacked it for display in the newly-papered sitting-room, and already the exhibition was creditable, since the Grandjeans had sent a whole dinner-service. (Miranda set out all sixty-seven pieces, and Aunt Bee had to dust them every day. 'When more come, we can stack up a little,' said Miranda.) The staff at Joyces had clubbed to buy fish-knives, and Miss Harris and Miss Molyneux to offer a mah-jong set; these gifts perhaps sent early to make sure of invitations to the wedding. So far Mr Joyce put his money on the Joan of Arc – or could she be a Valkyrie? – but he couldn't induce Harry to share his enthusiasm.

'Even knowing the shop, it must have cost a packet,' persuaded Mr Joyce.

But Harry Gibson, after one glance, wouldn't so much as look again. It became difficult to get him into the sitting-room at all, and after he had dropped a sauce-boat – by a mercy without breaking it, for as Miranda pointed out, the Grandjeans would have noticed at once – after this near-accident a daily inspection wasn't insisted on. 'Won't he see 'em all every day of his life?' Mr Joyce reminded his daughter – as usual taking Harry's part. 'Why should he want to stare now, like in a shop-window?' 'But things are coming in new all the time, Dadda!' protested Miranda. 'A lovely set of wine-glasses—' 'Better keep him away from them,' advised Mr Joyce. 'Three of mine he's smashed already . . .'

Madame Grandjean's sauce-boat was lucky. Thrice within one week, as he peaceably drank port with Mr Joyce in the study, Harry's fingers had gripped so abruptly on a fragile stem as to snap it clean in two. Undoubtedly his nerves were in bad shape; Mr Joyce was sometimes quite anxious about him, and though he'd meant to keep his own gift to Harry a surprise, divulged it to cheer him up.

'You know what *I*'m buying you, Harry boy? A bag of golf-clubs! So you will get out more in the open air! And one for me too, of course,' added Mr Joyce.

2

'Nasty weather,' remarked Mr Punshon. 'Nasty month, November. Turn out in all sorts, don't you?'

The observation was justified. For the third morning in succession Martha had come plodding through the rain to stuff herself in between the end of his work-bench and the shutter hung with bootlaces; and she was so damp about the shoulders, where her mackintosh leaked, that her jacket as it dried off made her smell like a wet dog. Combined with the reek of Mr Punshon's tobacco, and the wholesome aroma of leather, and a whiff of fish-and-chips, this made, in the narrow shop, for a very special atmosphere.

'In fact, you don't seem to spend much time at home,' added Mr Punshon thoughtfully, 'these days.'

Martha looked up from her drawing and as usual took a few moments to recover general awareness. The effort of concentration, besides raising her temperature, always put her in a slight trance;

Mr Punshon's words penetrated slowly; but when they had, they commanded her full, and uneasy, attention.

'Do you *mind* me here?' asked Martha uneasily.

Mr Punshon hesitated. He was a man who liked his own company, Martha all day and every day was more than he'd bargained for; but her troubled stare, so uncharacteristic in a young Pachyderm, disarmed him.

'Not now you've laid off glaring at the customers I don't,' said Mr Punshon. 'I just passed an idle remark.'

Martha took a good look at him, as though he was something to draw, and decided he could be believed. It was important, because the freedom of his shop, and not on Saturday afternoons alone, had become very necessary to her. Mr Punshon was correct; she was spending as little time at home as possible, to keep out of Dolores' way.

During the last weeks their relation had sadly deteriorated into one of mutual and permanent irritation.

The cause of Martha's irritation was simple: she wanted to get on with her work. Frustration on this point was indeed all that ever irritated her – no child more placid than Martha, even in the lean post-Gibson pre-Phillips days, drawing kippers and then consuming them. All she needed to retranquillise her now was the use of the kitchen-table. But for some reason the mere sight of her seemed to vex Dolores, no sooner had Martha got her elbows squared and her nose down than Dolores sent her off to take a walk, or run some errand, or to perform unnecessary dusting in the dining-room. More illogically still, when Martha tried to *use* the dining-room, Miss Diver sharply forbade it on the grounds that she'd make a mess. 'Then there'd be something *for* me to dust,' pointed out Martha; but was merely scolded afresh for arguing.

The cause of Miss Diver's irritation was more complex. It was also pathetic. The child Martha, who had guessed that Mr Phillips wanted to be rid of her, never guessed how the same thought troubled Dolores, nor what dilemma it presented to the woman. Dolores was well aware that Mr Phillips' offer of marriage held a proviso. He wouldn't take on any encumbrances . . .

'Martha does a lot for me in the house,' said Dolores.

'A char once a week would do more,' said Mr Phillips, 'and these days they're two a penny.'

'When Martha came, she was just a little tot,' recalled Miss Diver. 'I'm sometimes quite surprised to find her so big and useful . . .'

Why did she bother to say such things at all, when she didn't mean to accept him? She didn't mean to, but at the back of her mind, never taken out and looked at in the light of day, was the fear that she might be driven to it. Her hundred pounds in the Post Office was somehow dwindled to thirty, the lease of the little house had only a month or so more to run, after that she would have to pay rent; moreover a phrase let fall by Mr Phillips had thoroughly frightened her. 'I'm not hurrying you,' said Mr Phillips, 'but considering the state of my feelings, it's do I go or do I stay?' Dolores trembled – for where would she find such a Regular again? It had been a fluke getting Mr Phillips in the first place; the prospect of another such search appalled her. This thought too Dolores kept as much as possible in the twilight; but it was undoubtedly influencing her subconscious mind.

As was also the thought of being looked after again.

Already, now that fires were started, Mr Phillips besides emptying the garbage carried in the coal for her. He also made her a present of a sieve to riddle the cinders, an economy Dolores had never before practised, refusing to deduct the price from his weekly bill. 'It's a present,' insisted Mr Phillips, 'from me to you.' 'How kind!' said Dolores, sincerely. . . .

It was to turn his kindness back to Martha again, so that he should cease to think of her as an encumbrance, that she strove to say something nice about the child. (To blunt the horns of a dilemma not yet consciously accepted.) The attempt was all the more creditable in that Dolores was angry with Martha herself, she felt Martha well deserved to lose Mr Phillips' liking in the first place; the child was as sulky with him as possible. (Why could Martha *never* twine herself about a heart?) Yet Dolores remained loyal – as though she'd learnt loyalty from Mr Gibson. Her own single, brief impulse to turn Martha out was long forgotten. In her loneliness, what she remembered was that they were each other's only kin.

Unfortunately, the strain of all these conflicting emotions made Miss Diver more irritated by Martha than ever. The very sight of Martha irritated her. So Martha was harried out of the house.

Sundays were the worst, because on Sundays Mr Punshon didn't open. Martha kept as much as possible out of doors but even this had its dangers. For instance, the very Sunday after Mr Punshon passed his remark, on one seat in a bus sat the kind Librarian and his fiancée, and on the seat behind sat Martha – all bound for the National Gallery.

Martha didn't want to go, and Miss Hallows (the fiancée) didn't particularly want to take her; both were the victims of altruism. 'Darling, there's the little girl I told you about!' exclaimed Mr Agnew – spying Martha as she loitered after dinner along the Bayswater Road. He and Miss Hallows had been bound for Hyde Park; it wasn't a specially clement day, however, and the National Gallery (à deux) would have suited Miss Hallows just as well; she simply didn't want a third. She didn't either much take to Martha's looks, which was strange, since she was in general devoted to little girls. But when one is engaged to the kindest man in the world, some things have to be put up with, and to her fiancé's altruistic change of plan Miss Hallows did not demur.

Martha demurred as long as she could, but she had unfortunately cut the ground from beneath her feet by muttering first (as the Librarian's hand descended on her shoulder) that she was going for a walk; it was no use pretending afterwards that she was expected at home. 'You can be back for tea,' said Mr Agnew resolutely. 'By Jove, it's a chance not to be missed. Shy,' he explained (in a lower voice but no less resolutely) to Miss Hallows. 'Shy as a bird!' Like a bird of the fiercer species Martha made herself awkward in his grasp; but his hand was heavy; moreover they happened to be standing by a bus-stop; and the appropriate vehicle just then halting, the Librarian hoisted her on and hauled Miss Hallows after.

Twenty minutes later Martha had the wonderful experience of

encountering for the first time several hundred treasures of international art.

They bored her.

There were too many of them, and they were too big, and a lot couldn't be made head or tail of because they were too black. Martha was bored *instantly*.

She didn't behave as badly as she'd done at the cinema, with Dolores and Mr Phillips, though the circumstances were in many ways similar. She didn't actually hate the kind Librarian, and at least hadn't to sit still. But she was too bored to behave well. Boredom descended on her like a physical encumbrance, like something heavy and unwieldy she had to carry – as it might be a pile of wet blankets; and she inevitably dragged her feet.

Glumly Martha plodded on behind her benefactors, pausing as they paused, from masterpiece to masterpiece. Miss Hallows was too kind, and too much in love, to show any resentment of this hangdog at their heels; she wisely took the line of ignoring Martha altogether; but Mr Agnew, more committed, attempted many a kind device to stir appreciation. He showed Martha how to stand back at the proper distance, or to one side if the masterpiece was glazed, also which were the best bits to look at, with admirable persistence; alas, with no result save on his own part an increasing fatigue. He didn't drag his feet like Martha, but his step became less and less buoyant.

'Darling, let's sit down,' suggested Miss Hallows urgently. Her beloved could as a rule go through Religious Art like a knife through cheese; she was concerned.

'In a moment. I've an idea,' cried Mr Agnew, pulling himself together. He hurried them on to the Venetians. 'Doesn't *that* say anything to you?' he prompted – before an easy Canaletto.

Martha shook her head. She was by this time not only bored, but exhausted.

'But isn't it our own River Thames?'

'It doesn't look like it,' said Martha gloomily.

'Not *now*, of course; two hundred years ago. But can't you *imagine* it?'

'No,' said Martha.

146

Miss Hallows, watching her fiancé's face, perceived a flicker of despair. She was very sorry for his disappointment, but she really felt despair long overdue.

'Darling,' said Miss Hallows firmly – and she was obviously going to make an excellent wife – 'just give her her bus fare, and let her go home.'

3

Martha always looked back on this episode with a feeling of discomfort like indigestion. There had been only one picture she cared for at all, and that not one she was specially directed to: of a half-undressed woman between two men with all their clothes on. The woman had her arms out, one man was set higher than the other, and it all went into the shape of a pair of kitchen-scales.

This painful experience of Martha's took place on the Sunday before a Monday on which Miranda re-visited, for the first time in months, Harry Gibson's office.

CHAPTER TWENTY-TWO

I

Miranda was now too busy with wedding-preparations to come so often even to the Kensington show-room, where she had made such friends; as of course Miss Molyneux and Miss Harris quite understood. ('Who we'd *really* enjoy seeing more of,' remarked the latter, rather tactlessly, 'is Mr Joyce. . . .' The liking was reciprocated. Mr Joyce had formed a high opinion of La Harris, as for some reason he always referred to her, and often wished he had her at Bond Street.) Naturally Miranda didn't stay away altogether, but when she appeared one Monday about the middle of November – to the delight of the show-room, her parent with her – it was her first visit for a week.

It was her first appearance upstairs, in Harry's office, for several months, as she took the opportunity to remind him, by peeping with pretty trepidation round the door.

'May I?' coaxed Miranda. 'Dadda's been giving me lunch. I haven't come to *distract* you, Harry!'

In fact, Harry didn't mind her presence at all – or no more than he ever minded it – with Mr Joyce to chaperon them. The roguish look in her eye merely offended without alarming him. For the old man himself his welcome was genuine, and he ceded the chair behind the desk with good grace.

'All I want,' said Mr Joyce, 'is a look at the ledgers '29 to '31.'

Harry Gibson, in the act of placing a second chair for Miranda, froze. It was well for him that the ledgers had been seen already, by the Joyce accountants, so that his look couldn't be misinterpreted. He in fact made the point almost immediately.

'So I know they have,' agreed Mr Joyce. 'Now I just want a look myself. Where d'you keep 'em, son? In the safe?'

All the old Gibson ledgers were in the safe. Harry Gibson kept them there from habit. They were of no importance. There was nothing in the safe of importance, except a Spanish comb.

2

Harry had taken it out only that morning, just to hold in his hands a few moments: now as he fiddled clumsily with the lock (for he had no option, he couldn't refuse to open up), he tried desperately to remember where he'd put it back. On the bottom shelf, he thought, and behind, not in front of, the cash-box; he was almost certain he remembered a deep, thrusting motion of his hand – the gesture of one burying a treasure. And he was right. As the door swung open only a corner of the handkerchief-swaddling was visible, and might have been a scrap of crumpled paper.

Harry pulled out the ledgers from the shelf above and with a springing step carried them to the desk.

'Will you take them or look at them here?' he asked cheerfully.

'Here,' said Mr Joyce. 'I haven't come to rob you, son.'

'Did I think you had?' protested Harry Gibson – quite hurt.

'Just now, you looked as though you had a pistol at your head,' said Mr Joyce. 'And why not? No businessman likes to open up his safe, even to a partner.'

It was spoken with much kindness, particularly in the use of the word partner; even at that moment Harry Gibson felt the force of the old man's sympathy. As he sat down, glad of the opportunity to steady himself, he managed an appreciative smile. Indeed, he felt all right again almost immediately, all he needed was to turn his mind from the danger so narrowly escaped; the time to thank his stars would come later, when he was alone . . .

'Guess what I had for lunch!' began Miranda provocatively. 'Vol-au-vent of chicken and peach melba! Wasn't I *dreadfully* un-British!'

'Miranda, be quiet,' said Mr Joyce.

He began to go steadily through the books. Harry Gibson would have liked to ask what he was looking for. But for the presence of Miranda, he would have.

She was actually behaving very well. Mr Gibson noted with plea-sure her Dadda's restraining influence. She held her tongue, she didn't attempt to sit on his, Mr Gibson's, knee, and her *oeillades* he could avoid. She fidgeted no more than any woman might fidget – poked into a letter file, disarranged the stationery, exclaimed that there was no red ink in the red-ink-well. 'For bad debts, Harry no longer needs it,' murmured Mr Joyce, still looking for whatever it was he sought. 'Sit still, Miranda, or else go home!'

In the grateful hush that followed, broken only by the regular turning of a page, Harry Gibson sat relaxed. It didn't hurt him to see old Joyce going through the Gibson books; it even struck him to wish his own parent had been through them more often and as thor-oughly, to trace the disastrous results of auction-room quixotry. 'It was the pater Joyces should have taught business to!' thought Harry Gibson – and involuntarily, wryly, grinned, as he recalled the fanatic light in the pater's eye, the St. Vitus jerk of the pater's catalogue, as any detritus of the Romanoffs came up for sale. The pater had been unteachable . . .

Miranda sat still for at least five minutes. At least five minutes passed before she began to poke about again. The safe still stood open, to put the books back. Harry Gibson hadn't time, as Miranda suddenly pounced, to slam its door on her fingers.

'Oh, look what *I've* found!' cried Miranda Joyce.

3

The handkerchief fluttered away as she jumped up, holding the comb aloft in pretty glee. In a last ray of winter sunshine the carved butterfly-spread of tortoiseshell quivered as though with its own life, it looked like a great brown butterfly caught in her hand.

'Put that down!' shouted Harry Gibson.

'Oh, Harry, but why?' cried Miranda. 'Isn't it for me?'

'Put it back!' shouted Harry Gibson.

'*I* know! It was to be a surprise!' cried Miranda.

'All right, so it was to be a surprise!' shouted Harry recklessly. 'Put it back!'

She danced girlishly away from him, still holding the comb tantalisingly above her head. Mr Gibson could have taken it from her by force, but the scene was already violent enough; he was also instinctively aware that some such physical violence was what Miranda wanted to provoke. Even under the eye of her father, thought Harry Gibson with horror, she was ready to jump into a semi-amorous struggle. Luckily Mr Joyce, a man with remarkable powers of concentration, had now found whatever it was he looked for.

'Thank you, Harry boy,' said Mr Joyce. 'Miranda, what are you needling him about?'

His daughter at once looked penitent. The mild yet authoritative intervention produced such a drop in the emotional temperature, it was the best thing she could do. She nonetheless sketched a motion of slipping from Harry's grasp, as she darted to drop the comb under her father's nose. It happened to fall upon the still-open ledger. Harry Gibson wasn't a man much given to symbolism, but he saw the two halves of his life meet . . .

'Harry had a surprise for me, and I found it, and now he doesn't want me to see,' pouted Miranda.

Mr Joyce picked up the comb and looked at it. In his knowledgeable palm it weighed like a feather – but he examined it with increasing respect.

'Old,' pronounced Mr Joyce. 'Fine workmanship. I'd say this was a very old piece indeed. Where did you get it, son?'

Harry Gibson swallowed.

'It just happened to come into my hands . . .'

'He's lying!' cried Miranda – turning to vivacity again. 'Oh, what a liar my Harry is! He paid a fortune for it, and doesn't want me to know! Is it my wedding-present, Harry? Oh, Harry, do you see me such a Spanish type?'

'Now I'll have to buy her a Spanish shawl,' complained Mr Joyce humorously. 'Now we're going to live on Spanish-style chicken and rice.' His eye was still appreciative. 'You say it just came into your hands? Then I'm taking on a partner who can teach me something,' said old man Joyce. 'Want to tell me how much you really paid for it?'

'*With all my life!*' Harry Gibson might have answered. '*With all my life!*' He naturally couldn't say it. Fortunately his silence could as naturally be taken for that of a lover justifiably chagrined at the surprising, by his beloved, of his surprise for her. Mr Joyce dropped the question, which really interested him, of the comb's price, and looked at his daughter admonishingly.

'See how a pleasure is spoiled by too much noseying! Let Harry put it back where it belongs, until the proper time. Harry, it should be in a box.'

Still without speaking, Mr Gibson stooped, and picked up his handkerchief, and dropped it over the comb as it lay on the open ledger. He wouldn't touch it, while he was watched.

'That's not enough protection,' said Mr Joyce decisively. 'Remind me after dinner to-night, and I'll give you a cigar-box.'

Before they left Miranda apologised very prettily for making Harry cross, and promised never to mention the comb again – until the proper time. All she begged was that she might have it very very early on the wedding-day, for the florist to fix up with orange-blossom, to wear in her hair.

4

The results of this episode, in the event, were far-reaching beyond expectation upon the destinies of all concerned. Everything that now followed, followed from it. Dolores' bitterest tears followed, and Harry's bitterest anguish, and Miranda's moment of triumph, from this fortuitous bringing to light of the Spanish comb.

Harry Gibson sent it back next day. For the first time, he realised that what he'd borne away as a last gage of love was in fact an object of value; and he could imagine how Dolores might be pressed for money. (Where she herself had picked up the comb, he remembered her once telling him, was in the Caledonian Market; where famous bargains had been picked up before.) After night-long, agonising reflection, in the morning he sent it back, by special-messenger. (Also in Mr Joyce's cigar-box. Nothing he could find in the way of cardboard offered equal protection.) So the last link was broken, he had nothing left to remember her by, his Spanish rose; and the opening of the package reduced Dolores to despair.

There wasn't a line of writing with it. Mr Gibson, pen in hand for three hours, at the end of them had written nothing. What good would it do to either of them, to write, '*I love you, you are my only love*'? Yet what else could he write? So he wrote nothing; and Dolores, opening the package, laid her head down and wept.

PART III

CHAPTER TWENTY-THREE

I

As the last dislodged pebble unlooses the avalanche – as the last additional straw beats the camel to its knees – so acted upon Dolores' heart and situation the return of her Spanish comb in a cigar-box.

It had been a symbol of her personality as a Spanish rose. It had been the symbol of the mutual love she and her King Hal bore to each other. When Dolores missed it on the tragic morning after his departure, she still rejoiced to guess it in her lover's keeping. Thus its return broke her heart.

All her tragedy being shot with absurdity, the cigar-box broke her heart, so to speak, extra. A cigar-box also is a symbol – of carelessly-puffing prosperity. Mr Gibson in his new good fortune, it seemed to Dolores, threw that new good fortune in her face. She was utterly mistaken – down to the detail that even Mr Joyce no longer smoked cigars, having taken to a pipe like Harry; but she could not know, and her last, lingering, foolish spark of hope was quenched.

Once only she set the comb in her coiled hair again, and sat before the mirror perhaps half-an-hour. Her enormous dark eyes stared back at her dolorously; for the first time the meaning of her taken-name occurred to her, she realised vaguely that it meant something sad – an unlucky name perhaps to have chosen?

Dolorous were the lines about her mouth, dolorous her hollowing cheeks: King Hal's Spanish rose had withered indeed. All that remained of her was the flare of carved tortoiseshell, elegant, erect and glossy, mocking the grey in the once-black hair. 'Passée,' thought Dolores. 'I'm passée . . .' The tears started under her lids; after she had cried a little she looked worse.

She drew the tortoiseshell from her braids and shut it not in her dressing-table, but in the long wardrobe-drawer, among the pot-pourri, under Mr Gibson's dressing-gown. At some future date, she dimly acknowledged, that drawer might have to be emptied; but not yet. The photograph by the bed she also left in place. (Not yet, not yet!) – She looked at it as long as she'd looked at her own reflection; though it was many years since Mr Gibson, save to the eye of love, had much resembled that martial image, she had no doubt that it was a true and continuing likeness. Only she herself had withered; King Hal could not . . .

During the following days Mr Phillips noted the change in her with satisfaction. He found her far less uppish, far less lah-di-dah. In fact, for a few days at least she went about as though she'd been beaten. Mr Phillips had no idea what caused this welcome phenomenon, he hadn't been there when the packet arrived, and put it down to a general coming to her senses. Though subdued, she was evidently trying to please him; and when he tired of seeing her long face, and jocosely told her to cheer up, she smiled.

2

On the Saturday of the same week Miranda took Miss Harris out to lunch.

Miranda hadn't believed the pretty myth of a surprise wedding-gift for one moment. She knew it to be her own invention. (It was also a credit, in the circumstances, to her wit.) She had successfully taken in both her father and Harry Gibson, but she hadn't taken in herself. She couldn't – not before Harry's last look of all, his look as she'd petitioned, so prettily, to wear the comb among her orange-blossom . . .

Miranda in fact rightly guessed the Spanish comb to have been the property of Harry's unknown Past.

He kept it in his safe.

He couldn't bear to see it handled, or even looked at.

His mother claimed to know how he spent every minute of the day, and this Miranda accepted, especially after making such friends with the show-room; she knew herself how he spent his evenings. She didn't imagine Harry still saw his Past; but she was certain that he still thought about her, and in a way most offensive to a fiancée's feelings. Miranda's jealousy and curiosity, that had never been quietened altogether, now gave her no peace.

It was all very well to say let sleeping dogs lie; that was a man's point of view.

Miranda didn't hire detectives. She hadn't the courage to, without her father's backing, and Dadda's earlier lack of sympathy with such a project would scarcely have diminished. On the contrary – Miranda was perfectly aware that at the first hint he would at once begin to defend Harry, cover up for Harry, even warn Harry what was afoot. ('Like two schoolboys!' thought Miranda angrily. 'Harry could steal apples, Dadda would keep guard!') She knew better than to invoke so corrupted an ally; so she took Miss Harris out to lunch.

The latter had no thought of being disloyal. She was too good a sort. But her loyalties were now divided between Gibson and Joyce; moreover she realistically saw Mr Gibson's marriage as a splendid way out of all his difficulties. She thought Miss Joyce very chic. Miss Harris wasn't bought by a West End lunch; she simply wanted to do her best for all parties, and fortunately this proved quite straightforward.

'Oh, *no*, Miss Joyce,' declared Miss Harris, 'there's never been *any* lady about the place before! Which is why, if I may say so, both Miss Molyneux and me so appreciate you taking an interest – especially you so knowing what is what.'

Miranda accepted the compliment with a friendly smile.

'Of course I take an interest – in my fiancé's business! But I see I didn't make myself clear. The person I was thinking of, the person Mrs Gibson mentioned, was someone more like a secretary – an old employee of some sort – we'd like to surprise Mr Gibson by inviting to the wedding . . .'

'If I may say so again,' said Miss Harris, 'Mr Gibson is a very lucky man. I call that a very beautiful thought indeed, Miss Joyce. It just so happens I don't recall beyond a charlady or two, who really come and go like the wind, anyone at all answering to the description.'

Miss Joyce reflected, while they finished their *tripes à la mode de Caen*.

'Perhaps somewhere among the old letters,' she mused, 'there might be an address?'

'Well, I suppose there *might*,' said Miss Harris doubtfully. 'It's not exactly in my department. In fact, I don't *know* that we keep any old letters at all . . .' She hesitated; as she said afterward to Miss Molyneux, Miss Joyce was evidently quite *set*; and it really was a beautiful thought. 'I tell you what,' said Miss Harris, 'if it's really got to be a surprise—'

'Oh, but it must!' cried Miranda girlishly.

'—Friday evenings, half-past five to six, the charlady comes in to do the office, so Mr Gibson leaves it open and I stay a little late to put the lock down afterwards. If you care to come in next Friday and look round—'

'What a wonderful idea!' cried Miranda. 'Oh, but what would the charwoman think?'

'Pop in as she's leaving,' said Miss Harris practically. 'Which in my experience is nearer a quarter-to. Then *I* could leave *you* to put the lock down – couldn't I, Miss Joyce?'

Miranda ordered *Crêpes Suzette*. Miss Harris consumed them cheerfully. She hadn't been bought. Was her suggestion *quite* straightforward? Well, perhaps not *quite*, admitted Miss Harris; but she felt certain it could do no harm. Privately, she thought Miss Joyce would be wasting her time. In any case, there could be nothing in Mr Gibson's office that Joyces hadn't seen already; the Joyce accountants, in Miss Harris's recollection, having made a remarkably thorough job.

3

Until Friday was longer than Miranda wanted to wait; but she had no choice. In the interval she behaved rather discreetly with Harry, and kept her word about never mentioning the comb to him again. She didn't mention it to anyone – obviously: or why should old Mrs Gibson have been so surprised, at the latest alterations to the wedding-array?

'Can you imagine what Miranda has thought of now?' demanded old Mrs Gibson of her son. 'For instead of a veil?'

'No,' said Harry.

They were at the breakfast-table. Since they dined so regularly in Knightsbridge, breakfast had become more than ever the time for any intimate conversation, and Mr Gibson regretted it. It had been bad enough to start the day on reminiscences of Moscow: to start on his approaching nuptials was far worse. 'No,' said Harry Gibson, repressively . . .

'She wants to wear – but you would never guess!'

'Am I trying to?' asked Harry Gibson.

'A mantilla!' proclaimed his mother. 'Now I ask you! A white mantilla! Which might look I admit very nice, very unusual – but with the beautiful Honiton, so Buy British, already ordered! "What foolishness!" I said at once. "Are you a Spanish girl?" I asked. "Is my Harry a Spanish boy? Do you go to bull-fights?" Yet she is now quite set on a mantilla!'

Obviously Miranda had kept her word. What she would say on the wedding-morn, when no Spanish comb arrived to be twined with orange-blossom, Mr Gibson refused to imagine. It was only by keeping the strictest hold on his imagination that he managed to retain any sanity at all.

4

'So what has Miranda thought of now?' demanded Mr Joyce, that night in the study. 'A mantilla!'

'I know,' said Harry Gibson. 'The mater told me.'

'Also the bridesmaids are to wear mantillas! Those girls will look like dust-sheets on hangers.'

'Their mothers will stop it,' said Harry Gibson, perceiving a ray of hope.

'You forget who is paying,' retorted Mr Joyce. 'I am the chappie who is paying. All dresses are the gift of the bride's father. So Miranda has her way. But this is all your work, Harry boy, buying Miranda that Spanish comb.'

Harry Gibson splashed more port into his glass. It was a comparatively quiet night, only Rachel or it might be Denise in the drawing-room, no mothers: Mr Joyce reached companionably for the decanter in turn.

'You still don't want to tell me how much you paid for it? Okay, okay!' said Mr Joyce good-naturedly. 'But don't go back to the same shop, son, unless they come cheaper by the half-dozen!'

—How inevitably the spirit of the grotesque intervened! leaving not even the most sacred emblem unfingered! To Harry, Dolores' comb had always been something unique, he thought of it as the only one in the world, a rarity as singular as precious; was he now to go out and buy half-a-dozen, cheap, a job-lot?

'For the bridesmaids,' explained Mr Joyce, chuckling. '*Your* gift to the bridesmaids, Harry boy! To be the hooks on top of the hangers!'

5

In Alcock Road no less bridal-thoughts hovered. It struck Mr Phillips as a good time, while his intended was so down in the mouth, to jockey things along a bit. Nothing had as yet happened about the Midlands post, but something might at any moment; and though, as has been said, he felt little doubt as to his ultimate success as a wooer, he felt also that it was time to jockey things along.

'See here,' said Mr Phillips, 'I'm not to be kept hanging about for ever. I made a fair, I may say very fair proposition, and I want an answer. Make your mind up.'

Even as the plea of an impatient suitor, the locution was rough. Dolores, remembering how she couldn't possibly manage without a

Regular, swallowed her pride and hedged. She had in any case little pride left.

'I've only known you such a short time, Mr Phillips . . .'

'The name's Arnold,' said Mr Phillips. 'Call me Arn.'

She subdued her tongue to it.

'Arn, then . . . I haven't known you more than a few months, have I?'

'Fare farther and fare worse,' suggested Mr Phillips jocosely. 'You know what I'm going to call *you*? Dot. The other's too daft.'

'I haven't asked you—' began Dolores – and broke off helplessly. How could she stop him calling her Dot, if he wanted to? Unless she gave him notice, as she didn't dare? It was in any case less unendurable than hearing 'Dolores' perpetually on his lips . . .

'That's right,' said Mr Phillips, watching her. 'I see I'd better make your mind up for you.'

6

'Word of six letters first two f, l,' ordered Mr Phillips.

He was engaged not in solving a cross-word, but in composing one. The mysterious, silent occupation of his early days as a lodger, upstairs in his bedroom, was at last disclosed; as a contriver of these ingenuities Mr Phillips made half-a-guinea a time. They weren't eminently ingenious, Mr Phillips not catering, as he frequently pointed out, for highbrows; the journals that employed him bore such reassuring names as 'Home Hints' and 'Snippets'. Now he brought the dictionary down to the sitting-room and turned it over to Dolores, training her to assist him.

'*Floral,*' offered Dolores.

'Too fancy,' objected Mr Phillips. 'I keep telling you.'

So the evenings passed as it were in a foretaste of domestic ease. Mr Phillips had made up Dolores' mind for her – or rather he had made his own mind up, and took hers as read. Indeed, Dolores never spoke out to disabuse him; she was afraid of the consequences. When Mr Phillips said they'd be married at a registrar's, cheaper and less fuss than in church, she said nothing at all; when he suggested that a month should see everything straight, by which he meant that a month should see Martha settled in an orphanage, Dolores said nothing to that either. Her tongue was heavy in her head; she was too worn out – her sleep broken and unrefreshing, each day a long miserable toil – to think at all, with any real coherence. . . .

Sometimes he was quite kind.

'You'll be able to go and see her, don't forget,' said Mr Phillips.

'See who?' asked Dolores vaguely.

'Martha. They've days when the kids can be taken out.'

Dolores' consenting silence was on this point almost rational. When her mind was working best, and remembering her own fruit-less attempts to find work, it sometimes occurred to her that Martha would have to be sent to an orphanage in any case – supposing Mr Phillips in some way escaped. When the lease of the little house ran out, without a house how could she even look for lodgers again? Dolores felt incapable of fending even for herself, unless someone looked after her. . . .

Once or twice, when the thought of being looked after again came uppermost, she nearly opened this subject of the lease to Mr Phillips, so that he could tell her what to do. But she didn't, because it was too much effort. She had no idea that in time she might be accused of chicanery; having no idea how confounded Mr Phillips would be, and how justifiably angered, by the discovery that his wife didn't own a house.

CHAPTER TWENTY-FOUR

I

Miranda took no chances, that next Friday evening, but waited until she saw Harry Gibson leave. (She knew where he was going. On Fridays, because he left early, he always took his mother to a cinema before dinner. It was all right.) Miranda waited from just after five, behind a chestnut-tree at the corner of Almaviva Place – not a very dignified station, but the nearest cover, and she was too well furred to suffer much discomfort from the cold. (Her hands were in fur-lined gloves; only her feet gradually numbed.) No one remarked her, in that quiet cul-de-sac. A stray pigeon or two waddled up as though looking for crumbs, but that was all her distraction.

Mr Gibson came out at twenty-five to six, and took a taxi off the rank. To occupy the next ten minutes, and restore her circulation, Miranda walked briskly down Kensington High Street, as far as an artist's supply-shop, and briskly back. Her calculations proved exact; within, she crossed first the charwoman bundling downstairs, then Miss Harris on the flight above. Miss Harris, like the charwoman, was already hatted. 'Don't forget to put the lock down, don't get me sacked!' breathed Miss Harris – a gay accomplice. Miranda nodded gaily in return.

It gave her, immediately, such pleasure to have penetrated into Harry's sanctum, behind Harry's back, that for the first few minutes she almost played. Miranda's girlishness was perfectly genuine; alas that only to the eye of love could it have seemed engaging. As she sat herself in Harry's chair behind the desk – opened Harry's blotter, laid a finger to Harry's telephone – how endearing the spectacle might have been, to a lover! But even her Dadda would have told her not to meddle, for however he indulged his daughter, old Joyce saw her objectively; and every action which performed by Miss Diver would have driven Harry Gibson to rapture, had he seen Miranda performing them would have driven him to fury.

She didn't play the childish game more than a few minutes. She wasn't there to play, she was there to hunt for some clue that would lead her to Harry's Past.

As Miss Harris could have foretold, she wasted a great deal of time. The safe was inviolable, the drawers of the desk were so casually unlocked as to quench curiosity. Miranda went through them nonetheless; and learned only that Harry for some reason hoarded a quantity of Gibson-and-Son-headed notepaper. A file of invoices headed Joyce of Bond Street and Kensington testified to an increasing if modest prosperity; another, of old letters, to certain extramural follies on the part of Mr Gibson senior. (It wasn't auctions alone had been old Mr Gibson's undoing: upon splendidly-monogrammed notepaper equerries to certain princely names thanked him for his visit and enclosed a receipt.) Miranda observed that there were no autographs worth having, put the file back where she found it, and returned to the desk.

The uppermost sheet in the blotter showed only a repeated scrawl, too evidently Mr Gibson's signature to be of interest; and none of the undersheets had been used at all. By the telephone lay a list of numbers, obviously those Mr Gibson most frequently used; but as obviously all connected with the business, for each had a name alongside, and each name Miranda recognised; and when she checked them in the Directory, all were correct, not one was a cunning alibi. She put the telephone directories back too, resent-fully.

It was hard to admit that she had drawn blank.

It was so hard to admit that as a last, foolish resort Miranda looked about for a mirror, intending to read Mr Gibson's signature through the glass, to make certain (what indeed she knew to be certain) it was that and nothing more. There was a mirror hooked behind the door, beside a second hook from which depended a tweed jacket – Harry's office jacket, thought Miranda; she didn't remember seeing him in it. Until that moment, concentrating on the desk and the files, she hadn't consciously noticed it. Nor did it now seem probable to her as a hiding-place for anything Harry wished to conceal. Miranda took it down and went through the pockets without any particular hope, simply because it was there; and so found a receipt for a quarter's gas at an address in Paddington.

Mr Gibson had forgotten it.

At a certain moment, as he bade his beloved farewell, it had been a sensible comfort to him. Then he forgot all about it. He had worn the jacket since, without finding it. It was in the inside breast-pocket.

Only his own name appeared, as the official occupier: Miranda learnt nothing but an address. But it was enough, she dropped the lock behind her and ran downstairs, well satisfied with the results of her excursion.

Dinner was usually a little late on Fridays, on account of Harry taking his mater to the cinema; it was also, usually, steak-and-kidney pie – as less susceptible than roast beef to the hazards of over-cooking.

'Jolly good grub all the same,' commended Mr Joyce.

'First chop,' agreed Harry Gibson.

'Am I never to cook goulash again?' complained Auntie Bee.

'So much the boys enjoy their pie, don't they earn it?' cried old Mrs Gibson.

Miranda said nothing. She was exceptionally quiet all evening – busy with her thoughts.

3

In Miranda's elegantly-appointed bedroom stood a particularly elegant little writing-desk furnished with particularly recherché notepaper; and of this, over the week-end, she wasted a great deal.

The time was over when Miranda wished merely to know the facts about Harry's Past, just in case Harry needed help. She now urgently required some personal encounter from which she, Miranda, would come off best.

'*Dear Miss—*' (wrote Miranda)

'*As an old friend of Harry's, and I am sure truly interested in his welfare, may I say how much I should like to pay you a visit? It would be so nice to have a friendly chat. Please telephone me if you agree, as I sincerely hope you will, and believe me,*

in all sincerity,

'*Miranda Joyce*'

Then she tore it up. Though she had her own telephone by the bed, it was only an extension: suppose Dadda took the call!

'*Dear Miss—*' (began Miranda again)

'*As a woman of the world, I have no hesitation in saying how much I should like to make your acquaintance. May I call, or would you prefer lunch at the Ritz? I hope for a line from you very soon.*

'*Sincerely,*

'*Miranda Joyce*'

She tore that up too, as too stodgy, and wrote very fast:

'*Dear Miss—,*

'*Oughtn't we to meet? After all this IS the Twentieth Century! Drop me a line!*

'*Yours,*

'*Miranda Joyce. (Harry's fiancée.)*'

Many more such drafts did Miranda pen – some formal, some informal, some sympathetic, some almost menacing, but all ending in her paper-basket. None of them did. None of them, Miranda felt, properly projected her personality. Quite apart from the awkwardness of addressing an envelope to Miss Blank, this difficulty again and again baffled her – and was a cardinal one: insufficiently impressed, Miss Blank might snub. Certainly handwriting alone was known to tell much, and Miranda took pride in her curlicue script; but could Miss Blank read handwriting? Could she read from Miranda's elaborate capitals, for instance, how free from prejudice Miranda was? From her long-tailed y's, how attractive and well-dressed? Could even a practising expert, to put it plainly, deduce Miranda's new skunk coat from the loop of an f? Miranda fancied not; and equally mistrusted her own literary skill . . .

By Sunday night she had made up her mind to the only certain course; and early on Monday morning, unheralded, set out for Paddington.

CHAPTER TWENTY-FIVE

I

At the corner of Alcock Road Miss Joyce was passed by a plain, stocky little girl who looked at her, she felt, suspiciously. In fact, the eye of Martha was caught merely by Miranda's hat; its shape exactly duplicated, on a larger scale, the lid of Mr Punshon's tobacco-jar. Miranda however quickened her step. She in any case felt conspicuous in Alcock Road, a natural target for conjecture and suspicion, because in so seedy a little thoroughfare she was aware she must look out of place.

The seediness of Alcock Road in fact quite disconcerted her. She had never imagined Harry's Past housed in extravagant luxury, but she did expect something smarter than Alcock Road – simply as the scene of illicit amours in general. (If illicit love hadn't *chic*, hadn't glamour, thought Miranda, what had it?) In Alcock Road, she noted with distaste, the inhabitants didn't even clean their brass properly; all about the plate of a Miss Taylor, chiropodist, smears of dried metal polish marked the paint. Even the municipal authorities, it seemed, neglected Alcock Road; its letter-box still carried VR for monogram, and there were bits of newspaper unswept. As for the taste of those inhabitants – passing an open front-door Miranda glimpsed within a china-frog umbrella-stand almost perverse in its hideousness. . . .

She didn't notice the grating in the gutter, that Martha's eye of love could turn into a Greek temple. If she had, she would have observed only that it was blocked by two banana-skins and a sucked orange.

Miss Joyce walked rapidly, nervously, distastefully on.

The number five clear in her mind, she had kept to the opposite, the even-numbered side, to reconnoitre first at a sufficient distance. Actually opposite Number 5, she was disconcerted again by a seedy little house with faded pink curtains. The card in the window advertising apartments struck her as pathetically in keeping; but that such an establishment could be the target of her Harry's thoughts was unbelievable. 'It's a mistake,' thought Miranda Joyce. 'I've made a mistake . . .'

She would have turned and walked back again, and found a taxi to take her home again, only at that moment the door opened and a woman came out.

2

She wore, the woman, a dirty overall, and a duster tied over her hair. Since her purpose was to shake the front-door-mat, the costume wasn't unsuitable; it was in fact a uniform – the uniform proper to the landlady, or servant, of so seedy an establishment, at that hour of the morning.

It was also a uniform peculiarly unbecoming to Miss Diver. The overall, tying behind, was so tightly knotted about her lean shape, that her hip-bones showed prominent through the flimsy cotton: the yellow duster at once concealed her jetty hair and jaundiced her sallow cheeks. At that moment she didn't look like a Spanish rose, nor even like Old Madrid; her sole achievement in the way of appearance was that an on-looker such as Miss Joyce took her for landlady rather than servant.

It still didn't for a moment enter Miranda's mind that this scarecrow, this poor creature so denuded of all feminine grace, could be the rival she feared.

The sole reason she crossed the road was because she had inherited her father's instinct to make perfectly sure before cutting a loss.

The address was undoubtedly the address on the receipted gas-account; however seedy the actual dwelling, it was still within the bounds of possibility that Harry's ex-mistress either lodged, or had lodged, under its roof. . . .

'Good morning,' said Miranda. 'I see you let rooms?'

Dolores let the mat drop. The long-hoped-for enquiry, the words she'd given up expecting to hear, took her so completely by surprise that she even glanced backward over her shoulder, as though for confirmation, at Martha's beautifully-lettered card. It was still there, it hadn't, as it so easily might have, dropped down inside unnoticed. Dolores had heard aright – and looked back at the enquirer.

In old plays, old romances, they'd have recognised each other at once. But no more than Miss Joyce did Dolores know her rival. She too, in fact, saw a scarecrow – one very well-dressed, indeed, but as regarded general boniness and unappetisingness, a scarecrow. 'Buyer,' thought Dolores swiftly. 'Ladies' and Children's Wear; West End – with that coat . . .' It never for a moment crossed her mind that this poor creature so denuded of all feminine grace could be the rival to whom she'd ceded all rights in her King Hal. They were so far on equal terms.

'Or don't you take ladies?' suggested Miranda. (It was all she wanted to know.)

'I'm sure I could make a lady very comfortable,' said Dolores. Her brain had started to function again – feverishly. Another lodger, and Mr Phillips could go or stay as he pleased – could be given notice! – what a wonderful, what a miraculous issue from her troubles! 'Either with lunch or without,' elaborated Dolores eagerly. 'Even a packed lunch, if it suited, or hot supper if late. For three pounds a week, I'm sure I could make a lady very comfortable indeed!'

'But have you ever taken one before?' pressed Miranda – it was all she wanted to find out.

'No,' admitted Dolores. It didn't surprise her to see a look of withdrawal, she never now expected anything to be easy. 'But the gentleman here at present,' she added recklessly, 'if you don't care for a gentleman in the house, mayn't be staying much longer – owing to his business calling him away.'

She spoke just like a landlady. Miranda at least had excuse for blindness: tragically, Mr Gibson's, King Hal's Spanish rose now talked just like a landlady. She behaved like a landlady. Miss Joyce, having learnt all she needed, desired merely to end the conversation and go. Dolores wouldn't let her.

'Thank you, I won't come in,' said Miss Joyce. 'Perhaps another time—'

Dolores edged between her prospect and the gate.

'As you're here, I *would just like you to see the room*. . . . It's really quite exceptional.'

(So it was indeed. It was her own. Within the last few seconds Dolores had made up her mind to surrender her own bedroom, if by doing so she could get rid of Mr Phillips.)

'I'm afraid I haven't time,' said Miranda, making a movement towards the gate. But Dolores stood firm in her path.

'It won't take a moment. Now that you're here.'

Simply because it now seemed her shortest way out of Alcock Road, Miss Joyce allowed herself to be shepherded within. It was entirely Dolores' doing, that she entered the house.

3

At least the small bare hall offered nothing to detain her; nor did her tiresome cicerone linger in it. Dolores being at least as conscious as Miss Joyce that the hall looked bare: her trump card was the bedroom, and she hurried on upstairs. 'I'm sure any lady would be comfortable *here*,' said Dolores, throwing open the door.

Miss Joyce admitted it freely. The comforts displayed – the big double bed, the commodious dressing-table, the long mirror centring the commodious wardrobe – were unexpected. 'It's certainly very nice indeed,' said Miss Joyce. 'Perhaps I'll come back later.'

'The bathroom's just across the landing. With lavatory separate,' persuaded King Hal's Spanish rose.

'Perhaps I'll come back later,' repeated Miss Joyce.

Dolores recognised defeat. Even her own beautiful room, her ultimate sacrifice, hadn't availed. Sadly she stood aside at the door.

'Thank you for letting me look,' added Miranda kindly.

She was actually half across the threshold, when her eye fell on the photograph beside the bed.

Miranda paused.

It was unmistakably a photograph of Harry Gibson – younger, in uniform, but unmistakable; on the table by the bed.

At the same moment, Miss Diver remembered the duster about her head and pushed it back. Her night-coloured hair had always been her chief beauty; she still dressed it with care. Now a ray of sunlight between the pink curtains burnished it black and sleek and Spanish. All it lacked was a butterfly-shaped tortoiseshell comb.

Miranda paused.

'I'll write to you,' she said abruptly. 'What's your name?'

'Diver,' said Dolores. 'Miss.'

'I'll write to you,' repeated Miranda Joyce.

4

She believed it only out of inherited instinct. If the facts were incontrovertible, one had to credit them. (So old man Joyce, buying another business than Gibsons, had once been forced to cut a loss: the facts proving incontrovertible, he let the firm go bankrupt and got out.) Miranda was luckier. The incontrovertible facts, however immediately painful, could be made use of.

For she couldn't imagine Harry ever again regarding his Past with the eye of love.

5

'Arn.'

'Well, what is it?' asked Mr Phillips, frowning over his cross-word.

'There's been a lady to look at a room.'

Dolores had meant to give this piece of news boldly, as a bold reminder, so to speak, that he wasn't the only pebble on the beach. But even to her own ears the effort was unsuccessful, and Mr Phillips snubbed it at once.

'They're no good, more trouble than they're worth. Besides, what room would you put her in, with Martha still here?'

'I showed her mine . . .'

'Oh ho! There'll be other uses for *that*,' said Mr Phillips, with pleasant meaning. 'She didn't take it?'

'She said she'd write. . . .'

'There you are: shilly-shally,' said Mr Phillips. 'Find me a word of six letters, first w, last t – and not too fancy.'

Dolores turned obediently back to the dictionary. She hadn't really hoped. Even at the time of the morning's encounter, she hadn't really hoped anything would come of it.

CHAPTER TWENTY-SIX

I

'Another party!' groaned Mr Joyce. 'A fortnight only to the wedding, and Miranda wants to give another party! I ask you!'

But it was no use asking Harry; for once Harry had no advice, no sympathy even, to offer. To avoid thinking of the dreadful event so swiftly rushing towards him, he had to keep his mind, except for matters of business, as much as possible in a coma. He asked, 'Why?' but it was simply an opening and closing of the lips.

'She says it will be nice to ask your girls, also some of our staff from Bond Street.' Mr Joyce groaned again. 'Very nice I say too, let them come to the reception, drink all the champagne they want, I shall be pleased to see them. But no, Miranda says, they must come to a cocktail-party as well, if not they will be disappointed. Is that right, Harry boy?'

'I dare say,' said Harry Gibson.

'Well, would La Harris be disappointed?' argued Mr Joyce. 'Mind you, there is no one I like better! But how can she be disappointed, not coming to a party she doesn't know to expect?'

'I don't know,' said Harry Gibson.

'I don't either!' said Mr Joyce fiercely. 'And so I shall tell Miranda!'

Miranda nonetheless got her way. The superabundant festivity was essential to her new-laid scheme; though inviting the staff was merely an excuse, for she intended it to be a very smart party indeed, it was an excuse she could lean on, and she did. Within twenty-four hours her parent had given in; and the invitations were sent out for Wednesday week.

One went to Miss Diver at 5, Alcock Road. Since Miranda had no doubt but that Harry needed only to set eyes on her again, to be finally released from amorous bondage, obviously the best and kindest thing was to bring this, if possible, about.

Actually Miranda was confident of Miss Diver's acceptance. Judging the feelings of Harry's Past by her own, she relied equally on curiosity and jealousy to bring Miss Diver to Knightsbridge.

Then she and Harry could have a good laugh together afterwards – for what Miss Diver would look like, in the Joyce drawing-room, among all the smart people, was something Miranda could easily and pleasurably imagine.

2

Jealousy and curiosity are among the more vigorous emotions. Both curious and jealous was Dolores indeed – in the earlier days of her loss. For neither emotion had she now the energy. Receiving Miss Joyce's invitation, she spent all her strength in suffering. Luckily it arrived, the gay little card (Miranda went in for little cocks embossed in colour, cherries brightly embossed on crossed cherrysticks) after Mr Phillips had left; Dolores needed an hour even to stop crying.

For to Dolores, it seemed that Miss Joyce could have no possible way of knowing her address, unless Harry gave it: therefore Harry joined in the bidding. He was willing to display himself before her in his quality as Miss Joyce's betrothed. She did him bitter justice; most probably this aspect of the situation hadn't even occurred to him; on the contrary, love, and with it memory, thought Dolores, between fresh bouts of tears, had so thoroughly withered from his heart that a little indifferent good-will could spring there instead: he'd thought perhaps she'd like to come to a party – and why not?

In its indifferent kindness, it was as hard a blow as the return of her Spanish comb.

Of course she would not go.

3

By evening she was dry-eyed; but no amount of make-up could restore even her usual looks.

'Have you been upsetting your aunt again?' enquired Mr Phillips gravely.

'No,' said Martha.

'Well, I think you have,' said Mr Phillips.

'Well, I haven't,' said rude Martha.

How rude she had grown!

'Do you know what happens to little girls who contradict? They get whipped,' said Mr Phillips, 'as I dare say you'll soon find out.'

Martha stamped from the kitchen, where they now ate their evening meal all together, before she could be told to leave the room, thus frustrating Mr Phillips' next intention. Dolores took no notice. She didn't even glance, as she usually did, during such all-too-frequent scenes, to see whether the child had emptied her plate. Dolores' fingers inside her apron-pocket were still twisting and tormenting a square of pasteboard gay with cherry-sticks – now not so gay, having been so wept upon.

4

Of course she would not go.

Even to show herself equally indifferent, she would not.

Even out of curiosity to behold her supplanter – slightly the emotion revived! – she would not.

There was only one possible reason why she might consider going.

To see Harry again.

To see her Big Harry again, just once more, to feast her eyes on

King Hal for the last time, Dolores would have walked, like the Little Mermaid in the tale, on knives.

She'd known from the first moment that she would go.

In the morning, after a night of so little sleep that she rose sick and faint, Miss Diver penned a note of acceptance – as formal as the invitation, in the third person, and herself went out to post it. Then she took a pair of scissors and laid them to her Spanish shawl.

At the pillar-box, she unexpectedly encountered Martha, engaged in tracing out the VR monogram with a careful forefinger.

'Whatever are you doing *now*?' scolded Dolores automatically.

'It's lucky,' mumbled Martha. 'If you like, I'll show you the way. . . .'

Dolores laughed harshly and went back to the house, and cut up her Spanish shawl.

5

This was actually an offer of sympathy on Martha's part, in their common predicament. How critical that predicament was she didn't exactly know, but she was very uneasy. Her plan to become self-supporting she recognised a failure: even in her best week, after the first, her earnings fell too sadly below the pound she ate. Actually for whole days at a time Martha had tried to eat less, but though her strength of mind was great her appetite was greater. Her savings would have been greater too, but for her appetite; sad to relate, she often blew as much as fourpence at a go on cocoanut-ice. In short, Martha was by now only too well aware that if Mr Phillips stopped hinting and came out with a plain eviction order, she hadn't an economic leg to stand on.

How mad the dreams of youth! It must be revealed that Martha once actually dreamed of earning enough to evict Mr Phillips – heard, in rosy dreams, Dolores giving him his notice, as she herself, in true Ma Battleaxe style, hurled his bags over the banisters. Now she was both wiser and sadder; and at the same time, as for the first time, saw her aunt equally involved, and equally unhappy, in her economic defeat.

'Do you *like* Mr Phillips?' asked Martha, suddenly in the middle of lunch.

'No,' said Dolores.

'I don't either,' said Martha.

Across the kitchen-table Dolores raised her head. Her long thin neck, wasted like all the rest of her person, reared scraggier than ever: her fine dark eyes, sunken from sleeplessness, made charcoal holes in the pallid mask of her face. Martha – again for a first time – regarded her aunt appreciatively. At that moment, she would have liked to try and draw her. But it obviously wasn't the right time to get a chalk.

'When things are too much for you,' said Dolores deliberately, 'you have to give way and take your best chance. Try and remember that.'

'Am I going somewhere?' asked Martha uneasily.

'I expect so,' said Dolores. 'I can't help it. Remember that too.'

Extraordinarily, her mouth full of kipper, Martha choked. More extraordinarily still, she thrust back her chair, and stumped round the table, and pushed her head into her aunt's lap.

'I can earn half-a-crown a week, regularly,' muttered Martha, 'for writing cards in shops. Or nearly half-a-crown, anyway one-and-nine. I've been doing it. I have tried. . . .'

'Have you? Harry always told me you'd be a comfort,' said Miss Diver sadly. 'Really a whole one-and-nine?'

'I know it isn't enough,' muttered Martha.

Dolores didn't pretend. They were both of them past pretending.

'Just remember we've been fond of each other,' said Dolores, sadly.

Miss Diver posted her letter on the Friday. During the next five days, except for the week-end period when Mr Phillips required her attendance, she kept almost entirely to her bedroom, and when Martha tried to come in sent her off on an errand. (To buy a reel of silk at the Praed Street draper's. Martha was feeling so depressed she didn't even turn from the Haberdashery into the Veilings, where she still kept up good relations.) Though no time had been happy for her, of late, in Alcock Road, this was by far the unhappiest. Mr

Phillips, however, as Martha grew daily more subdued, appeared to notice nothing save a welcome, halcyon calm.

'Mind you, it's too late now,' he warned.

'What is?' asked Dolores.

'Martha behaving as though butter wouldn't melt in her mouth.'

'Everything's too late,' said Dolores.

'And may I ask what you mean by that?' enquired Mr Phillips sharply.

'Nothing,' said Dolores. (Only that roses withered, only that the tide of love ebbed, only that a mistress too undemanding must look to be discarded ... nothing.) 'Nothing,' repeated Dolores; and opened the dictionary where he'd just told her to, at L for love, with placative haste. 'Did you say a word of six letters or seven, Arn?'

6

It took her a long time to get ready, when Wednesday arrived, for she wished to look her best; even so she was out of the house before six, before Mr Phillips returned. She should thus have reached Knightsbridge in very good time, and in fact did so.

At the entrance to the block of flats, however, her courage failed, and she walked away again. It wasn't only that the uniformed commissionaire intimidated her – guarding the portals to a world of such evident wealth and luxury; now that she was so near to coming face to face with her King Hal again, she was overtaken by panic. 'I must be calm and dignified,' thought Dolores – walking on while she mastered the hysteria of her nerves. 'I must show how little I care ...' She walked until she was tired out, gathering her courage and losing it again, summoning her poise and panicking again; and in the end was the last guest to arrive.

CHAPTER TWENTY-SEVEN

I

The first guests to arrive had been Miss Harris and Miss Molyneux. They'd looked forward to the party immensely, and meant to crown the evening by going to a cinema together afterwards, unless Miss Molyneux clicked. (Miss Harris never clicked. As she recognised herself, she hadn't the figure.) 'We won't stick together all evening, dear,' murmured Miss Molyneux, as they entered, 'we'll just meet downstairs afterwards, *unless*.' Neither of them had any idea of not staying till the very end.

Someone has to be first, or how would any party start? – and how graciously Miss Joyce received them! How well she looked! ('Blue's certainly your colour, Miss Joyce,' said Miss Harris admiringly. 'If I may say so, it certainly *is*!') Mr Gibson too they admired, in a handsome dark suit; his manner was slightly absent, which was not to be wondered at, so near the happy day, but perfectly kind, and as for Mr Joyce, he greeted them like old friends. 'Here come my two young ladies from Kensington!' cried Mr Joyce, introducing them to Miss Joyce's aunt. 'Why ever must I be in Bond Street?' It was all as jolly as could be, and with further cordial exchanges, and all the lovely buffet to look at before it was spoiled, the time fairly flew until more people came. . . .

Soon they were coming in a rush, the drawing-room filled. All the bridesmaids turned up, and their parents, the Grandjeans and the Conrads, and old Mr Demetrios, and a sufficiency of un-attached men, and several of the staff from Joyces, democrat-ically mingling. The noise was like the noise in a swimming-bath, the atmosphere, as each lady added her quota of scent, like that of a high-class florist's. Mr Joyce, as the champagne-cocktails resolved into neat champagne, developed a tendency to make speeches. 'Do I know why we're putting on this party? I don't,' proclaimed Mr Joyce, amid universal plaudits. 'In one week, it will be put on again. All fathers with daughters going to marry I warn here and now – not one wedding-party they'll want, but two or three! So they push around their old Papas!' Miranda, again to applause, hid behind her fiancé. No one took Harry's lesser vivacity amiss, he was by now accepted as a bit of a dull dog, and it was famous that he spent every evening at Knightsbridge. 'A son-in-law in a thousand!' people told Mr Joyce; who from time to time nipped behind the buffet to open more champagne himself.

It was very late when Miss Diver entered; but when she did, nothing could have given Miranda greater satisfaction than, in every sense, her appearance.

2

It was to a certain degree fashionable. Gay jumpers were in fashion, and Dolores' was gay as a Spanish shawl. In fact it was made from a Spanish shawl; she had made it herself. Tiny tilted hats were in fash-ion, and she had bought a new one. Black fox was still a fashionable fur, all women were wearing a good deal of make-up: Miranda was still well satisfied by Miss Diver's appearance.

She caught sight of her at once, across the length of the room; not for an instant, in the thickest of the party, had she forgotten to watch the door. Dolores paused just within, as it happened beside Miss Harris and Miss Molyneux, momentarily converging to compare notes. ('I believe it *will* be the movies, dear,' mur-mured the latter philosophically. 'So far I've just given my telephone-number . . .') They eyed the newcomer curiously – Miss Molyneux with a lift of the brows. 'Are you from Joyces?' asked Miss Harris kindly. Dolores shook her head – and continued to stare across the room at where Harry Gibson stood.

To feast her eyes on him, for the last time, was her only admitted motive in coming; and if there had been foolish hopes, hopeless dreams, unadmitted, they died now, killed by the brilliance of the company and the luxury of the room. She didn't distinguish, to recognise, Miss Joyce; it was a scene, to Dolores, simply overpowering – and Mr Gibson stood at its centre. To this world of brilliance and luxury, it broke on her, he rightly belonged. This was the moment when she finally surrendered him. Dolores feasted her eyes indeed, but did not, now, even want him to see her. . . .

Harry didn't see her.

Miranda watched him impatiently – they were a little separated. He had actually been facing towards the door; now he turned, giving way before a cluster of guests. Miranda couldn't wait a moment longer. In a moment, she managed to regain his side.

'There's someone you know, Harry!' whispered Miranda playfully. 'See, an old friend!' – and pointed Miss Diver out to him.

3

Thus to Miss Diver's moment of defeat succeeded Miranda's moment of triumph. Watching Harry's face, she saw her plan so successful, she almost laughed with pleasure. How appalled poor Harry looked! and what wonder! For it was hard to say which was most grotesque, the ill-cut garish jumper, or the ropy old black fox, or the fashionable hat perched uneasily on such coils of ropy hair, or the long bedaubed countenance beneath. Perhaps the last: Miss Diver having indeed laid on her cosmetics with a liberal, and shaking, hand.

'Go and speak to her, Harry!' urged Miranda. 'Go and say something nice!' She thought he would never move.

He moved then. Stiffly, one stiff step after the other, Mr Gibson crossed the room: as stiffly Miss Diver stood and watched him come: alone, for the girls beside her had drifted away. Miranda glanced round for her parent, and edged through the crowd to slip behind the buffet.

'Look, Dadda, over there!'

'Look at what?' asked Mr Joyce, with his nose in a champagne-bucket.

'At Harry's *Past*!' whispered Miranda. 'She's here, I invited her! Haven't I been clever?'

From Mr Joyce's expression, as he slowly straightened and turned, he was about to tell his daughter that on the contrary she had been a great fool – he looked as appalled as Harry. But at that moment a shifting in the crowd gave him a clear view to the door, and though of Harry he could see only the broad back, it was plain towards what person he advanced. No more than a yard or so now separated them, and Miss Diver, standing alone, was in full view.

Mr Joyce stared unbelievingly.

'Holy smoke!'

Miranda giggled.

'It *is*, Dadda! Harry's Past! I can't *think* what he's going to say to her! Come and hear!'

'Not on your life,' said Mr Joyce promptly – still staring in a trance of mingled amazement and compassion. 'Poor old Harry!' he marvelled. 'A skeleton! A bag-of-bones! A kiss of death! And you don't go either,' he added swiftly. 'Let Harry tell her good evening, and I'll send a boy to break it up . . .'

But Miranda didn't want to miss the fun; she started away; and as Mr Joyce caught her by the wrist, on the other side of the room, with an identical motion, Mr Gibson grasped the wrist of Dolores, and pulled her outside and shut the door.

It was all over in a moment.

To those guests who noticed it, Mr Gibson's behaviour appeared, to say the least, unrestrained. They should have given him credit for his self-control. Not in the public eye had King Hal taken his Rose to his heart again – not though, like two drops of water, they could scarcely touch without coalescing; nor even in the hallway. It was in the study that Mr Joyce caught up with them, standing locked in each other's arms.

<h2 style="text-align:center">4</h2>

They had said nothing but each other's names: *King Hal, Big Harry, Dolores, my Spanish Rose: Dolores, Big Harry, my Spanish Rose, my King Hal*. When Mr Joyce entered, that was all they had said.

Mr Joyce's situation was extremely difficult. He had followed only partly to prevent Miranda following; it was also in his mind that Harry had foreseen his Past about to create a disturbance – what a fool Miranda was! – and might now need moral support. True friend in need, Mr Joyce came prepared to reason, to browbeat, to soothe with port and call a taxi – anything to help poor Harry. The sight that met him in his study necessitated a complete reorientation. Being also a man of delicacy, he felt himself an intruder. That it was in his own study the scandal was taking place offended his delicacy again but differently. It was a very difficult situation.

'Harry boy,' said Mr Joyce, 'break it up, will you? Oblige me.'

They didn't start apart. Harry Gibson merely raised his head and stared blankly over the crown of Miss Diver's hat. (It was crushed to a pancake. Part of her hair was coming down.) For a moment he appeared to have difficulty in remembering who Mr Joyce was; then he gently turned Dolores about, still within his protecting arm, so that they faced him side by side. Mr Joyce received the extraordinary impression that he was expected to be dazzled.

'She's here,' said Harry Gibson – as though in full explanation.

'I know that,' said Mr Joyce. 'Also I know how, and why. Which is plenty,' he added hastily. It struck him that Harry was perhaps taking a wise line; the less said the better. The great thing was to finish. 'Tell me nothing, there is nothing I want to hear,' begged Mr

186

Joyce. 'Just for God's sake finish, say good-bye, come back to the party. . . .'

Miss Diver immediately began to sob. Harry immediately re-embraced her – Mr Joyce mightn't have been there. As for Harry's blubbered words of consolation, they were at once so idiotic and so outrageous he could hardly believe his ears. 'No good-bye ever again!' Mr Joyce distinguished; also, 'My Spanish rose!' Nor did Miss Diver remain silent, both their tongues were unloosed at once, a man couldn't get a word in edgeways. 'I'll never leave you again!' cried Harry Gibson. 'I swear it!' 'How can you?' cried Dolores. 'Never while I live!' affirmed Harry. 'Now that I know what hell it is—'

'Oh, was it for you too, my darling?' cried Miss Diver.

'Was it for *you?*' cried Mr Gibson – in joyful agony.

'I just wanted to die,' wept Miss Diver. 'Oh, Harry, I've had to take a lodger!'

'Look,' said Mr Joyce urgently, 'why not write to each other? In a letter—'

'A chap?' demanded Harry Gibson – aflame with jealousy.

'I couldn't help it. And, oh, Harry—'

'I knew it!' groaned Mr Gibson. 'I should never have left you, you're too attractive! But I'll never leave you again, my darling! Say you believe me!'

'How can I?' sobbed Dolores.

'Yes, how can she?' put in Mr Joyce.

'Because I swear it!' shouted Harry Gibson.

'Then you are swearing what is not true,' said Mr Joyce gravely. 'Wait, and think, before you swear any more.'

At last, his words produced a brief silence. For the first time, he had gained their attention. 'I must hit hard,' thought Mr Joyce. He waited as long as he dared, until he saw Harry on the very verge of breaking out again, before he went sternly on.

'You are wrong to say such things, Harry,' rebuked Mr Joyce. 'I wouldn't have thought it of you. How can you bring yourself to say them, when in a week you are going to be married?'

Again there was a pause. He had spoken impressively enough, he thought, to bring them to their senses; but judged it wise (though he was a kind man) to re-administer the bitter, dream-dispelling dose. He deliberately addressed himself to the poor woman.

'When in a week he is going to marry my girl Miranda,' said Mr Joyce.

'No, I'm not,' said Harry Gibson.

5

Once when Mr Joyce was a little boy holidaying with his parents in the Black Forest, the tree under which they all sheltered from a storm had been struck by lightning. All escaped harm, but it was the small boy who kept his head – remembered where the carriage was, remembered to collect the picnic-basket. (Jumped and capered, and made his father jump and caper, to convince Mama they were still alive.) The years had brought no weakening of this fibre: even at the thunderbolt-instant of Harry's astounding perfidy, Mr Joyce kept his head.

He thought rapidly and coherently. There were a great many points to think of; but first things first, and the first point was that just across the hall was a party in full swing. Or perhaps breaking up: Mr Joyce looked at his watch, partly to check this and partly to see how long he had been away. As he suspected, it was after eight o'clock; also the passionate and dismaying interlude had occupied barely ten minutes. There was still time to save the immediate bacon.

'Harry boy,' said Mr Joyce, with a certain greatness, 'come back with me now to the party and help Miranda say good-bye.'

As well he might, Harry Gibson stared.

'Didn't you hear what I said?'

'I heard all right,' agreed Mr Joyce mildly. 'And of course it must be talked about. But not now. Just now I will not see Miranda look a fool.'

'I won't do it,' said Harry Gibson.

'Must you behave badly all through?'

'All right; I can't,' said Harry, more honestly.

Mr Joyce considered him. Emotion always made Harry sweat, and his eye was very wild.

'Then I will go back by myself, and say you have had a little too much champagne,' decided Mr Joyce. 'You had better lock yourself in. Then when they are all gone, we can have our talk. The lady—' He paused; the lady was indeed a problem. 'The lady, I am sorry, I ask to leave.'

'Not without me,' said Harry stubbornly. 'If you think I'm going to let her out of my sight again, I'm not.'

Mr Joyce sighed.

'It is a miracle Miranda is not here already. Do you want a real hair-pulling?'

'Lock *her* – Miss Diver – in too.'

'Miranda will know she is in the house. Don't ask me how, she will. Harry,' said Mr Joyce sorrowfully, 'I am doing the best I can for you, when I should be screaming for a horse-whip. When I could be a cry-baby myself, to see you suddenly so ungrateful. Oblige me!'

It was Dolores who acted. Another miracle; the last few minutes had restored her personality as a Spanish rose – a Spanish Queen: the beloved of a King. With a consciously graceful and swan-like motion – to Mr Joyce it looked like a swimming-stroke – she disentangled herself from Harry's arm and kissed him gently on his blubbered cheek.

'Yes, my darling: I do believe you,' she said tenderly. 'But you owe this gentleman an explanation, and it's far, far better that I shouldn't be present. Let me go now, then come.'

She swam queen-like, swan-like, towards the door. Harry with far less poise blundered after.

'That chap—!' he began uncontrollably.

There are moments when every woman is right to lie.

'Mr Phillips? I scarcely see him, my darling,' soothed Dolores.

Harry Gibson wavered.

'I shall still chuck him out to-morrow . . .'

'Yes: to-morrow,' agreed Dolores serenely. 'Until to-morrow – King Hal.'

6

Mr Joyce still felt it wiser to lock the door from without; the hall was too full of people leaving to risk any belated Lochinvar-like eruption. He locked it, and put the key in his pocket. It was also necessary to start the champagne-fable: catching the eye of old Demetrios, Mr Joyce winked towards the study and murmured, 'Flat out!' Most of all he was concerned to speed Miss Diver, who for all her new-found poise looked to him scarcely capable of getting away alone. (Old Demetrios, observing her swan-like motion, offered a wink on his own account; this Mr Joyce repelled. Harry's Past was theoretically an object of detestation to him, yet he couldn't help feeling sorry for her.) Most fortunately, just then entering the lift he spied that good sort La Harris; Mr Joyce practically thrust his charge into her arms and bade her find the lady a taxi. ('Heat,' murmured Mr Joyce. 'Feeling faint.' 'Poor thing, I noticed it,' rejoined the invaluable Miss Harris.) Then he returned to the drawing-room and Miranda.

It brought a first moment of relief to realise that the fable which did for the guests would also do for his daughter.

'Where is Harry?' whispered Miranda at once.

'Flat out,' reported Mr Joyce, rather loudly. He caught as many masculine eyes as he could, and grinned. 'Flat out is Harry on my champagne! To all the ladies he apologises! – not to you chaps!' It was an amusing enough hit: the champagne had flowed. 'Mamma Gibson, I will telephone a hire-car for you!' called Mr Joyce – spreading the jest further; also attending to detail. 'I think your boy will spend the night on my sofa!' Out of the tail of his eye he saw Miranda slip from the room and a moment later return looking baffled. 'Thank God for La Harris!' thought Mr Joyce piously, and returned to his business of mirth-making. He was so waggish, indeed, the party ended on a note of extra hilarity – husbands moved to describe their own youthful exploits, wives squealing reprobation, the bachelors looking knowing and giggled at by the maidens. 'Mr Joyce, I can see you're without a care!' gasped Mrs Grandjean at last. 'Simply a man without a care!'

When they were all gone, Mr Joyce wiped his forehead and dealt with Miranda.

It hadn't been difficult to avoid her hitherto; after her return she stopped trying to corner him; she was evidently holding her fire. But Mr Joyce's brain was still working at top speed, and he had no intention of submitting to any fresh bombardment. 'For one night, I've had enough,' thought Mr Joyce – and with a groan remembered that the worst of the night might still lie before him. He dealt with Miranda summarily.

'Listen to me,' ordered Mr Joyce – the door scarcely shut behind the Grandjeans. 'Without interrupting. Harry's Past is gone. She has been gone since before I came back. You have been a great fool, but there is nothing for you to worry about. Harry is as I said, flat out in my study. You are not to go to him, he doesn't want you and he doesn't look very nice. If all that is understood, put me some cold beef in the dining-room and go to bed.'

Every now and again there came a time when Miranda knew argument vain; this was one of them. Every now and again, a time when her Dadda put his foot down, she knew there would be no moving him; it was such a time now. However discontentedly, she submitted.

'I never thought there *was* anything to worry about,' said Miranda sulkily. 'I'm not such a fool as that!'

Mr Joyce looked at her, and said nothing.

7

In the dining-room he ate alone. Miranda had evidently reported the storm-signals to Auntie Bee, they both kept out of his way. Mr Joyce made a good meal; he suddenly found himself famished. When he thought of Harry cooling his heels in the study, he cut himself another slice of beef.

The whole flat was now very still. There were none of the clearing-up sounds that usually succeeded a party; for once all was being left till morning. ('"Came the dawn,"' thought Mr Joyce, for some reason.) Where had been brilliance and gaiety, darkness and silence brooded; the lights were out, the guests were gone.

Or all save one – and she not actually on the premises. Miss Molyneux was down in the lobby. Poor Miss Molyneux! – still waiting for Miss Harris, who almost an hour earlier had promised to be back in two ticks.

CHAPTER TWENTY-EIGHT

I

If Miss Molyneux hadn't *seen* Miss Harris nip out, she'd have thought her still up in the flat, perhaps kept behind for a word on business – but Miss Molyneux had seen her. At the lift they'd been separated, but Miss Harris came down with the next load – and then nipped straight out into the street saying that about two ticks. They were going to a cinema as arranged, because Miss Molyneux hadn't clicked.

For the first ten minutes or so waiting had been quite enjoyable: there were all the rest of the guests to watch as they went out, and she got a good view of the ladies' wraps. (A better class of skin all round Miss Molyneux had rarely seen.) Then the stream dwindled and died (Mrs Grandjean, in sables, a splendid finale) and she began to feel conspicuous to the porter's eye. 'I'm waiting for my friend,' said Miss Molyneux crossly – and wishing there were some way to express the feminine gender; 'girl-friend' she considered common. At this stage irritation at least prevented her from worrying about Miss Harris, but of course she soon began to worry as well, because though it wasn't *like* Miss Harris to get run over, no more was it like her to leave a person in the lurch . . .

After picturing her friend under a bus, under a car, and in hospital, when Miss Harris at last appeared Miss Molyneux naturally went for her.

'I know, dear, and I'm ever so sorry, but I couldn't help it,' panted Miss Harris. (They were hurrying to the Regal, just round the corner, to save time.) 'Mr Joyce asked me get a taxi, and could I find one? And when I *did* find one—'

'You can't tell me it took an hour!' snapped Miss Molyneux.

'No, but I've been to Paddington and back in it,' explained Miss Harris. 'I took it back, dear, so as not to keep you waiting. It was for that poor old Black Fox by the door – remember? It was her Mr Joyce asked me to get a cab for, on account of her feeling faint.'

'You ought to be in the Boy Scouts,' grumbled Miss Molyneux.

'And when I *did* at last catch one and put her in, she really acted so – so peculiarly, I felt I had to go along.'

'St. John's Ambulance,' glossed Miss Molyneux unkindly. 'How d'you mean, peculiar? Was she tiddly?'

'Oh, *no*, dear. At least I don't think so, I really don't. I mean, she didn't *talk*. In fact, beyond saying where to, she didn't utter the whole way. It was more—' Miss Harris paused, partly to draw breath, partly because the special quality of her taxi-companion's peculiarness, though it had left a strong impression on her, was difficult to describe. 'Well, you remember that tatty bit of fox she had?' essayed Miss Harris.

'Do I not!' agreed Miss Molyneux. 'Moth-eaten from the Ark.'

'She sort of draped it round her as if it was ermine. As though she thought she was a Queen or something. It was more, if you know what I mean, dear, as though she didn't know what *was* from what wasn't.'

'Loony,' said Miss Molyneux. 'If it had been me I'd have been worried stiff.'

'Well, I was a bit, dear, I admit it. *She* wasn't, though,' added Miss Harris thoughtfully. 'Whatever else she was, she wasn't worried. Here we are.'

They entered the Regal at just about the same time that Mr Joyce crossed the hall and unlocked the study door.

'Now we will have our talk,' said Mr Joyce.

Harry Gibson looked up, blinking. The time had passed more swiftly for him than for anyone, for he had been asleep. He had made no attempt to tidy himself, his face was still smudged, his hair wild, his collar dishevelled; but he was more composed. He turned on Mr Joyce a look at once humble, and stubborn.

'Unless,' continued Mr Joyce, 'there is no need to talk at all. Miranda was to blame for inviting her—'

'How did she know where she lived?' demanded Harry Gibson jealously.

'Maybe detectives, what does it matter?' Mr Joyce sensibly brushed the point aside. 'Miranda was to blame, perhaps you had more champagne than we thought; if you tell me, "All was a dream. Forget it," then it can be forgotten.'

'I'm sorry,' said Harry Gibson.

Mr Joyce smiled wryly.

'You might have said that before – even in a dream.'

'I mean I'm sorry, it's no use,' said Harry Gibson heavily.

Miranda's father sat down. He should have known, he told himself, that it couldn't be so easy; but he had hoped. Now the night was still before him. He resigned himself.

'You don't know—' began Harry Gibson.

'All right; tell me,' sighed Mr Joyce.

So it was, in those unlikely surroundings, to those unlikely ears, that Harry Gibson at last poured out the story of his love.

He wanted to pour it out. He wanted to tell it, not only in self-justification, but also because it was so beautiful. It was so beautiful, the wonder of it still struck him afresh. 'I called her my Spanish rose,' said Harry Gibson. 'You wouldn't think a chap like me could think of it, would you?' He went back – and it was well Mr Joyce had resigned himself, for in the cinema round the corner Miss Molyneux and Miss Harris saw a third of the big picture, before Harry Gibson stopped talking – he went back to the Chelsea Arts Ball, with its *coup de foudre*; to the moment when they lost each other afterwards, which now seemed like a warning, and to their astounding, fated reunion. He dwelt like the lover that he was on the ten magical years in their secret garden, describing in detail the poem Dolores had made of the sitting-room, the pink curtains sewn by her own hands. ('I could see 'em as soon as I turned the corner,' yearned Harry Gibson. 'Sometimes I almost ran down the road.') Martha he barely mentioned, she appeared only as Miss Diver's orphan niece, only to display the exquisite tenderness of Miss Diver's nature; indeed it had always been the spell of the little house that it existed for its King alone. 'It was a Kingdom of Love Divine,' recorded Harry Gibson solemnly, 'exactly as the song-chappie says. You wouldn't think this either, but when she called me, sometimes, her King Hal, it didn't seem cracked. It just made me feel like a King . . .'

Miranda's father listened with – envy.

It wasn't the emotion he'd expected to feel. He'd let Harry have his head from a sense that it would be better to get the facts; but what he'd heard were facts only insofar as they adumbrated a date or two, cleared up a point or two relative to the choice of a curtain-colour, or the provenance of a Spanish comb; otherwise, moonshine. It was the moonshine he envied.

For who had ever called Mr Joyce their King? Certainly not Miranda's extremely well-dowered Mamma.

'You were right,' sighed Mr Joyce at last. 'I didn't know . . .'

'I've often wanted to tell you,' Harry Gibson said truthfully. 'But how could you understand, unless you'd seen her?'

Mr Joyce unconsciously shook his head. The physical appearance of that Spanish rose was still definite to his mental eye. 'All moonshine!' thought Mr Joyce . . .

Yet what was moonshine but a belittling name for love? Employed only by the envious? 'My poor Harry and his Kiss of Death, they love each other,' thought Mr Joyce uneasily. He gazed earnestly at his friend and tried to make him look like a King. It was no use, Harry had begun to sweat again. The eye of friendship couldn't do it, only the eye of love . . . So love it was.

Mr Joyce pulled himself together.

'For myself, I sympathise with you,' he said. 'Believe me, you have my sympathy.' (It didn't occur to him to ask why Harry hadn't married his Rose in the first place. Like Harry himself, he took the original omission for granted. The only point unusual was that he appeared determined to marry her now.) 'But I have my daughter to think of,' went on Mr Joyce. 'How can I let you jilt Miranda practically on the honeymoon? How can you, Harry, even think of such a wicked thing?'

Harry Gibson groaned.

'Because I can't help it. Do I want to behave like a cad?'

'It is the most caddish thing a man can do. Harry,' said Mr Joyce sternly, 'it's un-British.'

Mr Gibson bowed his head on his chest – as upon the barrack-square, while all his buttons are cut off, bows his head the Outcast of the Regiment. Then he lifted it again.

'What sort of a husband should I make, to Miranda, thinking all the time of another woman?'

'A very good husband,' said Mr Joyce stubbornly. 'Did I never think of another woman, married to Miranda's mother?'

'Not all the time.'

'For many years, every day,' affirmed Mr Joyce rashly. 'A girl I knew when I was a young boy. So pretty, no money—'

'Tell me,' said Harry Gibson.

4

She had evidently been far more obviously attractive than Dolores – Mr Joyce's first love. But though Harry (their rôles now reversed) listened with genuine sympathy, he couldn't help feeling also a certain disdain. To fall for a brown shoulder and a white blouse – how naïf, how calfish! Yet that, it seemed, was what Mr Joyce remembered best . . .

'You don't see them now, those blouses,' mourned Mr Joyce. 'Anyway not in Bond Street . . . gathered full and very low round the neck, so one shoulder always slipping out, like a little brown pigeon. Maybe you wouldn't think that of *me*,' added Mr Joyce, with a faint smile, 'but it was what came into my mind. To squeeze, it was just like a plump little bird.'

Harry Gibson nodded – thinking with passion of Miss Diver's collar-bones. How slender, how fragile, his own Spanish rose! How *unbucolic*!

'Hilda,' pronounced Mr Joyce softly. 'Her name was Hilda. Every summer my grandmother took a châlet in the Black Forest, and there we spent our holidays, and there Hilda lived. An educated girl too: some French, some English, nice manners, everything. Everything except a penny. For dowry perhaps a herd of pigs. Was my father in the pig-business? Harry boy,' said Mr Joyce resolutely, 'I tell you this to show my sympathy, but all I assure you has been for the best. To-day that girl is a fat old woman, seven sons and seven daughters maybe, and here am I like Mrs Grandjean said, without a care in the world but what you yourself load down on me.'

Regretfully – as regretfully as Mr Joyce returned from the Black Forest – Harry Gibson returned from Alcock Road. The idyllic interlude was over.

'I'm sorry,' he said heavily. The very words, the very accent, of an hour earlier! Mr Joyce groaned.

'Damn it, what is the use to say you're sorry? Show you are sorry! Think, consider!' implored Mr Joyce. 'Have some port! Sit quiet for ten minutes and consider!'

'I have considered,' said Harry stubbornly.

'When? When I came in, you were asleep. You haven't considered anything! Give me some port too!' shouted Mr Joyce. 'Have you no affection? Have you thought what life Miranda will lead *me*? And what can I do to you back? Even just to satisfy Miranda, what can I do to you?'

'You can ruin me,' said Mr Gibson.

5

Now they were down to business.

It was a situation in which Mr Joyce held every advantage. He had Harry where he wanted him. For all his talk of partnership, the business in Kensington was as much his own property as the business in Bond Street. Harry Gibson dismissed from his employ, he could as easily keep him out of another berth in the fur-trade as he could if necessary find him one. Otherwise, in the depression, Harry hadn't a hope. Mr Joyce held every advantage – save one.

He was fond of Harry. Harry was his friend. When he looked at Harry solemnly pouring out the port, when he remembered the consolatory hours they'd spent together, in that very study – sharing that very decanter – the drawing-room full of women – also the good British grub Harry had introduced him to, so annoying to old Beatrice, and his encouragement over the new hairy overcoat – when Mr Joyce remembered all this, his heart failed.

'You can ruin me,' repeated Harry Gibson. 'Chin-chin.'

'I don't want to ruin you,' said Mr Joyce irritably.

Harry Gibson smiled – a smile of pure affection. But he said nothing, while Mr Joyce regarded him with increasing exasperation.

'How will you live, if I ruin you?'

'God knows,' said Harry Gibson.

'How will your mother live?' demanded Mr Joyce.

Harry shrugged his big shoulders. To Mr Joyce it was appallingly like the gesture of a man shrugging off a load.

'From seventeen years old,' said Harry thoughtfully, 'that question has been asked me . . . whenever I wanted to do anything different; when I wanted to go to the War. But I went to the War.' He smiled again. 'I dare say she will come and live here,' he offered helpfully. 'The mater is a great chum of Auntie Bee.'

'Are you mad?' demanded Mr Joyce – justifiably.

'They could have the new sitting-room, then it wouldn't be wasted,' joked – actually joked! – Harry.

'You *are* mad,' said Mr Joyce, in no mood for humour. 'Miranda would do murder. Sooner than that, I would give a little pension—' He broke off, too late; the fatal suggestion had been made, Harry was looking brighter every minute. To wipe the brightness from his face Mr Joyce hit hard.

'And the woman, and the orphan-child you speak of, how are they to live?' he asked grimly. 'God knows, you say for yourself – out goes noble Harry to starve! Are they to starve too? Or is *she* to keep you all, poor woman, taking lodgers? At least in the shop you earned your bread!' cried Mr Joyce bitterly. 'Not like a kept man!'

Harry might have been armoured in moonshine. Even this last, sharpest arrow glanced off his moonshine armour. It might have been shot from Cupid's bow – with a message of hope tied to the shaft.

'If I earn my bread there, why not some other place? Bath, or Cheltenham?' suggested Harry Gibson resourcefully. 'In both places we have connections. Start up a small branch, no need to tell Miranda—'

At this point Mr Joyce took his head in his hands and felt it gently all over, as though feeling for a crack in his skull.

'First you try to jilt my daughter,' he recapitulated, 'then you ask me to set you up in business. One of us is mad.'

'It wouldn't be *my* business,' pointed out Harry. 'I'd be on salary.'

Mr Joyce came up from his attitude of prayer with a grim smile.

'Put that out of your head, Harry boy. It was a good idea, but put it out of your head. Say toodle-oo to it.'

'Righty-ho,' said Harry Gibson. 'But you won't make me change my mind.'

Unexpectedly—

'You must be hungry,' said Mr Joyce. 'I'll get you some cold beef.'

6

He took his time about it. Crossing the hall to the dining-room, cutting a nice plateful – trimming it up with some bits of green stuff – Mr Joyce didn't hurry. He needed a respite. This was not, however, the chief motive of his butler-work, as neither was it solicitude for Harry's stomach. He had come to the conclusion that his best ally, in bringing Harry to his senses, was now the mere clockwork passage of time.

Whatever folly a man swears at night, by the cold light of day is not uncommonly foresworn; moreover the situation Harry Gibson faced in the morning was simply, in Mr Joyce's opinion, unfaceable.

So Harry, he believed, would find. In cold blood (and by daylight) he would find it utterly beyond him to throw overboard livelihood and honour, gratitude and filial affection, also make fresh arrangements about his laundry. (Mr Joyce ticked off this last point quite without cynicism. He simply and gratefully recognised how deflating to a fit of heroics such material pinpricks could be.) The essential, Mr Joyce now considered, was to get through the night without any irretrievable *act* performed – without Harry rushing off, for example, back to Paddington. Thus it was something to have salvaged ten minutes; also in furtherance of this aim Mr Joyce was prepared to go on talking to Harry Gibson, or listening to Harry Gibson, until morning.

'"Came the dawn,"' thought Mr Joyce, with a long, yet not hopeless sigh; and provisioned himself also.

'There is more I have remembered about Hilda,' announced Mr Joyce, returning in an evidently nostalgic mood. 'Her hair—'

It wasn't that Harry wouldn't listen. Harry's gratitude and affection were by no means dead, on the contrary, and to show this he would have listened willingly. The interruption came from without, when the door opened on Miranda. Both Mr Joyce and Mr Gibson had forgotten that the door was now unlocked.

'Dadda!' exclaimed Miranda. 'Harry! Dadda, why ever don't you come to bed? What ever are you *doing*?' demanded Miranda Joyce.

CHAPTER TWENTY-NINE

I

As Mr Joyce had remarked in another context, it was a miracle she hadn't appeared sooner. For hours she had lain with her door ajar, listening for him to come upstairs: planning to slip down herself for a delicious midnight interview with Harry. (Or if not entirely delicious, at any rate exciting.) All she heard was Mr Joyce cross the hall to the dining-room, and return to the study, and it was now almost one o'clock. It was a miracle indeed that her impatience and curiosity had been so long bridled.

'Whatever are you *doing*?' demanded Miranda.

On the face of it, though this by no means placated her, Mr Joyce and Mr Gibson were having a midnight snack. Their plates and glasses at once caught her eye. But they had no air of enjoyment, their dishevelment – for Mr Joyce too by this time had loosed his collar; Harry had taken off his waistcoat – their dishevelment appeared as no genial unbuttoning, but rather the effect of some desperate passage. They looked as though they'd been *through* something; and Miranda, who immediately thought she knew what, prepared with pleasure to join in and calm them both down.

Graceful, feminine and becoming is the rôle of peacemaker.

'Go back to bed!' said Mr Joyce.

They were the first words he had spoken; nor had Harry spoken.

Miranda looked from one to the other of them understandingly, and sat down. She was wearing a negligée that strictly belonged to her trousseau, pale blue velvet; its long wide skirts dropped in graceful folds, beneath which the toe of a pale blue mule peeped provocatively forth. Miranda naturally couldn't see it from Harry's viewpoint, but she felt there was to be a deliciousness about the interview after all.

'I shan't,' said Miranda – half-woman, half-child! 'I know what's been going on. Dadda, you've been scolding poor Harry. Haven't I told you there's nothing to worry about?'

'It was what I told you,' said Mr Joyce. 'I was wrong. Please go back to bed.'

Miranda swung a pretty toe.

'Not till you've made it up. Poor Harry! If I've forgiven him, that's all that matters. Dadda, you must make it up.'

Mr Joyce looked at her helplessly. He almost looked at Harry, for help; but obviously this wouldn't do. In the course of a whole evening that had been one long difficult situation, this was the second peak – the first being when he surprised Miss Diver in Harry's arms. There was literally nothing he could think of to say that mightn't precipitate a crisis – except 'Go to bed,' and Miranda wouldn't. With horror he heard Harry clear his throat.

'He can't forgive me,' stated Harry Gibson. 'You wouldn't want him to.'

Miranda smiled her understanding smile.

'But of course I do, darling! When I have!'

'You won't either,' said Harry Gibson.

'But I tell you I have!' insisted Miranda – now with a trifle of impatience. 'Oh, Harry, didn't you confess to me yourself?'

'Yes, but I've got to confess again,' said Harry.

There was a doggedness about him which even at that moment stirred Mr Joyce's admiration. 'The bull-dog breed!' thought Mr Joyce admiringly. But that doggedness was hurrying them all to disaster, and in alarm he made haste to interpose.

'Wait till morning,' interposed Mr Joyce swiftly. 'Something so important, wait till morning!'

'I can't,' said Harry. 'Miranda's got to know now.'

'I ask it as a personal favour! I beg you! Harry boy,' said Mr Joyce earnestly, 'if you have any fondness for me at all, if you feel I have behaved at all well to you, oblige me in this last thing I ask. Remember I have troubles too, and oblige me.'

It was a moving appeal. Harry was moved. Mr Joyce, seeing him waver, without the least concern for his own dignity, caught him by the sleeve and pulled at it.

'Haven't we been friends, Harry boy?' pleaded Mr Joyce. 'Haven't we been real pals? Can't you do me one small kindness? Wait till morning, Harry; wait till morning!'

Harry Gibson wavered. He might have given way. But Miranda had been too long out of the conversation for her liking, and felt it time to reassume control.

'Dadda, Harry!' she cried gaily. 'What a fuss! Whatever Harry wants to tell I want to hear! Did you kiss her good-bye, Harry, after all? If you did, I'm not jealous! How could I be,' laughed Miranda, 'of such a scarecrow?'

As Mr Joyce subsequently remarked, in one of his new slangy phrases, that tore it.

2

For a moment, Harry didn't comprehend; then the blood rushed up to his face, and all his love, and his fury, burst forth in one outraged cry.

'How dare you!' roared Harry Gibson. 'Not jealous! What else but jealousy is that lie?'

Miranda instantly jumped up. If he was furious, so now was she.

'What lie? Calling that creature a scarecrow?' She laughed again, but on a very different note. 'Let me tell you, Dadda called her far worse! A skeleton, a bag-of-bones—'

'Miranda, for God's sake!' implored Mr Joyce.

'—a kiss of death!' finished Miranda recklessly. 'And I say so too!'

'Keep your tongue off her!' shouted Harry Gibson. 'Now *I*'ll tell *you* something!'

'Stop!' shouted Mr Joyce. 'He's mad!' he added rapidly, to Miranda. 'Don't listen to him! Go to bed! Leave it to me!'

'I'm going to marry her,' said Harry Gibson, suddenly calm. 'Now you know.'

There followed an abrupt silence, sudden, and as generally disconcerting, as Harry's new demeanour. The air of the study seemed to quiver with it: for a moment, it seemed, as in a heat-haze, the outlines of solid objects swam. Then Miranda looked at her parent. She had every reason for disbelief, but what she saw in his face shook her.

'I told you, he's mad,' said Mr Joyce. 'Leave him alone, let it pass.'

Miranda frowned uncertainly.

'What he said, Dadda . . . of course is nonsense. How could he marry anyone, without—?'

She paused; almost pathetically, the words refused to be uttered. But Harry Gibson had no compunction. He had heard his Spanish rose called a scarecrow, and a bag-of-bones, and a skeleton and a kiss of death.

'Jilting you,' he supplied baldly. 'That's right: I'm jilting you.'

Miranda turned. There was no love in her eyes. There was still incredulity – but of a new sort. She had seen Miss Diver twice, and once no doubt at her smartest . . .

'For *that* thing?'

'For the lady whose name is Miss Diver,' returned Harry dangerously. 'Yes.'

Miranda drew a long, hissing breath. Her face was very white, but set, not tremulous.

'Dadda's right: you *are* mad,' she said contemptuously. She was bearing herself, in the circumstances, with considerable courage. She still didn't hazard any more criticism of Miss Diver's person. 'Is that what you were fighting about, Dadda?'

Mr Joyce nodded miserably. He was feeling extraordinarily tired, and he didn't like the look in Miranda's eye.

'He wanted to horse-whip me,' offered Harry – who still retained some sparks of loyalty.

'I think he can do better than that – can't you, Dadda?'

Mr Joyce sighed.

'If necessary, daughter. But why talk about it? In the morning, it will all be different,' said Mr Joyce pleadingly. By this time he didn't know exactly who it was he pled with – he didn't want his daughter to be jilted, he didn't want to ruin his friend; he didn't want to *lose* his friend. 'In the morning, you keep out of the way,' said Mr Joyce earnestly, 'and I'll try again.'

Undoubtedly he was very tired; but undoubtedly it was the worst thing he could have said. He was so tired, he repeated it.

'Just *you* keep out of the way—' repeated Mr Joyce; and precipitated a crisis indeed, as Miranda lost her temper.

3

She had lost it once, and recovered it; now she lost it irretrievably. She spoke the irretrievable words.

'Keep out of the way, *I* keep out of the way?' cried Miranda furiously. 'Why? Because when he sees me Harry feels sick? You think *I* want to see *him*? Because I don't screech and scream you think *I'm* not disgusted? Let me tell you, Dadda, now I know what tastes he has, it is I who break off our engagement, not Harry! If he was the last man in the world—'

Quite definitely, Mr Joyce was now pleading with Miranda.

'Stop!' cried Mr Joyce. 'Wait!' (All night, it seemed to him, he had been battering with those two words at ears as deaf as adders'.) 'Think, Miranda, for God's sake think! You are just giving Harry an out! Remember the wedding, all the preparations! How will you look, not getting married, after all this? What will your friends say?'

But Miranda was struggling with her engagement-ring, forcing it over her knuckle, obviously preparing to hurl it in Harry's face. Mr Joyce shot out a hand and fielded it just in time. 'Give it back to him!' cried Miranda – quite forgetting, the passionate girl, who had paid for it. '*I* don't want it! Let him give it to *her*, how snappy it will look on her skinny finger!' Mr Joyce slipped his two hundred pounds'-worth into a pocket and gamely worried on.

'What about the wedding-presents, all to be returned? Mrs Grandjean's beautiful dinner-service—'

'I don't want it!' cried Miranda again. She was ready to fling back diamonds, what were dinner-services to her? 'And as for what people say—' Here indeed she hesitated, as her father had known, it was the crux; but her temper carried her over it, 'They will say I have shown spirit!' cried Miranda defiantly. 'My friends didn't think so much of Harry, I can tell you! They thought he was an old stick-in-the-mud, and that I was throwing myself away!'

She shot Harry one last disdainful look, and swept from the room.

4

The peace was beautiful.

It had been Miranda's aim to make peace; at least she left peace behind her.

Several minutes passed before either man spoke. They were both exhausted; also the peace was too beautiful to spoil. Harry Gibson sank back on the sofa, Mr Joyce in his big leather chair. It was so obviously the moment for a pipe, both got out their pipes. Mr Joyce's was still raw, but as though in sympathy with the moment it drew better than ever before.

'You're getting the hang of it,' said Harry Gibson.

'I have that new tobacco you said,' explained Mr Joyce.

Casting his mind back over the recent to-and-fro, he thought Harry hadn't realised the provenance of the worst slanders on his beloved, and was glad. He was sorry for them now himself.

They smoked in grateful silence for some minutes more; but obviously something had to be said on another subject than brands of tobacco. Mr Joyce opened his mouth; but at the thought of all there was to say, closed it again. To reproach Harry with ingratitude, to harrow him with pictures of Miranda languishing in despair – what use now? Besides, Miranda hadn't looked despairing, as she flounced out; she'd looked furious. Justifiably. Mr Joyce didn't think

Miranda now wanted her beloved back, he thought she wanted him, her Dadda, to ruin her beloved. What was the use of going into that either?

'It's milder on the tongue,' said Mr Joyce, experimentally sucking.

'It's the mildest I know,' said Harry Gibson. 'But ask. They might put you up a special mixture.'

He too felt there should be more said; but he neither could think what, of any use. He knew he was behaving like a cad, but he'd admitted it already.

'I'm dashed grateful,' offered Harry Gibson at last.

'To me?' asked Mr Joyce wryly.

'To Miranda. I've never thought so well of her. And to you too,' said Harry, with his good, loving smile.

'If I think well of Miranda, if she thinks well of me, in the next few weeks, we shall both be ready for heaven,' sighed Mr Joyce. 'What you leave me with, Harry boy!'

'I'll give you a tip,' said Harry. 'Keep the mind a blank. You'll be surprised how it helps.'

He stood up, and began to put on his waistcoat. His pipe wasn't yet smoked out, but he could wait no longer. Symbolically, it had served its turn: a pipe of peace. . . .

'Are you going?' asked Mr Joyce foolishly. It was plain that Harry couldn't stay to be found there in the morning; he was still taken by surprise. 'I told your mother I would keep you here,' said Mr Joyce worriedly. 'Now at this time of night, where will you go?'

'Back,' said Harry Gibson.

5

They parted, the two friends, on the pavement. Harry had got into his big hairy overcoat, of which the twin hung in the hall; Mr Joyce, helping him on, rubbed a palm over the splendidly masculine fabric and heaved a final sigh.

'We could have been so cosy, Harry boy!'

But Mr Gibson shook his head.

'It wouldn't have worked,' he said solemnly. 'Something terrible would have happened. Don't ask me what, but it would have been something terrible.'

This was in the hall. Mr Joyce came down with him – they had to use the service-stairs, the lift had long ceased running – and out on to the pavement. It was about two in the morning, very cold and dark.

'D'you want me to look in at the shop to-morrow?' Harry asked. 'Just to leave things straight?'

'Perhaps yes,' agreed Mr Joyce. 'Turn your collar up.'

'I'll tell the girls I'm sacked, then you can tell Miranda.'

'Thank you, Harry. Leave me your address.'

'I'll give it to La Harris.'

Mr Joyce peered anxiously out at the December night.

'It's very dark. How will you go?'

'I'll pick up a taxi,' Harry reassured him. 'Toodle-oo!'

6

Mr Joyce waited till he was out of sight, in the cold, in the dark, then slowly went in and closed the big doors. How different it would all have been, he thought, if he could have made Harry wait till morning! (If he could have made Miranda go back to bed! If Miranda had *stayed* in bed!) Harry said it wouldn't have worked out, but what could he mean, something terrible? 'Maybe I should keep the mind a blank,' thought Mr Joyce, and wearily set about remounting the service-stairs.

He was more tired than he had ever been in his life, he was out on his feet; but back in the flat, though he longed with all his heart to go straight to bed, outside his daughter's room he paused. He was dead beat; but his daughter was his daughter. 'No more punishment can I take to-night!' thought Mr Joyce, pitying himself; but his pity for his daughter was stronger. Suppose Miranda was weeping, lying on her bed sobbing, as she'd sometimes lain and sobbed when she was a little girl? (Usually after a fit of temper, Mr Joyce recalled.) The last thing he felt capable of was consolation, he needed consoling himself. Nonetheless, as his ear detected, within the room, some confused yet continuous sound, he quietly opened the door.

Miranda wasn't sobbing, she was telephoning. Flung down across the bed, still in her blue velvet draperies, she fairly throttled the receiver. Whom had she rung up, wondered Mr Joyce, what household had she recklessly disturbed, at two o'clock in the morning? Was it Marion, perhaps, listening in sleepy excitement, or Mrs Gibson in hysterics, or Mr Conrad in a damned bad temper?

It was evidently Rachel.

'Marion and Denise I'll phone in the morning, they don't answer!' Mr Joyce heard his daughter finish. 'Come round as early as you like, come right after breakfast! *Then*, my goodness, what you're all going to hear!'

Tempestuously as the dawn promised, things might have been worse. Mr Joyce gently closed the door again, and went to bed.

CHAPTER THIRTY

I

Meanwhile Mr Gibson, like a homing pigeon, was batting his way north.

It was no smooth passage. He couldn't find a taxi, there was no other means of transport, he had to walk. Part of the way he ran. More than one policeman on the beat, startled by the sight of so portly a figure breaking into an elephantine trot, considered some arrestive action. Fortunately Mr Gibson didn't look like a criminal, and no one pursued him; he was allowed to thud by unchallenged. It was fortunate also that he'd had a nap – what a lifetime ago! – in Mr Joyce's study; he was out of condition to begin with, his lungs were sore before he reached Church Street, at Notting Hill he developed a stitch – he had to go the long way round because the Gardens were shut – at Queen's Road he almost collapsed before getting his second wind; but he made it. He got there. Long before there was light to distinguish the colour of a curtain, Mr Gibson reached the house in Alcock Road.

He didn't knock, or ring. He threw a handful of gravel up at Dolores' window; and in a moment she leaned forth.

Like a rose, like a Spanish rose, nodding on its trellis. . . .

'It's me, King Hal,' panted Mr Gibson. 'I'm back.'

There are some situations whose very blatancy is their saving grace. What is blatant at least requires no elucidation.

Such was the situation at 5, Alcock Road, on the morning following the re-possessing by King Hal of his secret garden.

Though every muscle ached, he was up and visible; and if only dressing-gowned, this added blatancy. (It had been the happiest moment of Mr Gibson's life when Dolores opened the wardrobe-drawer and showed him his dressing-gown and pyjamas laid up in pot-pourri. What a moment! What a succession of moments! His photograph still by her bed! How could he ever have left her? But he'd come back! O bliss, O incoherence!) When in the morning Mr Gibson appeared in his dressing-gown, Mr Phillips could have no doubt what had happened – incidentally, to himself.

Mr Gibson didn't have to throw him out. There was this to be said for Mr Phillips: he knew what was what. Moreover, from a personal point of view, he was scarcely more anxious to marry Miss Diver than had been Harry Gibson to marry Miss Joyce. Mercenary considerations alone had prompted his wooing; and there was still the chance of promotion to Birmingham. Mercenary considerations also ridded Dolores of him that same day. It was Thursday, midweek; and he got out of a whole week's payment.

'Since I shall no doubt be requested,' said Mr Phillips pointedly, 'to leave without delay, I can hardly be asked for my week?'

He said it loudly enough for Dolores to overhear; he saw the door from which Mr Gibson had just emerged still ajar. They encountered each other, the two suitors of that Spanish rose, on the landing outside the bathroom – Harry Gibson, as has been said, in his dressing-gown, Mr Phillips neatly accoutred to face the commercial world. He had had an extremely sketchy breakfast – milk and a fragment of cold ham, produced by Martha after he'd had to shout for it. At least it was a warning that the house wasn't running as usual; when he encountered his supplanter on the landing, Mr Phillips' shock was accordingly the less. 'Wherever he's been, he's come back,' thought Mr Phillips telescopically . . . His second reaction, as he pulled himself together, usefully paralleled Miranda's: if Miss Diver preferred such a chap to himself – bag-of-bones, bag-of-lard, what difference? – he didn't think much of her taste . . .

However, since the bag-of-lard was presumably well-heeled, Mr Phillips confined himself to irony.

'Two being company and three none,' added Mr Phillips. 'Or shall I stay my week out?'

'Pack your bags and say where to send 'em,' returned Harry Gibson – glad enough that no physical force was to be needed. For Dolores' sake he'd have chucked the chap out neck and crop, but every muscle applauded moderation.

'I'll collect this evening,' said Mr Phillips resentfully. '*I* shan't have any difficulty, finding another billet.'

'Fine,' agreed Harry Gibson.

'There's just a thing or two I'd like to say to my . . . *landlady* first,' said Mr Phillips.

'I'll tell you something,' said Harry Gibson, forgetting his weariness, 'if you annoy her again, I'll break your bloody neck.'

He spoke (to Dolores, listening behind her door) in the very accents of a King. To Mr Phillips they were the accents of a bully; but he took a look at Harry Gibson's big frame, larded with fat as it was, and recognised that half a week's lodging was the most he could get away with.

'I'll be back to-night with a taxi,' said Mr Phillips sulkily. 'I'm still not sure I couldn't get damages . . .'

Martha did more good than she knew by at that moment joining them; she put an end to what might have been a very nasty moment. Martha had heard Mr Gibson's voice from the kitchen, and came pounding up the stairs to welcome him back – not with any exuberance of affection, not with much surprise – as she hadn't been particularly surprised when he left – but with genuine welcome. Like Dolores, she trusted him to put things right: he was putting things right already; Mr Phillips' last words, familiar from the days of Ma Battleaxe, fell like music on her ear . . . She looked at Mr Gibson regardfully, and for the first time in their acquaintance pushed her hand up through his arm.

Harry Gibson stared down at her, and cleared his throat.

'Hey, Martha! Where's Mary?'

'In the Bible,' replied Martha.

'Best place for her,' said Mr Gibson.

With an exasperated mumble Mr Phillips pushed past them to the stairs. Martha turned round and watched him put on his hat in the hall, and noted for the last time how his head from the back looked like a can stuck on a pole, and watched the door shut behind him. Then she stumped into his room, and staggered back with the suitcase he kept his spare underwear in, and heaved it over the banisters.

3

Later that morning Mr Gibson went off to Kensington. He returned, in the evening, early. Dolores had steak for him. In the near future, she recognised, they might starve together, but the prospect held no terrors for her, and in the meantime she feasted her King. (Martha looked no further than her plate; Martha stuffed without a care.) In Miss Diver's hair gleamed the Spanish comb again, she wore the jumper made from her Spanish shawl, than which Mr Gibson had never seen anything more exquisite, and after dinner he put a new bulb in the bowl of glass fruit. Dolores' eyes filled with tears as she watched; that morning they'd spent barely ten minutes in the sitting-room, but he'd noticed, her Big Harry, when she tried and failed to make the fruits light up for him, and remembered to buy a bulb . . .

Tender was their talk in that variegated, jujube-coloured light. Mr Gibson's every moment of agony, during the past six months, was laid bare before his love; the explanation of how he'd felt forced to return her comb reduced Dolores again to happy tears. 'As if I'd ever have sold it, ever!' she wept. 'You might have had to!' groaned Harry Gibson. 'You had to take that chap as a lodger – and what came of that? Don't tell me he wasn't after you! You might have married him!' cried Harry Gibson – clutching her jealously back to his bosom. This wasn't an altogether distressing moment, for Dolores. With whatever repugnance, she might indeed have wedded

Mr Phillips, and now that the danger had passed it wasn't in feminine nature not to present him in the most favourable light possible.

'He was very kind, Harry. After you'd gone—'

'Say no more, don't break my heart!' cried Mr Gibson. 'Haven't I come back?'

CHAPTER THIRTY-ONE

I

Precariously still upon the sea of delight rode the bark of their bliss. In their Garden of Love Divine grew spiritual fruits only, and Mr Gibson (to say nothing of Martha) had a large corporeal appetite. Dolores' small bank account was running out, the lease of the little house was running out, more uneasily, each day, Harry scanned the lists of Situations Vacant in every paper at the Free Library. It was well for all of them that Mr Joyce couldn't endure to think of his friend starving.

For that was what he really feared it might come to – and Miranda was certain of it. 'Of course he'll *starve!*' she told all her friends, with a humorous grimace; and indeed did her best to make this likely by a neat piece of dove-tailing in the eagerly-awaited revelations. Dadda had found out something really *awful* about poor Harry, whispered Miranda, to Rachel and Marion and Denise – who would undoubtedly pass the word back to their fathers; Miranda didn't know exactly *what* – but hadn't Dadda sacked him out of hand? – and *then* it was that she'd jumped at the chance of freeing herself from such an old stick-in-the-mud, whom she'd only accepted in the first place because Dadda was so set on it. This double libel Mr Joyce bore with patience: though he didn't care for being branded as either a harsh parent or a poor judge of character, he felt Miranda in the circumstances entitled to do the best she could for herself; and recognised with pleasure that in the character of a girl who could have got married, but chose not to, she was on to a very nice thing.

For himself, he not only worried about Harry, he missed Harry. Miranda seemed not to miss Harry at all. Mr Joyce missed him all the time. Not to see his friend across the dinner-table, not to snug down with him in the study afterwards, to Mr Joyce made it scarcely worth while coming home. When old Mrs Gibson crept weeping to Bond Street, a letter from Harry in her hand – no address, just saying he'd be round to see her soon – Mr Joyce almost dropped a tear on it himself. The rash promise rose to his lips spontaneously. 'Don't worry, Mamma Gibson,' promised Mr Joyce. 'I'll find him a job somewhere . . .' 'But near!' wept Mrs Gibson. 'Not that Leeds again! I want my boy where I can see him!' 'So do I,' said Mr Joyce. . . .

Fortunately he had very good connections; not much more than a week passed before he was lunching his friend Conrad at the Ritz. Mr Joyce never minded doing things obviously. From the moment he saw the caviare, Mr Conrad knew he was to be asked a favour, and could think over the advantages of granting it while he ate. Its nature indeed startled him (he was the father of Denise) but not (also, perhaps, because he was the father of Denise) as much as might have been expected.

'I hear you want a manager for that branch of yours at Richmond,' said Mr Joyce, over the cigars.

'You hear right,' agreed Mr Conrad – thinking 'Ah ha!' to himself. The surprise was yet to come.

'Then why not Harry Gibson?' asked Mr Joyce.

Mr Conrad stared. Then, he stared.

'You want a job for that chap there's been all the trouble over? First he cooks your books, then you want to send him to cook mine?'

'He did not cook the books,' said Mr Joyce angrily. 'Harry is honest as the day. Conscientious, hard-working. Just the man you need. I dare say we could do a little business.'

'If he's as good as all that, why did you sack him?' asked Mr Conrad reasonably.

Mr Joyce shrugged.

'It was an affair of the women . . .'

'Ah,' said Mr Conrad. He had from the first mistrusted certain of his daughter's reports; after respecting old Joyce's acumen for some twenty years, hadn't been able to see him going so wrong at last over a son-in-law . . . An affair of the women, then! One might have known! 'When that girl of yours changes her mind,' said Mr Conrad, with something like admiration, 'she makes a thorough job of it. All right, send him round.'

2

Mr Joyce arrived at the house in Alcock Road not exactly furtively (he took a taxi), but having dropped in at Bond Street first to leave word that if Miranda telephoned, he was at an auction. It was the first step towards what he hoped would be a very happy double life – he had already discovered, for instance, that at Richmond was a golf-course, and meant to play there with Harry on Sundays under cover of taking Turkish baths. The immediate prospect, of relieving his friend's anxieties and saving him from starvation, was of course more delightful still; but as the taxi bore him down Alcock Road, it was a toss-up which took priority in Mr Joyce's excited mind.

How astounding, therefore, that within an instant of his ringing the bell, both should have been even momentarily forgotten! To Mr Joyce's amazement, the child who opened the door was a child he recognised. Short, stocky, fair-haired and grey-eyed – wearing the same jersey – actually with a stick of charcoal in her fist – there stood his faithless protégée of Almaviva Place.

'But this is crazy!' ejaculated Mr Joyce – even as he spoke grabbing hold of her. 'Why didn't your mother come to see me?'

'Oh, it's you,' said Martha stolidly. 'I haven't got a mother. I'm an orphan.'

'But you told me— An orphan!' cried Mr Joyce. 'Harry!' shouted

Mr Joyce, thrusting her before him into the house. 'Are you there, Harry?' Out burst Harry from the sitting-room; Mr Joyce thumped him gladly with the hand that wasn't grasping Martha and hurried on. 'Whose is this child, Harry? What is she doing here? I have a job for you, Conrad's, Richmond,' added Mr Joyce rapidly. 'Who is this child?'

'I told you about her, that's Martha, Miss Diver's niece,' said Harry Gibson, in natural astonishment, and thumping his friend back. 'Did you say Conrad's?'

'At Richmond, we will play golf, but never mind that now,' exclaimed Mr Joyce impatiently. 'She told me her mother was Mrs Brown.' He shook Martha up and down. 'Was it wrong? Why did you tell me wrong? Good afternoon, Miss Diver, have you a sister-in-law Mrs Brown?'

'No, Hogg,' said Miss Diver, adding to the confusion. 'I'm afraid she's dead. Oh, Harry, did I hear him say—?'

'Yes, he has!' exulted Harry Gibson.

'But she lives here, you look after her?' persisted Mr Joyce.

'Who, Martha? Of course,' said Dolores. 'Oh, Mr Joyce, won't you come into the sitting-room? Martha can come too—'

But Martha had had enough of being pulled about. She wrenched herself free and glowered all round.

'I don't want to come into the sitting-room. I'd rather not,' said Martha, very plainly.

'Martha, do as you're told!' cried Dolores. When their benefactor, their saviour, was taking an interest in her! 'When Mr Joyce is being so kind!' cried Dolores – an unfortunate echo. Martha started off towards the kitchen; Dolores glanced in desperate apology towards Mr Joyce, and was surprised to see on his face a look not of anger or offence, but merely one of peculiar attentiveness.

'Stop a moment,' said Mr Joyce mildly.

Remarkably, Martha stopped.

'What do you want to do?'

'Draw,' said Martha.

'That's right,' said Mr Joyce. 'Get along, don't waste time.'

3

It astonished both Miss Diver and Harry Gibson, in the sitting-room, how he kept recurring to the child, as though she was of importance. 'Conrad's won't be any goldmine,' said Mr Joyce, 'but enough for you both – and Mamma Gibson. (No pension for Mamma Gibson now!' chuckled Mr Joyce, in parenthesis.) 'But the one to think for, of course, is the child. If she's happy with her aunt, it would be a mistake to disturb her.' 'I'm sure Martha's always seemed perfectly happy,' said Miss Diver, uncomprehendingly. 'And she's been such a little comfort, we wouldn't dream of parting with her – would we, Harry?' 'By Jove, no!' said Harry Gibson. 'I wasn't thinking of that,' said Mr Joyce impatiently. 'All I want is that she shouldn't be put off.' 'Put off what?' asked Harry. Both he and Dolores were anxious to meet Mr Joyce's wishes in every possible way, but they didn't know what he was driving at. Even when he proposed to pay for Martha's keep and education, in return for the pick of her drawings year by year, they saw only another proof of his surpassing benevolence. 'I'll make her draw you something really *pretty*!' promised Dolores.

At that Mr Joyce laid down the law.

'On the contrary, I ask you please not to make any suggestion to her at all. Not to bother her at all about her drawings, or even look at them, unless she wants. Also not to try and make her be grateful to me, because she won't. Martha would chop us all up for india-rubber, if we were made of india-rubber,' said Mr Joyce, without apparent disapproval. 'Do you understand me at all?'

'Well, really, I'm not sure,' said Dolores. 'I'm afraid I'll just go on treating her as I always have.'

'That'll do,' said Mr Joyce.

4

It was inevitable in one of Harry Gibson's temperament that he should wish to celebrate rescue from financial catastrophe, the gift of a fair future – in short, the fulfilment of all his loving hopes for himself and Dolores – by going out to get a drink. ('You won't mind a pub just for once?' asked chivalrous Harry. 'Of course not, with you, dearest,' replied Dolores, as it were folding herself under his wing.) Mr Joyce took this further step towards a double life with alacrity; only Martha remained behind, refusing even the lure of fizzy lemonade. 'But she eats well?' enquired Mr Joyce, in a last burst of solicitude, walking down Alcock Road. 'Jolly nearly as much as I do,' Harry reassured him. 'Fine,' approved Mr Joyce. 'Good meat, good puddings, build up strength. D'you know what they feed *me* now?' he added wistfully. 'Eternal goulash. I put up with it because of you-know-why.'

This was the last word of reproach he ever uttered, to his defaulting son-in-law. He was a man of remarkable magnanimity.

'But on Sundays, at the golf-club, we will get some good British grub,' forecast Mr Joyce, cheering up.

5

When they were all gone Martha went out into the back-garden. It was several months now since she had frequented there; drawing hard outlines in Indian ink, and latterly in charcoal, had kept her within-doors; also Mr Phillips might have surprised her – Mr Phillips clanking about with garbage-pail and coal-bucket. There was no danger of this now.

It was quite dark. Head-on, head-down to the knotted grasses, one couldn't have seen an inch beyond one's nose. All Martha could make out was the shape of the coal-shed, square and peaked, and the cylindrical shape, beside it, of the dust-bin.

They formed a rather satisfactory combination. Martha, cautiously circling to find the best angle, meditated in terms of charcoal. When there was more light, thought Martha; not full daylight, but when it got shadowy; the top of the shed hard against the sky, and perhaps the dust-bin lid (which might be cocked) and the lower-down part blotty. Beautiful was the coal-shed, beautiful the dust-bin, at that moment, to Martha's eye of love; she forgot to be cold, out in the December dark without a coat, as she rapturously contemplated them. Then suddenly down from the fence leapt a cat – grey-furred by the night, discs of mica for eyes – and scared her out of her wits.

'You frightened me!' cried Martha indignantly; and like the child she still was, chased it away.

THE END

VIRAGO MODERN CLASSICS

&

CLASSIC NON-FICTION

Some of the authors included in these two series –

Lisa Alther, Elizabeth von Arnim, Dorothy Baker, Pat Barker, Nina Bawden, Nicola Beauman, Isabel Bolton, Kay Boyle, Vera Brittain, Leonora Carrington, Angela Carter, Willa Cather, Colette, Ivy Compton-Burnett, Barbara Comyns, E.M. Delafield, Maureen Duffy, Elaine Dundy, Nell Dunn, Emily Eden, George Eliot, Miles Franklin, Mrs Gaskell, Charlotte Perkins Gilman, Victoria Glendinning Elizabeth Forsythe Hailey, Radclyffe Hall, Shirley Hazzard, Dorothy Hewett, Mary Hocking, Alice Hoffman, Winifred Holtby, Janette Turner Hospital, Zora Neale Hurston, Elizabeth Jenkins, F. Tennyson Jesse, Molly Keane, Margaret Laurence, Maura Laverty, Rosamond Lehmann, Rose Macaulay, Shena Mackay, Olivia Manning, Paule Marshall, F.M. Mayor, Anais Nin, Mary Norton, Kate O'Brien, Olivia, Grace Paley, Mollie Panter-Downes, Dawn Powell, Dorothy Richardson, E. Arnot Robertson, Jacqueline Rose, Vita Sackville-West, Elaine Showalter, May Sinclair, Agnes Smedley, Dodie Smith, Stevie Smith, Christina Stead, Carolyn Steedman, Gertrude Stein, Jan Struther, Han Suyin, Elizabeth Taylor, Sylvia Townsend Warner, Mary Webb, Eudora Welty, Mae West, Rebecca West, Edith Wharton, Antonia White, Christa Wolf, Virginia Woolf, E.H. Young

'Found on all the best bookshelves' – *Penny Vincenzi*

'Their huge success is solid proof of the fact that literary fashion is a snare and a delusion – people like a good old-fashioned read' – *Good Housekeeping*

VIRAGO MODERN CLASSICS

&

CLASSIC NON-FICTION

The first Virago Modern Classic, *Frost in May* by Antonia White, was published in 1978. It launched a list dedicated to the celebration of women writers and to the rediscovery and reprinting of their works. Its aim was, and is, to demonstrate the existence of a female tradition in fiction, and to broaden the sometimes narrow definition of a 'classic' which has often led to the neglect of interesting novels and short stories. Published with new introductions by some of today's best writers, the books are chosen for many reasons: they may be great works of fiction; they may be wonderful period pieces; they may reveal particular aspects of women's lives; they may be classics of comedy or storytelling.

The companion series, Virago Classic Non-Fiction, includes diaries, letters, literary criticism, and biographies – often by and about authors published in the Virago Modern Classics.

'A continuingly magnificent imprint' – *Joanna Trollope*

'The Virago Modern Classics have reshaped literary history and enriched the reading of us all. No library is complete without them' – *Margaret Drabble*

'The writers are formidable, the production handsome. The whole enterprise is thoroughly grand' – *Louise Erdrich*

'The Virago Modern Classics are one of the best things in Britain today' – *Alison Lurie*

'Good news for everyone writing and reading today' – *Hilary Mantel*

'Masterful works' – *Vogue*

THE ENCHANTED APRIL

By Elizabeth von Arnim

With an Introduction by Terence de Vere White

To Those who Appreciate Wistaria and Sunshine.
   Small mediaeval Italian Castle on the shores
   of the Mediterranean to be Let Furnished
   for the month of April. Necessary servants
   remain.

A discreet advertisement in *The Times* lures four very different
women away from the dismal British weather to San Salvatore, a
castle high above a bay on the sunny Italian Riviera. There, the
Mediterranean spirit stirs the souls of Mrs Arbuthnot, Mrs Wilkins,
Lady Caroline Dester and Mrs Fisher, and remarkable changes
occur . . .

'A restful, funny, sumptuous, and invigorating vacation for
the mind and soul . . refreshing, charming and romantic'
500 Great Books by Women

Now you can order superb titles directly from Virago

☐ Mrs Palfrey at the Claremont	Elizabeth Taylor	£7.99
☐ Our Spoons Came From Woolworths	Barbara Comyns	£7.99
☐ The Enchanted April	Elizabeth von Arnim	£7.99
☐ The Diary of a Provincial Lady	E.M. Delafield	£7.99
☐ Provincial Daughter	R.M. Dashwood	£7.99

The prices shown above are correct at time of going to press. However, the publishers reserve the right to increase prices on covers from those previously advertised, without further notice.

Virago

Please allow for postage and packing: **Free UK delivery.**
Europe: add 25% of retail price; Rest of World: 45% of retail price.

To order any of the above or any other Virago titles, please call our credit card orderline or fill in this coupon and send/fax it to:

Virago, PO Box 121, Kettering, Northants NN14 4ZQ
Fax: 01832 733076   Tel: 01832 737526
Email: aspenhouse@FSBDial.co.uk

☐ I enclose a UK bank cheque made payable to Virago for £ . . . .
☐ Please charge £ . . . . . . to my Visa/Access/Mastercard/Eurocard

Expiry Date ☐☐☐☐   Switch Issue No. ☐☐

NAME (BLOCK LETTERS please) . . . .

ADDRESS . . . .

. . . .

. . . .

Postcode . . . . Telephone . . . .

Signature . . . .

Please allow 28 days for delivery within the UK. Offer subject to price and availability.
Please do not send any further mailings from companies carefully selected by Virago ☐